ONE WILD RIDE

CAKE LOVE Series Book 3

Elizabeth Lynx

One Wild Ride
Copyright © 2018 by Elizabeth Lynx.

For information contact:
lynxelizabeth1@gmail.com
http://www.elizabeth-lynx.com

Book and Cover design by Elizabeth Lynx
Photography by Innervision
Formatting template by Derek Murphy of Creativindie Design
ISBN-13: 978-0-9992799-0-8

DEDICATION

To the ones that say yes. Sometimes it's harder to say yes, but it can make the world a little easier to deal with, too.

Table of Contents

ONE

Aria

"I peed myself," my best friend, Morgana Drake, whispered to me.

We sat in a cold, dim room. Despite the darkness, my skin prickled from the glare I knew was coming from the towering, muscle-bound man standing by the door. The hoodie he wore shadowed his face, making him appear even more menacing. Like some thug waiting for a pretty young blond like myself to take a wrong turn down a dark alley.

Only, we weren't in an alley. We were somewhere much worse. Somewhere, that if Morgana, Evaleen Bechmann, and I screamed at the top of our lungs no one but this thug and his equally menacing friend would hear.

We were in downtown Chicago in one of the tallest building in the city where the top floor was the home of the wealthiest resident: A. Hawthorne.

But we were in the basement garage of that building in a tiny room surrounded by cinder blocks and one door. In other words, I should be scared.

I smirked. "Why are you hiding by the door? Afraid I might bite?" I wasn't frightened.

Growling for added effect, I kept my eyes trained on the hoodie guy by the door.

"Aria," Morgana whisper-screamed at me.

I laughed at our ridiculous situation. Laughed because these guys only wanted to scare us. We weren't tied to these chairs. They looked tough, but I've been around men who were the stuff of nightmares. Hoodie and his friend, Buzz Cut, were like boy scouts compared to them.

"What are they going to do to us, Morgana? Take us to some warehouse and brainwash us to take over the government? Come on." I snorted and rolled my eyes at my redheaded friend.

"You never answered us. Why are you here with the paintings?" Buzz Cut moved forward and into the light. His dirty blond spikes almost disappearing under the harsh glow of the hanging lamp.

"That's none of your business. Why would we tell you anything? We don't even know who you are." Evaleen's blue eyes narrowed as she leaned toward him.

I liked Evaleen. She worked with my roommate, Morgana, so I've only known her less than two months but she's tough and loyal. The perfect person to have with me when I decided to infiltrate a wealthy recluse's home.

Despite her blond hair always pulled back into a frumpy schoolmarm style and dressing like one too, she had a no-nonsense approach to life that fit perfectly now.

"My name's Bradley. That's all you need to know. Now tell me why you were with the delivery of A. Hawthorne's paintings or I'll have you all arrested for trespassing," he said as his dark eyes narrowed.

Evaleen snorted while Morgana whimpered.

Hoodie moved closer, hiding the most stellar gray eyes I'd ever seen beneath his hood. He concealed that secret weapon well. When

Morgana, Evaleen, and I first arrived and got out of the delivery van, Hoodie was the one who grabbed me and pulled me into this room.

The light in the garage was faint but his gaze hit me like a bolt through thick smoke. Those pale gray eyes caused me to make a wish—to kiss him.

Unfortunately, I never got the chance to make good on my wish.

The men thought it odd that three women were helping to deliver some paintings when the actual delivery guy and his assistant were perfectly capable of doing it themselves. At least Hoodie and Buzz Cut weren't dumb. I knew it was risky to pass ourselves off as part of the delivery team, but I had to come here.

When the wealthiest man in the city, if not the country, buys your paintings, you want to shake his hand. And I was giddy to catch a glimpse of the famously withdrawn A. Hawthorne.

"That's funny, Bradley. Since when is being in a garage trespassing. For all the police know we were only looking for our car. Besides, you two strong-armed us ladies into a dark, closed off room. Even if A. Hawthorne can buy off the police to cover this up, I don't think he can do a thing about us keeping it off social media." Evaleen smirked.

That's my girl.

Thugs may have muscles, but brains will always win in the end. A smart person would know not to let fear and emotions cloud their judgment. Bullies rely too heavily on their emotions to know better.

Bradley didn't seem to like what Evaleen had to say. His eyes widened, and he went over to Hoodie. They whispered and as much as I leaned forward I couldn't make out their words.

Hoodie finally came into the light. His eyes, turning to me, burned and seemed to brighten the room just enough to cause my heart to take notice.

He pulled down his hood to reveal thick dark hair that dusted his ears. And his skin, smooth and tan. I wondered if he lived in a country full of sun and sand and was forced to the cold, concrete-blanketed Chicago as punishment.

"Aria." His hypnotic eyes, the deep rumble of his voice, held me tight as he knelt in front of me.

"Yes?" I said transfixed.

"Why are you here?"

"To meet A. Hawthorne. Those were my paintings he bought. I just want to thank him."

Way to spoil everything, Aria.

Where was my usual flirty snark? His eyes were a dangerous drug. If his eyes had the power to get me to reveal my secrets against my will in a dark room, imagine what his hands could do?

My heart stumbled at the thought.

I soon found out their power. He placed his palm on my arm. My resolve obliterated the moment his fingers dusted my skin. And my breath, it withered and died as I leaned into his hand.

He had to feel that. That heat. That electricity. Or did his eyes protect him from such mortal things?

After a moment he rose, letting his hand fall and leaving me desperate for his touch. I suddenly felt the early March air in my bones. It was bitter and unloved.

When I glanced at him, the corner of his mouth ticked up, just enough to bring some of that warmth back.

"I think I can make that happen." He reached a hand toward me to help me up and I took it. At that point, I would hand over my wallet and perhaps my ovaries to make him smile.

Bradley opened his mouth to speak, but Hypno-eyes halted him with one look.

Those eyes were weapons. Even Bradley did as they commanded. He shut his mouth and let Hypno-eyes lead us out of the room to a set of elevators.

Once we were all crowded into the lift, Hypno-eyes leaned forward and stared at a mirror. The doors closed, and the elevator began to rise.

"Wow. That was cool. Did the elevator just scan your eyes?" Morgana asked.

"Yes. Mr. Hawthorne had his private elevators equipped with the latest security technology," Bradley said.

"Like James Bond or—" Morgana said before being cut off by Evaleen.

"Or *Get Smart*." Evaleen smirked at Bradley. "Let me guess, his shoe is also a phone?"

Hypno-eyes snorted and everyone in the elevator turned with wide eyes.

He shrugged his broad shoulders. "What? It was funny. I love *Get Smart*."

The elevator stopped, and the doors opened causing my mouth to drop open. We stepped onto gray-tiled floors and into a small hall with bright white walls. But it's what covered those walls that had my eyes melting.

Works of art.

Not my artwork, but master works of art.

Stuff I had only seen in textbooks during my art history class at Northwestern. I remember falling in love with Native American art in school. To the point where I studied Native culture and even learned some Navajo.

I stood only inches from paper warped and molded decades before I was born by R. C. Gorman. Fear that my hot breath would wither its beauty but too in awe to move.

"Stunning. How does A. Hawthorne have such a piece? Shouldn't this be in a museum?"

That's when I felt the warmth from down in the basement return to my arm. I turned to discover Hypno-eyes and I were alone in the hallway. A large, dark wooden door sat wide-open at the end. Bradley must have escorted my friends away and I hadn't even noticed.

I should be worried, for them, for myself, but for some reason I felt safe. Those eyes and now, his touch, did strange things to me. Had me reacting to the world in a way I never had before, well, not since I was young. Not since I was innocent of the evils that existed in the hearts and hands of men.

His eyes crinkled with warmth. "It's much safer here than a museum basement. Most of the collection is loaned from time to time to galleries and museums around the world."

"A. Hawthorne may be a recluse but at least he's not a hoarder. I'm glad he allows the public to experience these treasures," I said with barely contained excitement.

Hypno-eyes frowned and abruptly turned his back to move toward the door. I guess Mr. Hawthorne's employees didn't like people calling him a recluse. It's a good thing I hadn't brought up the rumors that he prefers to sleep with prostitutes.

I'm not one to judge women on what they have to do to survive in this male-dominated world, but I would think a billionaire wouldn't need to add to the exploitation of women. But what did I know of the happenings behind closed doors of penthouses?

I walked through the door and it eerily closed behind me. I hoped it was the latest tech gadget closing that door and not a dead painter's ghost here to collect his lost work.

I quickened my step from the eerie door and was struck once again as I entered what appeared to be the love-child of a living room and a museum.

My friends sat on a what I thought to be a replica of an orange Florence Knolls sofa. But as I glanced around the room, I realized there were no replicas in this room. No knockoffs or vintage-inspired. Everything was original, from the George Nakashima end table to the Matisse hanging on the wall behind Evaleen.

I pointed to my friends and said, "When I die, I want to be cremated and my ashes scattered in this room."

"You got it." Morgana gave me thumbs up.

"Ah, Dixon, you can't just scatter your ashes anywhere you want. This is someone's home. They don't want a dead person's ashes on their couch."

Despite Evaleen's cute habit of calling people by their last name and sound logic, I chose to ignore her comment.

"Ms. Dixon, A. Hawthorne will meet with you now. He is down the hall; the second door on the right." Bradley pointed toward a hall that appeared to be in competition with the Louvre.

This was it—the point of the whole evening. To meet the man who didn't just buy my paintings but propelled me into the elite artistic circle. If A. Hawthorne showed interest in an artist, their career was set. Every gallery wanted to show their work.

I can finally get a chance to show my paintings, not just in Chicago but New York, Los Angeles, and perhaps even the world. No more slinging drinks for tips. No more drunk losers groping me, expecting me to smile when they take what I never told them they could have.

I left my final resting place and moved quickly down the hall. Standing in front of the door to the room that held my savior I paused and removed my puffy black coat. Smoothing my shoulder length hair and rubbing at my good luck charm around my neck—my sister's old heart pendant necklace—I reached over knocking on the door.

It opened, and I wondered if all the doors in this place were possessed. In the middle of a square room with a large wooden desk and a few black leather chairs stood Hypno-eyes.

He waved me inside. "Come in, Aria. It's nice to meet you. I'm Alexander Hawthorne."

TWO

Aria hated me.

I had seen that look before on a woman—my mother. The shock. The hurt.

I should have been honest with Aria from the beginning, but Bradley insisted we tell them nothing. He didn't know the women and, therefore, he didn't trust them. He believed it a security risk if we let them know who I was.

What Bradley really meant was my mother would be upset if anyone, especially women she hadn't vetted, came near me. As much as I considered my security guard, Bradley Gibson, a friend who happened to be my cousin, he still worked for my mother.

"Please, Aria, come in and take a seat. I promise these chairs are much more comfortable than the plastic ones in the basement."

Her eyes still wide, stared at me. An ache radiated through my chest and down my arms. My hand slid over the supple surface of the chair back. I lowered my eyes as thoughts of her caused my cheeks to warm.

Her beauty was addictive and painful.

"You're A. Hawthorne? But . . . uh, but—" She pointed back down the hall to where Bradley was keeping an eye on her friends.

I walked over to her and placed my hand on her back. A jolt shot up my arm. It wasn't static, just my heart seizing from fear, from heat, from the wild thoughts my mind threw at it. And it was like nothing I had felt before.

I had become accustomed to hiding my emotions, especially fear. To survive in my family, it was essential. But this was new. This was wonderful and challenging to hide.

"We had to make sure you weren't with the paparazzi or a weird art groupie," I said after guiding Aria to a chair and crouching down to face her.

Her deep brown eyes searched my face as she frowned. I wondered if I pushed her too far tonight. Trapping her and her friends in that basement was wrong. I might have to kill Bradley if he helped ruin the one chance I got with the woman I had lusted after for three years.

Her brow wrinkled in the most delectable way. "You have art groupies? I have been in the art world for over ten years and I never had any art groupies."

"They tend to go after famous artists and collectors or the talented." Instant regret caused me to frown.

I shook my head and tried to open my mouth to explain my poor choice of words, but it was too late. Aria jerked away and up out of the chair.

"Oh, well, if I'm not talented then why did you buy my paintings, Mr. Hawthorne?" Aria asked as if the words left a dreadful taste in her mouth.

She moved backward toward the door before her eye caught the small Picasso drawing on the wall. With abrupt flare, she stopped.

"I didn't mean you weren't talented. Of course you are or I wouldn't have been fascinated by your work. I just meant artists and collectors who they deem talented," I said cringing at my even worse explanation.

Usually I could hold my own in just about any conversation. Even philosophical or political debates, while challenging, were enjoyable to me. But everything I said around Aria seemed wrong, felt wrong.

It was as if my penis told my brain to take a vacation. She challenged me in ways that I wasn't at all prepared for. It propelled me forward. I stood and walked toward her.

Aria turned to face me, her arms folded and eyes narrowed for what I knew would be a verbal attack. "I get that you are a little out of touch with us common folk with all your wealth to pad you from getting near us, but we don't really like to be insulted."

She smirked as she took a moment to gaze about the room. "Did you think you could dazzle me with your amazing art and killer body and hypnotic eyes and I would succumb to a giggle fit when you put down my work?"

Killer body? Blood raced through my veins the more she spoke. Her complimentary words, meant to disguise an insult, were all too familiar to me. It was a tactic my mother gave out like lollipops.

"Excuse me?" I said as I folded my arms over my chest.

"I'll make this real clear for you, Mr. Hawthorne. I don't like to be lied to or disrespected. Maybe in your fancy pants world, everyone lies all the time. Maybe it's a favorite game among the wealthy, who can conjure up the biggest fib while putting people down. Do you win a prize? A golden statue with the biggest dick?"

Aria stepped a little closer to me, her hands moved to her hips. I took a deep breath inhaling what I imagined a wild bed of flowers in a summer meadow would smell like.

My nose flared for more and I had to restrain my hand that only wanted to sink deep into her silky hair. I battled my senses to stay present and defend myself.

"You think this is a game? Some out of touch recluse that plays horrible tricks on people? Wow. This from a woman who hid in a delivery truck so she could sneak into someone's home."

Aria's eyes widened and her mouth opened at my accusation but I wasn't finished.

"Don't pretend you just wanted to shake my hand, Ms. Dixon. I'm well aware that there are lots of people who would do anything to meet me. Even a small-time artist looking to further her career," I said as the corner of my lips hitched.

She didn't like that. I believe I discovered what Aria actually looked like when she was mad and damn it, if it wasn't sexy. Her cheeks rosy as her chin tilted up. "You are so full of yourself, you know that, Mr. Hawthorne? *Oh, look at me, I'm someone who was born rich and never had to work a day in my life. I can make fun of anyone and they have to take it. La de da!*" Aria waved her hands in the air and started to hop about as she tried to mimic me.

I wanted to laugh but something about her, how she flushed at my words and her body came alive with reaction, kept me pushing her.

"Was that supposed to be me, Ms. Dixon? Because I have to say I have seen a better imitation from my five-year-old cousin when he tried to paint my Jackson Pollack painting." I gestured toward the door where on the hallway wall was, in fact, a Pollack that my cousin once said he could paint something just like that.

"Maybe you should stick with your day job," just before the word fell out of my mouth I knew I would regret it but I couldn't seem to stop myself, "bartending."

She gasped and something ghosted across her face for only a second but I knew it wasn't good.

Aria moved closer to me. Just an inch stood between us and I had to bend my head to look at her. My eyes dipped to her lips, thick and red and waiting to be tasted. Then to her long, creamy neck for a moment before returning to her eyes. She was petite, but I knew that even the slightest creatures could carry the biggest punch.

Her blow wasn't swift, and at first, I didn't realize she hurt me, but then it sunk in. It was deep enough that I knew the pain would linger.

She patted my arm and smiled. "You are so pretty. Tell me, is that why people want to know you," she tilted her head to the side, as if to really inspect me, "or is it just about the money?"

Memories of a dark time flickered in my head at her words. I took a breath and instead of telling her to get out, removing myself from her presence, I did the opposite.

As my arm burned from her touch, fire filled my veins. I stared back at her lips, the same color as her top. I could feel that red crawl up my neck and cover my ears. Every word that came out of her mouth reached into my chest and ripped it apart.

The more she spoke, the more I wanted to bite her. My fuel was her fire.

I pushed her arm from mine and turned my head. Trying to breathe, I focused on the Picasso. Art had always soothed me but for some reason as I closed my eyes, lines in the drawing seemed to morph into the curves of her body.

This game we were playing was petty, and I wanted it to end. How I wanted it to end was a problem. I kept picturing the solution. The beautiful resolution that only her thighs spread wide could solve.

But that was never going to happen.

"You see this line right here, Aria?" Opening my eyes, I pointed to the Picasso.

I glanced back for a second to find her brow wrinkled as she turned to gaze at the picture. "Yeah."

"Do you know why Pablo Picasso made that line?" I stared into her mocha eyes. They flickered between me and the line as her body stiffened in preparation for some impending attack from me.

"I know it's one of his lovers. I think she gave birth to two of his children."

"That's a fact, Aria. What I want was his heart when he drew that. There was a reason for every line he drew, and it had to do with what he felt for her. Why that line?"

Her hesitation melted from her face and she leaned closer. "It's where her hand meets her cheek. The line is clean, sharp, unlike the others that are messy."

I leaned closer to her ear and took a breath. My eyes closed as her sweet scent filled my lungs. "Perhaps there was a reason that line was different than the others."

She moved slightly, tilting her head to expose her neck causing me to weaken.

"I, uh . . . I don't know," she whispered.

"Because that's where he liked to touch her. Maybe to kiss her or bite her."

Aria turned her head, her eyes widened. "But what about her lips?" Aria's gaze dropped to my mouth. "Wouldn't he focus on that if he wanted to do those things?"

I brought my thumb up to her bottom lip and gently brushed it as I spoke, "He did focus on her mouth, but the lines are light, not heavily drawn. Maybe he was gentle there but savage everywhere else."

Her nostrils flared and I couldn't help myself. I had to take a bite. I moved closer but as I was an inch from her lips, the door to my office opened. We raised our heads to find Aria's friend, Evaleen, standing there with Morgana directly behind her. I could hear Bradley's voice growing louder as it came closer, about how they aren't allowed back here.

Before I could stop what was happening, Aria was pulled away, disappearing with Morgana down the hall. My eyes stayed on her until the last strand of platinum hair disappeared around the corner. I drew a heavy breath, finding it difficult to grasp that once again, she was disappearing from my life.

"Nothing better have happened to my friend. Your boss, Mr. Hawthorne, may know people. You may have money, but I have resources," Evaleen said as she poked her finger into my chest.

She turned and left with the other women. Bradley finally showed up. "I went to get Evaleen a glass of water because she started to cough and when I came back, they had sneaked down the hall. Are you okay, Alex? Did Aria do anything to you?"

I nodded. "Yes. And I want her to do it again."

THREE

Aria

"I'm rich now," I said as I slammed a fifty down.

Morgana reached over the wobbly booth table and gave me a high five.

"Despite all the money you got from the sale of your paintings, I'll still pay for my own drinks, Dixon." Evaleen lifted the glass tumbler of gin and tonic to her lips.

"That's very kind of you, Aria, but I wouldn't feel right taking your money like that." Tiffany Blackburn, the last to join our group of friends less than a month ago, reached over to pat me on my back. As she did so, her chestnut hair appeared to fly into both Evaleen and Morgana's faces. That woman had some thick hair.

"This is what? Our two-month anniversary of SWIM Meet. We should be celebrating. The last payment from Mr. Hawthorne deposited into my account today so I am in a partying mood." I lifted my whiskey up and spilled a little on the table. Just as I was about to lick the drops from my arm, I felt a hand on my shoulder.

I turned to find Evaleen staring at something across the room. "Dixon, doesn't that hoodie look familiar?"

Large black leather booths with round blond tables dominated the bar. A few tall tables with stools were in the center but most of the seating was along the walls with a large wooden bar lining the back.

Glancing toward the back of the darkened room to a booth on the other side tucked in the corner, a familiar and heart tumbling pair of gray eyes stared at me.

I pursed my lips. "Yes, that hoodie looks very familiar."

Once Evaleen and Morgana saved me from Alexander Hawthorne's grip two weeks ago, at least that's how they worded it, I haven't seen him since. His money, on the other hand, I have seen lots of. Which, technically, is my money now.

I stood from the booth but Evaleen's hand stopped me. "I wouldn't go over there, Dixon. What if he tries to strong-arm you again?"

She released my arm as I shook my head. "I told you, Evaleen, we were only discussing Picasso. He didn't do anything to me."

Except almost caused me to orgasm by talking about a line in a drawing.

I haven't been able to stop thinking about him. Both night and day. Many times, these past two weeks, I have woken during the night and had to use my vibrator to finish what he started in my head.

"Besides, I got my kick-ass SWIM Meet ladies here," I point to everyone in our booth but hesitate when I get to Morgana, "at least Evaleen and Tiff—"

I bite my lip when I mention Tiffany. I didn't know her as well as the others and with her having a twelve-year-old boy to take care of who's in and out of the hospital, I didn't want to put her at risk.

"I have Evaleen. You'll keep me safe," I said as I nodded toward her.

"Of course." She winked.

Strolling toward Alexander, I heard Tiffany say she forgot what SWIM stood for. Morgana mentioned, "It's an acronym for Smart Women with Idiot Men."

The closer I got to Alexander the more he straightened, his eyes fixed on me.

"If it isn't the most sought-after bachelor in the country," I said thick with sarcasm.

While all the single ladies within a thousand-mile radius wanted him, or at least wanted to know what he looked like so they could track him down and date him, I did not.

Sure, I wanted to rip all his clothes off and find out what it's like to ride a billionaire but that was just hormones and chemistry. His asshole attitude was the cold shower I needed to walk far away from him.

I learned long ago that when it came to men to never keep them in my life for too long. One-night stands were best but anything more and feelings started to spoil the fun. But with Alexander, as much as my body wanted that sex-filled night with him, the conversation I had at his place caused that slow burn to cool off quickly.

Except when he talked about Picasso.

Despite our mutual lust over art, Alexander tricked me and not just that, he hurt my feelings too. Maybe it was because I expected A. Hawthorne to be a weirdo with overly long fingernails and stringy hair; instead, I was shocked to find out he was tall, had thick muscles, and looked like he won genetic bingo a thousand times.

He's wealthy, handsome, and had a home I could die in. Then he insulted my talent.

"If it isn't the bartender." Alex's words cut deeper than I wanted them too. But I didn't let it show.

If a man wasn't attracted to me, I was fine with that. I could even handle if a guy was a bit of a jerk to me as I had dealt with much worse, but I had never had anyone tell me I had no talent.

Except my father, but I couldn't care less what my dad thought of me anymore. What he did to our family—to my sister—was unforgivable.

I waved at the booth seat across from him and he nodded for me to sit.

"Did you think I worked here? Is that why you came? Have some fun with the poor folk?"

I knew I had hit his sore spot as his jaw twitched and his hand rubbed over his face. Maybe he was one of those out of touch rich people who truly believed they were just like everyone else.

It was sort of a turn-on to tease him and poke the wild, sexy beast.

"No, I know you don't work here." His eyes stayed fixated on his hands as he twisted a paper napkin to death.

"I see. Had someone check up on me? Find out everything about me, huh? You can buy art from a talentless nobody but not a shady talentless nobody."

He groaned and shook his head.

"Can we just stop. Pretend like two weeks ago never happened. I didn't mean you didn't have any talent. I only meant that groupies don't understand what real art is. They don't see beauty and depth and emotion in works of art, they only see fame and popularity."

Surprise held me in place as he finished his speech.

"You may not be popular or famous, at least not yet, Aria, but your paintings have more soul and heart in them than all the art groupies in the world have in their bodies. That's why I bought them. That's what I meant to say but it didn't come out that way. I'm sorry."

Alexander's eyes lifted, sad as a cloudy sky, causing me to frown. I had judged him boldly, too quickly, and it was now his gaze that held my punishment.

"I didn't mean what I said . . . that you should stick to your day job as a bartender. I was angry and didn't mean that at all."

I nodded. "Good, because I quit."

His frown disappeared and turned into the slightest curve at the corner of his mouth. Damn it, but it was hot.

"Really?"

"Yes. I gave them my two weeks' notice last week. My boss was sad to see me go, so I promised to help out from time to time. She's a good person."

He nodded and then there was silence. We both sat there awkwardly. I played with the gold heart charm on my necklace and Alex strangled more napkins.

I should apologize too. I don't really know Alexander Hawthorne and it was unfair of me to assume he was some spoiled rich guy without a clue about real life struggles. But as I was about to say something he cut me off.

"It's best if you don't work anyway," he said as a big grin took over his face.

"What? Why shouldn't I work?"

That was weird. But I shrugged it off expecting him to explain himself.

His cheeks reddened, and it was sweet in a way. Like some boy about to ask a girl on a date. Maybe that was it? He wanted to go on a date with me. Though, that wouldn't explain the whole no work thing.

Would I go out with him? Yes, I think I would. When he explained what he meant just now about the art groupies . . . well, it was flattering. Alex's hot and obsessed with art as much as I am, I think that would be a great idea. If it goes well, I might suspend my one date rule and go out with him twice.

It would be refreshing to go out with someone I had something in common with.

"I, uh, wanted to hire you. To, um. I didn't think this would be so hard. I've never had to ask someone, usually someone else hires them to, you know . . ." His eyes dipped to my lips.

That's when it hit me.

"Like to have sex with?" I lowered my voice and leaned my head forward. "You think I'm a prostitute?"

The muscles in his jaw twitched as he leaned forward. "Who told you that? Did my mother talk to you?"

Of course, he wanted to go out on a date with me, a hired date.

I stood from the table but turned to him before I left. "And here I was about to apologize for assuming you were some spoiled brat. You know what?" His eyes grew wide as I took a step closer. "You aren't spoiled. I made that mistake and I am sorry for that. But you are a sleazy asshole. Did you think just because I'm an artist that I'd be willing to have sex with you for money? For someone who appreciates art I'd rather hang out with shallow art groupies than you. Goodbye, Mr. Hawthorne. It was nice almost getting to know you."

What a disgusting excuse of a man. I can't believe I used my vibrator last night imagining him on top of me. Or this past Monday when I imagined us in the middle of the National Portrait Gallery. Or that weird dream about us on a giant pizza.

I craved pizza after that one.

Instead of heading back to the SWIM Meet booth, I made my way to the bathroom. I needed some quiet time. My head was pounding from the highs and lows of the night.

A part of me was angry at myself for being attracted to such a loser. I should have known better and remembered those rumors about him.

As I made my way down the narrow hall behind the bar toward the bathrooms, a hand grabbed my arm. I turned to find Alexander towering over me. His steel eyes bore into mine and my heart began to race.

He pulled me back until he found a door with a brick propping it open to a broom closet and pushed me inside. I stumbled over a bucket but righted myself just as he pushed the brick out of the way. He turned on the light switch by the door before closing it. Alex stood in front of it and blocked my escape.

With his arms folded over his chest he became an impassable wall.

Heat traveled up my neck as I broke out into a sweat. Maybe Alex wasn't used to anyone telling him no. Maybe those rumors of prostitutes aren't really about prostitutes at all, but women he forced to be paid sex slaves.

Morgana had tried to warn me that no good would come of trying to see what the famous art recluse looked like, but I didn't listen. I may not have bills anymore, but it seemed like I may not live to enjoy my new debt free lifestyle either.

FOUR

Alexander

"What's happening here?" Aria asked with fear widening her eyes.

I made a terrible mistake.

Did you think shoving a woman into a dark, dirty room without anyone knowing was the right thing to do, Alex?

Why can't I think straight around her? And why do I keep forcing her into dark rooms?

"Look, I'm sorry. I panicked okay?" I held up my hands before turning to open the door.

That's when my heart plummeted. The handle wouldn't move and when I pushed it, I realized the door was locked.

Fuck. We were locked in here.

Fuck. Now I had to tell Aria we were trapped.

Fuck. She was going to hate me even more now.

I turned back to face her and smiled. The grin seemed to only make things worse as she frowned. I held up my hands. Aria wrapped her arms tightly around herself as dread began to roll off her.

This wasn't how I expected the night to go at all. I thought she would be excited by the opportunity I offered her, and then we would celebrate together. Instead, she called me an asshole, and I forced her into a broom closet.

Maybe I was an asshole?

"I didn't plan to come here tonight to rape you," I said and instantly regretted it.

Her mouth dropped open as tears streamed down her face.

"Shit, that isn't what I meant." I shook my hands and she flinched. "I mean, I never planned to hurt you."

Damn it. My mouth was making everything worse. I don't seem to be very good at putting women at ease. And I was even worse dealing with the most beautiful woman in the world.

"I just want to leave, okay?" Her voice trembled.

I stepped forward to comfort her, but she stumbled back slamming into the wall behind her.

"Look, Aria, I wanted a moment to explain myself. You walked off before I could say anything. I didn't realize this was a broom closet. I thought maybe it was an office or work room or something. Just a room with some privacy so I could explain."

She wiped her tears with her fingers. I reached into my pocket and gave her a handkerchief. I waved it in the air like a white flag and gave her a small grin. Aria hesitantly reached forward and grabbed it before blowing her nose into the cloth.

"Then why won't you open the door?" Aria asked, her voice small, and hiccupped before trying to hand me back the handkerchief. I waved it away letting her know she could keep it.

"The door won't open." There was no easy way to tell her so I let it out. "We're locked in here." I turned and showed her how the doorknob wouldn't move.

Finding her resolve, Aria pushed past me and tried her hand at the door—like I was completely inept in using something as simple as a doorknob. For a minute, she pushed and pulled at the doorknob with no success. Once she pounded on the door with her fist and began to yell, I joined her.

We tried for several minutes until Aria stepped back with rapid breath.

"I can't believe we are stuck in here. What were you thinking dragging me in here?" She slapped my arm, not hard, but enough to let me know she wasn't happy.

"I don't know. There's something about you. I get flustered and don't really know what to say or how to act."

Aria sat back on a stool. "I'm being serious, Mr. Hawthorne—"

"Please, call me Alex," I said and smiled.

She hesitated before taking a breath. "Okay, Alex. Someone like you doesn't get flustered around someone like me. I want the truth as to why you brought me in here."

"I'm serious, Aria. Why wouldn't someone like me be nervous around you?"

She rolled her eyes as she leaned back against the wall the stool was up against. "You're rich, Alex. From what I've learned in life, rich people get whatever they want. And even if you didn't have money, I'm sure there aren't many women who have told you no."

Stupid me. I forgot how Aria thought of me.

"You know, my mom and you have a lot in common." The corner of my mouth hitched as I shook my head. "You both think I don't have anything to offer the world besides my money and my smile. Thank you, Aria. I thought it was just my mom who was a terrible person for telling me those things all my life, but now I realize that maybe she was right."

I turned back to the door and began to shove my body against it, intending to break it down. It's not so much that I wanted out, but I had to hit something hard and the door was right there.

"Alex. Alex!"

I hesitated but refused to turn toward her. Even when she placed her hand on my arm, I wouldn't let her soft, warm touch sway me.

"I'm sorry, Alex. That's not what I meant."

I finally turned to find deep mocha eyes and a soft smile turned up toward me.

"Sorry?"

The only time my mother ever apologized was to get something from me. I realized Aria wasn't my mom, but the way she had been treating me since I met her had me wondering if I had some weird mother complex.

I felt nauseous.

"Yes, Alex. I am sorry I said that back at your place about people only liking you for your looks or money. It was mean, and I was hurt. But, that's no excuse. Maybe I'm not as confident in my art as I would like to be. When you bought my work, I felt validated that someone other than my friends liked my paintings."

"Your artwork is amazing, Aria. It's what first drew me to you."

She wrinkled her nose, and it was the most adorable thing I had ever seen.

"Really? Thank you." She took a breath and smiled at me. "And, I have to say, your place is to die for. I'm not just talking about how big it is or those hi-tech security gadgets, I mean your taste in art. I'm jealous."

"How about we start over?" I held out my hand to her. "Hi. I'm Alex Hawthorne. I'm a rich recluse who only buys artwork by the most talented artists the world has ever seen."

She smiled and took my hand to shake. "Hi, I'm Aria Dixon. I'm a not-so-struggling artist who just had a famous art collector buy all of her work."

I laughed and held her hand for a moment too long. I could tell because of the way she was staring at my hand and quickly pulled her arm away.

"Is that the second or third time we tried to start over?" Aria asked as she wrinkled her nose again and glanced at a broom in the corner.

"If we don't count the first time in the basement garage—"

"Technically, you never told me who you were in the basement. Bradley told us his name, but you never said anything."

I shoved my hands into my pockets also glancing at the broom in the corner. "Yeah, about that. Bradley, who happens to be the head of my security, wanted to make sure I was safe. We didn't mean to scare you. I didn't think it was a good idea to take you to that dark room but he insisted for safety."

Aria waved her hands. "Don't worry about it. I thought it was kind of fun. We were on an adventure and besides, I've dealt with worse. Morgana was the one who peed herself. But I made it up to her and bought her some cake so she was happy in the end."

I made two mental notes at that moment: 1. What had Aria dealt with that being trapped by two men in a dark basement wasn't the worst thing? And 2. I'll have to send Aria's roommate a cake from my personal baker.

"I never thought you were a prostitute."

As long as we were clearing the air I felt like that really needed to be cleaned up.

"Then why were you offering to pay me to have sex with you?" Aria pointed toward the door.

"That's not what I meant when I said I wanted to hire you. I wanted you to paint a mural in my bedroom. You're so talented and I wanted something unique just for me."

And I wanted a chance to get to know the woman I had been fantasizing about for three years.

I tried to look at Aria again but I felt the heat rising in my neck. My eyes landed on a large yellow bucket resting against the back wall.

"Wow. I was way off on that one." She grimaced. "Sorry."

I tried to laugh to ease the tension but it ended up as a snort. Glancing at Aria, she had her hand over her mouth obviously holding back a laugh.

"I know my reputation, Aria, and it really isn't what you think—"

"Alex, it's none of my business. Really, what you do in your bedroom is, well, I guess it is sort of my business now that I am going to paint a mural."

My eyes widened, and I thought my heart was going to pop out of my chest. "Really? So that's a yes to painting a mural for me?"

She nodded. Without thinking, I opened my arms and picked her up for a big hug. Aria was soft and smelled sweet and airy, like spring. I didn't normally go around hugging people but I was ecstatic.

"Alex?" Aria said, her voice muffled.

"Right. I'm sorry. I should put you down now."

Only I didn't. I squeezed her tighter. Not only that, but I sniffed her. Not a subtle intake of breath; no, my awkwardness around this woman had no bounds. It was the loud and obvious sniff variety. It was her hair, too. Her silky, honey hair was right by my nose so it's not like I could help myself.

I heard a creak from behind us as a cool rush of air filled the closet.

"Found them." A very male voice came from behind me. "And they still have their clothes on so it's okay to look."

I finally let go of Aria. Actually, I let her soft body slowly slide down mine trying to milk every second I could. When I turned, I saw stern blue eyes staring daggers at me. It was Aria's friend, Evaleen, and behind her was the owner of the male voice, the bartender.

"We meet again. I'll be taking my friend back." She reached inside and helped Aria move past me. Before she left, Evaleen turned back toward me. "I suggest for your own well-being you stop stalking my friend Aria. Or I might have to give your mother a call."

Evaleen knew who I was. But what surprised me even more was that she knew my mother was a threat.

FIVE

Aria

"It's so big." Tiffany's mouth fell open as her head dropped back taking in the full length.

"I know, it's as if the old stiff was compensating for something." I chuckled, tilting my head back to gaze up at the tip.

"Compensating? But it's a building. And I thought you told me Alexander Hawthorne wasn't old? You said he looked younger than you."

Turning my head, I found a confused Tiffany glancing between me and Alexander's building.

"Alexander didn't build this, he just owns it. It was built in the 1920s. I know enough about Chicago Architecture to know that whoever designed the Haute Tower was old, male, and has long since died. Being one of the tallest buildings at the time, I can almost guarantee he felt sad about his lack of manhood so he decided to take it out on the world by building a large phallic symbol."

Tiffany frowned. "I don't think I can ever walk into a building again without thinking of old men with penis issues."

"You're welcome." I curtsied. "Now, come help me design the crap out of the wall of a recluse's bedroom."

Tiffany nodded. We began to move toward the front entrance but as I was about to push through the revolving door, something made me stop. A shiver ran up my spine as if someone was staring at me so I turned. Searching the various people walking up and down the sidewalks of the city, I found no eyes turned my way.

I shook my head and shrugged it off along with the still bitter cold of an early spring day once we were inside. Glancing around, I was surprised by the small lobby. The slabs of dark marble that covered everything made it appear smaller than it should. My eyes landed on the two metal elevators behind a security desk.

Last time I was here, we came in through the garage. And, I was pretty sure staring at the elevator wall wasn't automatically going to take me to his floor like it did for Alex.

"Did he tell you to call him when we arrived?" Tiffany's innocent brown eyes darted around like a lost puppy.

"He doesn't know about this," I said.

"You didn't tell him I was coming? I thought he was okay with me helping layout the design on his walls?"

Tiffany went to school for design. She never graduated as her son David surprised her and her deceased husband. A year before she graduated she left school to become a mother and wife.

She works from home now doing graphic design, and I thought she would be the perfect person to help me with the layout of my mural.

"I never had a chance to talk to him about it. Don't worry, Tiffany, it's not like he's going to hold us against our will. He only did that once, and he has since apologized for it." I shook my head and patted Tiffany on the back.

Alex never contacted me after asking me to paint the mural last Thursday. It's Tuesday and since I still haven't heard from him, I figured I would stop by to pay him a visit. I figured the worst-case scenario would be him telling us to come back another day to start the work.

I tried to make my way toward the elevators before I heard a deep voice. "Can I help you two ladies?"

The security man, with graying hair and a thick neck, glanced in my direction through weary eyes.

"Yes, we are here to see Mr. Alexander Hawthorne."

His lip ticked up as he pushed back his black security hat. "Is that so."

I nodded but he didn't say anything, only folded his hands in front of his belly while leaning back in his chair.

"Do I take one of these elevators or do you need to call him?" I waved my hands at him because he wasn't doing anything. As far as security guards go, he wasn't very good.

"Oh, how rude of me. Just take that door right there. It should be obvious what to do next."

I glanced at the door near the far wall. "But . . . that has an Exit sign over it . . ."

He waved me over. I came to stand as close as I could with his wooden desk in the way. Leaning toward him, he lifted his hand as if to whisper something to me, "It's to fool all the reporters and unwanted people."

When I pulled away he winked.

Waving Tiffany over, we walked over to the Exit door and pushed. It was hard to open but we managed to shove through before stumbling onto the pavement.

"We're in an alley," Tiffany said.

"That asshole."

The door slammed behind us and I noticed we were standing next to a dumpster beside the building we were just in.

How am I supposed to paint Alex's bedroom if I can't even get into his place?

"I'm going back in there and tell that man exactly who I am and that Alex is going to be *very* upset that he prevented me from meeting him."

I realized I sounded terrible but I was mad. At the very least he could call Alex to make sure I could go up. That lazy guard couldn't even do that.

"Aria, no, I don't think that's—"

I threw my arms in the air. "He's going to be very sorry he messed with Aria Dixon. *Very sorry*. When I'm through with him, I'll—"

The door that we just came through swung open. A police officer stood in the middle of the doorframe and stared at us.

"Are you two ladies lost?" The tall, lanky officer who seemed too young to hold a badge stepped out into the alleyway and right behind him was the security guard twat.

"Oh, no, Officer, we were just leaving," Tiffany said as she grabbed my arm trying to pull me away but I was having none of that.

"Yes, we are lost. And when we asked this guard how to find our way, he led us to this alleyway. Seems a little bit suspicious to me." I tugged my arm away from Tiffany and folded my arms, firming my stance.

"Is that so?" the officer said as he pushed his hat back.

I narrowed my eyes, glancing at the officer and then at the security guard. "Are you two related?"

"Yes," they answered at the same time.

Now I'll never get into see Alex.

"Mr. Hawthorne has no visitors scheduled for today. The only way to see Mr. Hawthorne is with a scheduled visit, unless you are his mother." The guard leaned forward as to inspect us closer. "And neither of you two ladies look like his mother." The guard leaned back against the doorframe.

"But I am his mother." A deep feminine voice came from behind the security guard causing him to jump.

He turned and nodded his head profusely. "Yes, Mrs. Hawthorne. Forgive me, I didn't see you there."

"It's all right, Mitch. I can vouch for these ladies. I'll take them to see my son."

I smirked at the officer and guard as I passed them, walking back into the building. That was nice of Alex's mom to help us out. He must have told her about me. Maybe she had seen my paintings and wanted to be in on the design. While it's his room, I think a feminine perspective might be helpful.

"Thank you, Mrs. Hawthorne. I'm Aria Dixon," I said as I followed her past the elevators behind the guard desk to another door.

"I know who both of you are," Mrs. Hawthorne said.

My eyes widened as I turned my head to Tiffany. I understand how Mrs. Hawthorne would know who I was, but how would she know Tiffany?

Tiffany appeared as confused as me.

When we entered the other room, I noticed an elevator. It seemed to know Mrs. Hawthorne was coming as it opened as she drew near. The doors started to close so Tiffany and I picked up our pace to hop inside. The door nearly closed on Tiffany's red scarf, but she yanked it away in time.

As the lift began to move, I held my hand out to Mrs. Hawthorne. "It's so lovely to meet you."

She turned her head toward me and I noticed her eyes at once. So much like her son's but with age they seemed to darken to a worn iron. There was an air of polish about her, but with a little too much shine. Her high cheekbones held unusually tight, blemish free skin. Even her beautiful raven hair, that glistened in the florescent light of the elevator, appeared so perfectly coiffed into a French twist I had to stare at her roots to make sure it wasn't a wig.

There was a familiarity about Mrs. Hawthorne. I couldn't imagine she came to any of the bars I tended. Perhaps I saw her at an art show once.

She scrutinized me with precision before producing the tiniest smile and turning back to face the metal doors.

"I don't mean to be rude, but I prefer not to touch people if I don't have to."

Okay.

I slid my eyes toward Tiffany as she frowned. Tiffany pushed her hands into her pockets and I wondered if she had wanted to shake Mrs. Hawthorne's hand too.

The elevator stopped and the doors flew open. We followed Mrs. Hawthorne down the art-filled hall and through the haunted door, right into Alex's living room. It was even more beautiful in the daytime with light from the windows overlooking the river and the city. It was as if the window was one of the art pieces.

"Mom, what are you . . .? Aria?"

I turned to find Alex dressed in low hanging sweatpants and no shirt. Heat gathered between my legs and I immediately removed my puffy coat. I will, one day, want this room as my eternal resting place, I just didn't want that time to start today. If I left the coat on, I might perish due to heat exposure and possible ovary explosion.

"There's my boy." His mother walked over to him, cupping his cheeks and kissing both.

"Why are you all wet?" she asked and I instantly glanced down at my jeans for fear my ovaries had already burst.

"I just got out of the shower. Why are you here?"

With relief I realized Mrs. Hawthorne wasn't referring to what was between my legs. But that didn't stop my ovaries from threatening total meltdown when I saw Alex's hypno-eyes staring at me.

Heat was migrating up my body to my cheeks, and I knew I wasn't the only one taken in by this reclusive Adonis. I turned to find Tiffany staring at Alex's bare chest.

"To help you of course. I hear you wish to have a mural painted in your bedroom by your artist friend, Ms. Dixon." She waved her hand at me that glittered from the various diamond rings that littered her fingers.

"But it's *my* bedroom, Mother. I don't need your input." Alex folded his arms in front of his chest. You would think that would help cool me down, but the way his arms grew bigger, his muscles tighter, I almost drooled at the sight. I could hear Tiffany whimper beside me.

"Alexander, sweet boy, I let you live in this building. Where do you think your money comes from? If you wish to change something, I must have input on it. It's in the lease." She placed her hand on Alex's arm but immediately pulled it back and wiped her palm on her black, wool pencil skirt.

SIX

Alexander

"That's all wrong," my mother said for the tenth time today.

Mother had nixed every idea Aria had come up with so far. Aria and her friend, Tiffany, had been nice and accommodating but I could tell Aria was becoming frustrated. Not as frustrated as me, but I don't think it's humanly possible for anyone to get as frustrated as me.

"Mom, I appreciate your input. Maybe it would be easier for Aria if you told her what you would like to see on the wall." I ran my fingers through my hair.

Being this close to Aria made my fingers want to curl and tense. I settled on scratching my nails on my scalp—the only acceptable tension relief I could do in front of company.

I thought the mural would be a great way to do something personal, for *me*. Not just that, but spend some time with Aria. It's not that I got a lot of chances to hang out with sexy, talented women. It might be an excuse to have her near me, but now I wanted to tear everything down by hand.

My mom walked up to the wall and stood silently. I rubbed my face because I knew what she was doing. She didn't want this mural. She hated that I went behind her back to do something she didn't request personally.

Angry and humiliated, that as a twenty-six-year-old billionaire the only thing I was allowed to do without my mother getting involved was buy art. It's the one thing that she knew I had taste in.

Plus, it added value. Art was an investment, and she preferred anything that would give her more money.

"I'm thinking we leave things the way they are. I love this wallpaper. It's silk, you know." She turned with a smile meant to impress the women in this room.

"Then why am I here?" Aria pointed to the wall with one hand and waved her small sketch pad in the other.

"I'm sorry, Ms. Dixon, but my son gets ideas sometimes. And while I think they are cute, he has to realize he isn't eight anymore," she said.

I gritted my teeth as she walked over to me, adjusting the collar on the blue button-up shirt I put on after everyone came into my bedroom.

"That's right, Mother, I'm a grown man so I expect to be able to make a decision about my home without you or anyone taking over." I pushed her hands away.

Her eyes widened and she opened her mouth. I braced myself for the rainstorm of insults that always came. I knew she hated me standing up for myself. My mother still believed when we were in front of company I was expected to speak when spoken to and to do as I was told.

Despite the fact that every time I stood up for myself, ever since I was a kid, my mother ripped me apart, I did it anyway.

She's talented. Like Aria with her artwork, my mother knew how to find your soul with her words and shake it until it was nothing more than a regret-filled mess.

But this time was different. These weren't her friends, these were people I knew. People who came here specifically to see me, not her. I refused to let her hurt them or control them like she did everyone else in her life.

When she finally spoke, I was surprised by her words. What she said was strange, even for her.

"Alexander, you are right. It's time I let you spread your wings. What harm could come from this artist," she waved toward Aria but kept her eyes on me, "painting a wall? I'm sure whatever you two come up with will be lovely. I trust you, Alexander."

My mother patted my shoulder before heading toward the door. As she was about to turn toward the hall she turned back. "Ms. Dixon. I will have my lawyers fax over the lease so you can find out what is not allowed to be done to the walls of this place."

I stared at the door long after my mother disappeared.

"Are you okay, Alex?" Aria's voice and her light touch on my arm broke me from my shock. A shiver ran up my body and I turned to stare at her beautiful red lips.

"She trusts me. You both heard her, right? She said she trusted me," I said as I pointed to the empty doorframe.

"Yes, I heard it," Tiffany said.

"Of course. Why wouldn't she trust you?" Aria said before she chuckled and shook her head.

Because my mother hated me.

"Yes. Why wouldn't she trust me?" I tried to laugh too but it was a struggle.

"Mr. Hawthorne." Tiffany took the sketch pad out of Aria's hand and brought it to me. "Aria has come up with many designs this morning. Did you want to use any of them or do something else?"

I flipped through the pages and loved every single idea she had. There was one thing she drew that caught my eye but I wanted to change it slightly.

I glanced up to find two pair of eyes filled with anticipation staring at me.

"How about we discuss this over food? It's already noon."

"Actually, I have to go and get back to the hospital. I didn't realize it was already lunchtime." Tiffany gathered her coat from the bed.

"Which hospital?" I asked.

Aria glanced at Tiffany. They both went quiet and I wondered if I had said something wrong.

"The Children's Hospital just off of Michigan Avenue," Tiffany said as she shrugged on her thick black coat.

I smiled. "That's interesting you work there because I donate to them every year."

"Oh, I don't work there. My son is a patient."

Now I knew why they were silent. I felt terrible assuming she worked there.

"Forgive me. I didn't realize you had a son." I walked over to Tiffany.

"It's all right." She glanced up at me. Her deep brown eyes seemed to radiate sadness. It made me fear why he was in the hospital.

I recognized that pain in her eyes. It's the same thing I saw in my mother's eyes. Not so much anymore, but when I was young there were days she would lay in bed crying. I hated to see her like that but what was worse was how that sadness turned to hate.

I cupped Tiffany's hand between both of mine. "I'm sorry he has to be in there. I don't know him and I have only just met you, but I can tell you love him very much."

She nodded, biting her lip. Tiffany lowered her head and I noticed a tear falling to the floor.

"No matter what happens, Tiffany. Whether your boy walks out of that hospital tomorrow or never does, know that the absolute best thing in the world for him is your love."

"Thank you, Mr. Hawthorne," Tiffany said as she raised her head, tears streaming down her cheeks.

"Please, call me Alex."

She nodded and gave me a hug. "Thank you, Alex. I'm glad you are getting your mural and that you aren't a crazy recluse," she whispered before letting me go.

I needed to look into finding a good PR company. Does everyone assume I'm crazy?

Once Tiffany left, I turned to find Aria staring at me. The way her arms were folded over her chest and her eyelids narrowed I thought she might be upset with me.

"Is something wrong?"

"Yes," she said.

"Maybe you want to elaborate so I can understand what is upsetting you."

Aria shook her head and walked over to me. I noticed how her purple sweater seemed to cling to her curves. What I really focused on were her tits. I wondered if she was even wearing a bra. I knew I shouldn't be thinking that, but I kept imagining lifting that piece of cashmere and discovering only smooth skin underneath.

"Tiffany is a good person. She cares about her son very much, and I think it's shitty what you want to do with her."

"Where is this coming from?"

Did I say something I shouldn't have? Again?

"You know exactly what I am talking about, Mr. Hawthorne." Aria stuck her finger into my chest.

"No, I really don't, Aria. And stop calling me Mr. Hawthorne. Mr. Hawthorne was my father. I asked you to call me Alex."

She pushed her finger deeper into my chest and it was starting to hurt. "Do you always take advantage of women in pain? Don't think I haven't heard about you. About what happened to that young mother and her baby."

Not this again. Why was it when the press did find out something about me they only focused on the negative?

"You shouldn't believe everything you read." I grabbed her finger to pull it away from my chest, but I hadn't let go.

"I didn't, Alex. But from what I just witnessed, I'm starting to wonder if the article I read was right."

I never cared about what anyone said about me or the lies they spread about my family. Ridiculous lies about my parents and even more crazy ones about me. It never hurt before because my mom and dad agreed on only one thing while I was growing up and that was that the press said anything to get people to buy their papers or watch their news show. Journalists were never to be trusted.

If both my parents agreed on something, then it must be true because they never agreed on anything.

"If you believe that, Aria, then you might as well believe all the other crazy things the papers have said about my family. Like how my mother has a secret love child with my uncle, and my grandfather got angry and had his own son killed. Or, maybe the one where I have a twin out there that I don't know about. And the best one of all. The one where my mother had my father killed and is planning to take over the government. If Shakespeare were alive, he'd love to write a play based on those wild tales."

She held up her hands but kept her eyes on the ground. "Look, I get it—"

"No, Aria, you really don't get it. I may not know what it's like to struggle to pay bills or worry if I have enough money to eat or pay rent or put gas in the car to get to work. I'm lucky in life. Real lucky, but it doesn't mean I haven't gone through things in life."

I took a breath and grabbed her shoulders, forcing Aria to look at me. "And it doesn't mean I'm some cold, spoiled monster ready to take a young mother in with her small child, only to have them booted from the country."

SEVEN

Aria

*"**Firm and long**, just how I like it,"* I said as I pushed it past my lips. "Mmm. It's sweet too. Uh, it's dripping. Better lick that up." My tongue flicked at the tip to draw the sweet cream into my mouth.

I sucked on the cannoli as I stared at Alex. He wouldn't look at me. For the past fifteen minutes, we had been eating in his huge dining room. Me on one end of a massive, rectangular, dark wooden table and him at the other.

Alex had his head down, staring at his food as he ate. I pulled the pastry out of my mouth and placed it back on the white china dessert plate.

"I'm sorry, Alex. There, are you happy? That's the third time I had to apologize for misjudging you."

He lifted his head. "Here's an idea, Aria, why don't you stop judging people? Maybe, and I get this may be a novel concept for you, but maybe take the time to get to know them."

I clenched my jaw, pissed at him. Here I was trying to make amends and he had to rub my nose in it.

"Some of us don't have the luxury of getting to know men. Some of us have to do what we can to protect the people we love before we get to know strangers," I said and immediately wish I hadn't.

Alex raised his head even farther, sitting at his full height. I surprised him. I didn't mean to, but he seemed to know how to push my buttons.

I wish he had accepted my apology and moved on, or just kicked me out. Anything but the curious eyes of a recluse.

"Why would getting to know someone be a luxury? You appear to have friends, Aria. Tiffany and those two women from a few weeks ago, Morgana and Evaleen. You must have taken the time to get to know them?"

I took a bite of the cannoli. No point in pretending to give it a blow job anymore to get Alex's attention. I got it, and now I wish he would stare at his food again.

"That's different," I said after I swallowed the dessert.

"How is that different? Are they robots? Do they not count as people?"

Taking the napkin, I wiped my mouth before leaning back against the chair.

"What about you, Alex? Or should I call you Mr. Recluse?"

Alex pushed back his chair, got up, and walked over. I tried not to stare at his very worn and very fitted sweat pants but the closer he got, the more I focused on what I shouldn't.

My eyes became level with his as he sat in the seat next to me. "I wasn't talking about me. I was asking about you."

"If you get to ask about me, then I should get to ask about you." I raised my eyebrow.

The corner of his lip ticked up and he nodded. "On one condition."

"You have to take your clothes off," I said.

"What? No."

"I have to take my clothes off?"

"No. That's not what . . . uh, not unless . . . I mean no," he said as his Adam's apple bobbed up and down his neck.

"We both have to take off—"

"Aria, there will be no nakedness." Alex waved his hands at me.

"Fine, but this sounds kind of boring to me." I rolled my eyes.

"You were the one to suggest the questions to begin with."

I shrugged. "I figured you would turn it into a drinking game that required us to remove a piece of clothing for every question answered, or a non-drinking game that required us to remove a piece of clothing for every question."

"You sure do like to get naked." He laughed and it was the sexiest thing in the world.

He had laughed a few times since I met him, but they weren't intense belly laughs—the kind that came from deep within your soul. That was what he was doing now and it was mesmerizing.

"Only in front of men."

His laughter stopped. But it was how he stared at me that caused my smile to fade too. Those hypnotic eyes drifted to my lips and stayed. They sat so long glued to some imaginary string attached to my mouth that it wasn't until Bradley entered the room that Alex moved.

"Alex, a fax came from your mother."

He glanced up as Bradley walked over. Bradley's eyes bounced between us and I couldn't tell if he was surprised to see me here with Alex or worried.

"Yes, the lease. Here you go, Aria. You can read the bylaws about what is permissible here." Alex slid the paperwork over to me. When my fingers grazed his as I took the document, I was caught off guard. The spark shot up my arm and straight to my mouth, causing me to gasp.

"Alex, can I have a word with you?" Bradley said while staring at me.

"Of course. I'll be right back, Aria." Alex gave me a soft smile before he stood and walked off.

Once the two men left the room, I wiped my hands and lips with the cloth napkin from my cannoli show. The food we had for lunch was delicious. I figured Alex would order pizza but when he told me he had a personal chef, I almost swooned like a Victorian woman who wore her corset too tight and was prone to fainting.

I had to take advantage of that. When it came to food, I was a whore. There's no food that I would turn down. I had no shame as to what went into my mouth—from a cheap, street corner dirty-water dog to a tarted up steak at a classy restaurant, I didn't discriminate.

Sitting back against the surprisingly comfortable wooden chairs I massaged my belly as if it contained a precious baby and not a three-course meal. After reflecting wistfully at the empty plates, I grabbed the lease and perused it while Alex was out of the room.

Most of it was standard contract jargon that I was familiar with. I may only be an artist but my father was a lawyer. When my sister and I were young, we would play in his home office and he gave us old contracts to entertain ourselves. After a while we asked him what certain words or phrases would mean. I retained a lot of what he told me.

I also remember a lot of the terrible things he showed me.

I stopped when I noticed one paragraph in particular. It made me wonder about Mrs. Hawthorne's words from earlier. But before I could ponder more, Alex came back into the room. He reached a hand toward me.

"My mother wanted my lawyer to look at the lease. I wasn't meant to hand it off to you, Aria. Sorry."

I reluctantly lifted the contract and placed it into Alex's hand. "But she told me to look at it so I knew what not to do to the walls."

Alex glanced down at the papers in his hand. "That's my mom for you. She will tell you anything you want to hear to your face, but make everyone else force you to do what she really wants. Bradley just got confused when he handed over the lease."

He was about to walk away when I stopped him. "Do you own this building?"

Alex turned back to face me and lifted his arm to rest on the doorframe. The fabric of his shirt tightened around his bicep and I couldn't keep my eyes off it.

"No, actually, my mother owns the building. My mother is the one with all the money. When my father died twenty years ago, she got the bulk of his estate and money. That's why I can't do anything without her approval."

I shook my head confused and tried to piece together my thoughts. "But you're a billionaire. You're famous for being a billionaire."

Alex walked back over to the table and sat back in his seat, throwing the paperwork on the table. "Again, that's my mother. She wants the world to think I am the most eligible bachelor. She likes to control people, even me, and she controls how the world sees me. I'm surprised she let you and Tiffany in here today. As far as I knew, my mother didn't know about you."

"She knew who we were." I chuckled, turning my head toward the table.

"What?"

"Nothing." I shook my head and turned my attention back to him. "Alex, this may be none of my business but have you read that contract?"

"No. I have a lawyer for that. That's why I have to send it over to him."

Alex leaned forward about to get up. He placed his hand on top of the lease, hesitating when I gently laid my hand on top of his.

"Your lawyer has seen this lease before?" I don't mean to sound annoying asking so many questions but the more he answered them the more confused I became.

He nodded. "Of course. There have been small revisions over the years for building upgrades to meet city code regulations, but most of it has stayed the same. He has seen this many times."

"It's just . . . You know what? Never mind. I probably read something wrong. It's been years since I eagle-eyed a contract." I shook my head.

That must be it. I'm sure an experienced lawyer that got paid top dollar had a better handle on this lease than I did.

Alex paused for a second but finally stood taking the lease with him. When he got to the door he turned toward me. "Was there something in here that didn't seem right?"

I waved my hand at him. "I'm sure your lawyer would know more than me."

Instead of smiling for reassurance, I frowned. What I saw in that lease was either one hell of a typo or his lawyer needed to be fired.

His lifted his arm against the doorframe again. The combination of his thick, corded muscle straining against his shirt and his soulful gray eyes was too much for me to resist. He didn't have to utter a word and I broke. I tried to play it off. The last time I meddled in someone else's financial life they disappeared.

I swore then I would only ever worry about food, art, and hot men bringing me orgasms from that point on. Here I am with two and a half of the three satisfied.

And yet, with almost nothing to distract me from using my awesome contract superpower, I screwed with Alex's life. I told him something that was none of my business because sometimes I can't seem to shut up.

"According to that lease, your mother doesn't own the building. You do, Alex."

EIGHT

Alexander

"Congratulations, Mr. Hawthorne, you are the proud owner of the Haute Tower at 26 East Lake Street in Chicago Illinois," the man in the gray, oversized suit said as he sat across the conference table from me.

I stared at him in disbelief. How did I not know this? My lawyer never said a word to me. When Aria told me last Tuesday I didn't believe her. I mentioned wanting time to consider her sketches for the mural and told her I would call her when I was ready.

I spent the week since making phone calls and researching what I could. Most everyone gave me the run around when I asked them about the building. I finally told my lawyer he would be fired if he didn't tell me the truth. He repeated over and over again that he needed to see the lease to verify if anything had been changed.

So, I faxed it to him. When he called back, he told me that nothing had changed and my mother still owned the building but he did notice a small typo that might have thrown me off. Other than that, nothing had changed.

"Are you sure it's not a typo?" I asked leaning forward, resting my elbows on the smooth wooden table. The windows behind the man were dark and I caught my reflection in the glass. It looked like I hadn't slept in days. Probably because I hadn't.

Between my mother giving in so easily with the mural and the lease stating I owned the tower, my world felt upside down. Causing old issues to rear their controlling head. Aria wasn't far off when she stated I was a crazy recluse.

The door opened and a petite woman with short black hair walked in. She stared at me and something about her seemed familiar. She placed a water bottle in front of me and Mr. Reed.

"Thank you, Grace." He smiled up at her but her eyes were glued to me.

She scurried out before I could ask if I knew her. I shook my head and turned back to Mr. Reed.

"No, I don't see any typos. Your name is repeated not just in this paragraph, which states ownership, but in several other points throughout this contract. It's actually an Emma Hawthorne that leases the penthouse from you."

My mother.

"How long have I owned it? Can you tell if this is a recent change?"

He brought the paper close to his face and lifted his glasses. "The last change to this lease was dated five years ago. Before that I wouldn't know and would have to see the previous documents to answer further."

She lied to me. My mother has been lying all this time. I knew she was cruel and controlling and even manipulated my image to the public, but I thought she was at least honest with me about my inheritance. Based on how little my father wanted to do with me I figured she was right when she said he left me almost nothing.

"If you have no further questions, Mr. Hawthorne, it's after hours here at Mimir and I would like to go home to my wife for dinner." Mr. Reed, the property lawyer for the online retail giant, Mimir, pushed the contract back to me as I waved for him to go.

"I'll let your wife know we are done in here," he said as he made his way out of the room.

I was still in too much shock to correct his marital views about Aria.

After a few moments, there was movement from the door behind me. "Well, how did it go? Is that your second penis or not?" Aria said as her sweet scent drifted around and she took a seat next to me.

"Huh?" I said as I glanced over to her warm mocha eyes. I think I smiled, too.

Even if the first few times meeting Aria were chaotic, it felt good to finally have someone I could trust to talk to. After she left last week, I picked up her sketch book, the one she scrawled her phone number on, and I picked up my phone. I wanted to hear her voice, tell her everything but one word stopped me.

Crazy.

Those rumors about me being a crazy recluse who pays to hang out with women, it's all true.

Aria wrinkled her nose causing my smile to widen. "Do you own the building?"

She formed a circle with her hands and moved them up and down like she was giving a hand job to an abnormally large penis, "You know, phallic-shaped buildings. Ohh, yeah, I do love me some building. That's it, baby, work my *building*."

I grabbed her wrists stopping her and glanced around to make sure her friend, Evaleen, the one who let us use Mimir's lawyer and conference room, didn't walk in.

"Jesus, Aria. What are you, a teenager?"

"No, I'm twenty-nine but in my heart, I'm a horny eighteen-year-old." She winked at me.

My cock went hard instantly. The way she was so casual and free with sex and her artistic talent . . . she made me want to do things to her body I only fantasized about. Things that she might not like.

I cleared my throat, dropping her wrists. "Yes, I own the building."

She jumped up from the chair and threw her arms open. "That's wonderful, Alex! Now you can do whatever changes you want."

Aria stood there, her arms still wide and I knew she wanted to give me a hug. I wanted to do that too, but something stopped me. The same thing that stopped me from going up to her in that gallery when I first noticed her years ago.

I nodded. "Yes, I can pick one of your drawings now. Maybe even tear down the wall and make the room bigger."

My mind raced with ideas. I felt like a child let loose in an amusement park with no one there. Any ride free to enjoy but which to pick first? My gaze fell to her breasts.

"So, no hug then?" Aria's lips ticked up.

"We should keep this professional. How we started off meeting wasn't right. I want to keep things on track," I said as I focused on gathering the paperwork.

I was such a liar. Of course, I wanted to hug her. I wanted to do lots of things to her, but if she ever found out the truth about me I know I would lose her forever. I'd rather have Aria for a short time in my life than not at all.

"Fair enough. Let's at least shake on it."

Aria pushed her hand out. Setting the papers down, I turned in my seat but didn't stand. Staring at her fingers my imagination went wild. Thoughts of those digits pressing into me, pulling and using me for their pleasure.

Just shaking her hand was a summit to climb but I had to do it. She already thought I was odd being a recluse. I didn't want to add to it by being too afraid to touch her.

"Of course." I slid my fingers across her palm. Her skin as smooth and warm as I remembered.

Maybe even softer than before. I wondered if I firmed my grip, would she give?

"There, now was that so hard?" I noticed her eyes dip to where I actually was hard.

She knew. Aria wasn't stupid, she could tell I wanted her. That would mean one thing. She was going to try. Aria was going to give. Give me what she knew I wanted.

I shook my head, unable to form words.

She released my grip but moved both hands to cup my palm, tickling my wrist with her fingers.

"Wow, you have such smooth skin, Alex."

It hurt. My cock was in pain.

"Why are you doing this, Aria?" I said, my voice rough.

"Because I want you, Alex. It's that simple. When two people are attracted to each other, they should be together. They fuck. Get it out of their system or keep fucking, but they do something. To pretend there is no attraction because of some societal pressure is ridiculous. This isn't the nineteenth century."

Her words from before popped into my head—how people only wanted me for my money and looks. Was she like that? My mother warned me that's how women were. How she tried to protect me by making sure I met with the right kind of woman.

Which was never the right kind. They were the bought kind.

I pulled my hand away. "So what if I'm attracted to you. Yes, Aria, I think you're beautiful. I could fill a thousand canvases with the curves and shades of your eyes. And your lips, the dips and bends. How they plump and swell after you've bitten them while deep in thought. I'd use oils and brush with delicate strokes before smearing the color with my fingers."

Pushing the chair away as I stood, not caring my hard-on was clearly visible. She was pushing me and it was working. The words coming out of my mouth I never spoke to anyone.

"But that's cheap, isn't it? Maybe you like cheap." I inched closer forcing her up against the table. "Do you like it cheap, Aria? Pretty words about a pretty face you can't help but wear."

Her eyes fluttered as she grasped the edge of the table to hold herself up. "Maybe I do."

Aria tried to push back, stand taller, and it was cute and sexy and I wanted to laugh.

"But I have money. You pointed that out many times. It's the reason we're here, in this room. Why would I want to throw cheap things at you when I could give you anything you've ever dreamed of? Isn't that what you want from me? The wild ride. The one that takes your breath away and shines like gold."

Her chest rose and fell with a quickened pace the more I spoke. I shouldn't have said all that. But as much as I wanted her, as much as she thought she wanted me, I would never be used by a woman again.

"Yes," Aria whispered.

I leaned forward, ghosting the words across her neck. "As much as I want to give you the ride of your life, it's your talent that does it for me. It gets me hard and makes me weak. I want to see that gift when I wake in the morning and just as I drift to sleep at night. So, words are cheap and sex is primal, but your art is my life."

I don't know how I did it, but I turned and walked to the door. Before I opened it, I turned back to find her still leaning against the table, her cheeks flushed.

"I'll take you home. I want you rested and ready tomorrow when you bring your gift to life in my bedroom."

NINE

<u>Aria</u>

That was some vibrator worthy talk.

After Alex and I left the Mimir building last night, he had his car take me home. I went straight to my room and got out my beloved vibrator. I worked out a few orgasms before I felt like a normal human again and not some repressed teenager.

I wanted to fuck Alex so bad.

It's becoming frustratingly obvious that Alexander is unlike any guy I had been with. Not that I've been with him sexually. He eloquently stated why that won't happen.

I like cheap and he doesn't fuck cheap.

Why should I be surprised? I shouldn't, based on his money, his looks, and his power in the art world. He probably has supermodels with huge tits and long legs begging to come over so he can feed them his cannoli.

What did I have? A flat chest and body so petite that I'm not tall enough to go on some rides at amusement parks. Maybe that's why I sleep with so many men. I'm compensating for my lack of . . . well, everything.

What made this worse? That I had to see him every day so I could paint his mural. I hope I don't fuck this up. Literally.

Even now, as I ride the elevator up to his condo, I try my best to push last night out of my head. How he both complimented me and ripped me apart in just a few words.

I kept my head down as the doors opened. I wouldn't let his amazing art distract me. The door was left open and I did my best to remember where his bedroom was.

I think I made the wrong turn down a hall because I entered a small room with lots of television screens.

"What are you doing in here?" A deep voice came from behind.

I gasped, turning to find Bradley standing in the doorway.

I covered my rapidly beating heart. "You scared me. I seem to be lost. I thought this was Alex's bedroom."

"Sure you did." He stepped back and waved me out.

"What?" I said as I walked past him.

"Alex's bedroom is at the end of that hallway." He pointed to the other end of the hall where it turned to the right.

Before I could ask him again what he meant, he stepped into the room I recently left and closed the door.

Asshole.

After making it to the end of the correct hallway I noticed the door to Alex's bedroom was open so I gave a swift knock on the door and stepped inside. Glancing around, Alex was nowhere to be found but my sketch pad was on the padded leather bench at the end of his bed.

Walking over I picked it up. The page was turned to the sketch I was hoping he would pick. It was a risk since most people want pretty or serene murals. This was the opposite with so much going on. Color, movement, and chaos made it feel as if it was coming to life.

"Good, you're here." Alex's voice created a myriad of sensations colliding at once under my skin.

My head rose as I did my best to temper those thoughts, quash those feelings, and dampen my need.

"Yes. Just as you asked. You did say ten in the morning last night in the car, didn't you?"

I caught the wobble in my voice and hoped he hadn't.

He looked amazing today. Better than I fantasized about last night or the night before or every night since I met him. His light blue sweater fit him like it was made for him. Based on his account size, it probably was. And those jeans were tight enough that when he turned to look at the wall where the mural was going, I fist pumped the air.

That man had a great ass. Don't know why I was so excited about that. It wasn't like I was going to be able to touch it.

"I see you picked my Art History mural."

Alex turned back from inspecting the wall. "Yes. Clearly, it's the best. It shows my love of all art but you added your take on the great masters of the past. I have to say, Aria, I'm blown away."

Damn it. Why was he so nice, too? No man in the world was this perfect. I'm being set up.

I began walking around the room, picking up knickknacks and glancing under the bed.

"What are you doing?"

I stood after I had made sure under the bed was clear. "Looking for hidden cameras."

Alex folded his arms and shook his head. "What? Why would you do that?"

"Because you aren't real. None of this is real." I spread my arms out wide. "There is no man on this planet as perfect as you, Alexander Hawthorne." I came over to him and pointed at his chest.

Okay, maybe I didn't point. Maybe I smoothed my hand up and down his chest. But that's not the point. The point was he's tricking me in some manner.

He glanced down at my hand currently rubbing a hole in his sweater but he didn't remove it. "Why is this okay, Aria? Why do you think coming into my home and putting your hands on me is something okay to do? What if I did that to you?"

I stopped moving my hand but left it resting on his chest. "Then do it."

"What? You actually want me to rub your chest. You think that's fine to do? It's okay if a stranger comes up to you and starts to rub your chest?"

"I never said I was okay for a stranger to do it. I said I was okay for you to do it."

His eyes widened and I knew he would make an excuse. Alex lifted his hand toward mine but I grabbed his wrist before he could get to mine.

"Here, let me help you." I pulled his arm up and placed it on the center of my chest.

We both stood there not moving.

"I'm waiting," I said and couldn't help the smile that crept over my mouth.

This man wanted me as much as I did him, and his views on not being with a cheap woman or whatever excuse he used looked like they were about to falter.

I really hoped they crumbled.

"You want me to grope you?" Alex asked with wide eyes.

As much as I wanted this and much more, it was becoming frustrating. It seemed if I wanted him to touch my body in any way I would have to force him, and that was not okay. I may be a tiny woman and he may be a giant of a man, but I would never force anyone to do anything they didn't want to.

I lowered my hand. "I only want you to do what you want to do, Alex. If your physical attraction to me really disgusts you that much, then don't do anything. I'm not an idiot, I saw your boner last night so don't deny you're attracted to me."

Wrapping my fingers around his arm I tried to pull his hand off my chest, but he wouldn't move.

"I never said I was disgusted with you, Aria, or what feelings I have for you."

I rolled my eyes. "You said I was cheap."

Alex shook his head and puffed out a laugh. "No, I said I would never give you cheap. But what I have to give you might not like. You may run as far as you can from me. Then I would lose a chance to have your beautiful talent on my wall."

It seemed like Alex was about to say more but he stopped and dropped his hand from my chest.

"Why would I run? Is it really tiny?" I said as I crinkled my nose.

He dropped his eyes to the floor as his face grew pink. I thought it was cute that he embarrassed so easily.

"I don't think so."

I took a step back and focused my attention on his crotch. "Did you compare? Or maybe other women might have mentioned you were big? I have to warn you, if women have never mentioned your size before then it's probably small." I frowned and gave him a supportive slap on the arm.

He raised his hand to his face, covering his eyes. "Why would I compare my penis with other guys?"

Shrugging my shoulders, I went over to the leather bench and sat. "I don't know how guys are with each other. Maybe they compare length and girth?"

Alex dropped his hand and came to sit next to me on the bench. Leaning over he lowered his voice. "So, do, uh . . . women compare . . . you know . . . ?"

A bit confused, I tilted my head but realized what he was talking about as his eyes dipped to my chest. "Boobs? Yes and no. Not how you think. It's not like in porn where women get all grabby. Basically, we complain. Women with big boobs complain about back pain and finding a decent bra. While women more like me," I waved a hand over my petite chest, "well, we complain about clothes that are supposed to show cleavage but just end up causing us to flash people. We are united on one thing though . . . bathing suits. All women, no matter what shape or size, all complain about bathing suits."

"Never thought of that. I guess I always imagined the porn part." He rubbed the back of his neck.

"You never answered me, Alex." I turned toward him, scooting an inch closer.

"What?"

"What have women said about your . . ." I waved my finger around his jean-covered cock.

He straightened his back and stared at the wall. "Nothing. Women haven't said anything about my, uh, penis before."

Crap. I had to ask. It's not like a man with a small dick can't be creative in other ways. I once slept with a guy with a small cock who give me multiple orgasms. He was very creative.

I smiled and gave a swift pat on his leg. "Oh, well, I'm sure that doesn't mean—"

"But, then again, no woman has ever seen me naked," Alex said.

TEN

Alexander

"But this body?" Aria said waving her hands around me.

I shouldn't have told her about never being naked in front of a woman. Now, I'm going to have to explain why. That's when I'll lose her forever.

Perhaps if I had kissed her last night or any of the other nights I had the chance, I would have gotten something before she left. Not left with a sad conversation about my penis and a look of horror on her face.

"What about my body?" I said as I glanced down at the zipper on my jeans.

Aria stood and I took in how beautiful she was—savored it because I knew it would be my last chance to admire her this close. She had an amazing purple sweater on that clung to her and all I wanted to do was peel it off.

But that wasn't going to happen.

She knelt in front of me. "You have this beautiful, sexy body and you haven't let women see it? Even covered up with your top and jeans I can tell it's gorgeous underneath. What if I took all the art in your place and hid it away, saying you could never see it again? How would that make you feel?"

"I'm not an object, Aria. Paintings are objects to be admired—a person is not," I said, disappointed at her take on beauty and people.

"You're right, Alex. And I don't mean any woman has the right to feel you up whenever they want, or that you should wear revealing clothing. What I meant is, if you are intimate with someone you should trust them enough to show them. Did you not trust them?"

Aria tucked her legs under herself and sat on her haunches. Her soulful brown eyes wide, seeking answers. Answers I couldn't give her.

"Trust had nothing to do with it." I shook my head. "Why are we talking about this, Aria? Why does this concern you anyway? These are my issues. You are here to paint my mural, not delve into my psyche."

I picked up the sketch pad and handed it to her. She took what I offered, sighing as she studied her drawing. Aria didn't move and refused to lift her head. A minute crept by before her eyes rose, telling a story I was afraid to hear.

"You're right, Alex. I'm just your employee, here to do a job." She stood and turned to face the wall.

Gritting my teeth, I held onto everything that wanted to come out. Every detail of my life, of my frustration, and how she was the first person to get to know me that wasn't controlled by my mother.

I carried the weight but I had grown up learning how to hold that heavy burden. Aria was light and free—everything I wasn't. Everything that drew me to her sweet splendor kept me from reaching out for more.

I stood and walked up behind her. "I didn't mean that—"

She turned and all the warmth had drained from her eyes. "I know what you meant, Alex. Or would you prefer Mr. Hawthorne?"

"I want you to call me Alex. Just because you work for me doesn't mean we can't be friends."

She covered her heart with the pad of paper, cradling it. "Like Bradley? No thank you, Alex. Despite what you think, my friendship can't be bought. You may be used to paying people to be with you, but I have to be honest and tell you that's not healthy. And I won't contribute to that behavior."

Aria turned and headed toward the door of the bedroom. "Since you picked out the picture, it's going to take me a few days to make a large mock up for your wall. I won't be back until next week. Goodbye, Alex."

I watched her turn and walk down the hall before she disappeared. *Damn.*

That wasn't at all how it was supposed to go. I was stupid to think Aria would start to fall for me as she spent more time in this room near me. Like the mural was some aphrodisiac drawing us together. It's as if I have the imagination and emotional maturity of a sixteen-year-old.

And even if she fell for me, what would become of that? There was a battle being fought in my heart. Between life as it has always been and the risk of love. I wanted love to win and maybe that was why I tried to keep Aria near. Even though I knew at the end of whatever this was, life as I knew it would ultimately win.

Because life before this mural involved my mother. And my mother always won.

"Alex, can I speak with you?" Bradley appeared in the doorway.

Perfect timing. The one man I considered a friend was also hired help.

"Yes. What is it?"

Perhaps whatever Bradley had to tell me might distract me from my invisible love life. It might even cheer me up. Even if he was an employee, Bradley was still nice and friendly.

"It's about Aria. Something happened when she came here this morning and I wanted you to know about it." He took a step into my room but hesitated to move farther.

"What happened?"

"I know you like her, Alex, but as head of your security I must warn you."

"Okay . . ." I said a little confused.

His eyes flickered up to the corner of the wall where the mural would go. I began removing some of the wallpaper yesterday but a few strips remained.

"When she came in this morning, she went straight to the security room and walked inside. It's as if she knew where it was and began looking around."

Why would she do that? There had to be a mistake.

"Maybe she got lost and—" Before I could finish another voice cut me off.

"Alexander, my beautiful boy, I am so glad you are here." My mother's deep voice caused everyone in the room to straighten.

"Mom, what are you doing here?" I stood as she walked past Bradley and went straight to the wall.

"Why, I've come to see the progress on your little mural. I have to be honest, Alexander, it looks terrible."

"Aria hasn't started yet. I only picked out the picture today. As you can see, I am still tearing down the wallpaper." I waved my hand at the two remaining strips on the wall.

She gasped and swiftly walked over to me, taking my hands in hers. "Oh no. Tell me you didn't rip that paper down yourself?"

I shook my head. My mother and her spoiled ways. She believed manual labor was for the hired help, not for us.

"Of course, I did it myself. It's not that hard. You may revel in not ever having to lift a finger, but I'm not you."

She stood a little straighter and scoffed, "That is not something a Hawthorne does. Don't you understand, Alexander? This name means something or I wouldn't have put up with your father for as long as I did."

As much as I hated my mom's views on work and privilege, she was right about my father. She did tolerate much at his hands.

"I never asked you to stay with Dad." I put my hands on her shoulders causing her brows to lift. "You should have left long ago. We would have been fine. Just the two of us."

In that moment, something passed over her eyes. It was gone as quickly as it came, but I witnessed it. Regret. Pain. A need so great I wondered if my arms were wide enough to hold it.

As it disappeared, the mother I have come to know returned with her guarded and cold features. And I knew there was no point in getting her to understand anything.

"That was long ago and your father is no longer with us. We never need to worry about him again."

She pulled away from my arms. My touch was warm and loving, and she couldn't be reminded of something she no longer wanted.

"So, the mural. I'm glad we are changing this wall. You were right, Alex, this did need something fresh."

"Alex, I'll come back later so we can discuss Ms. Dixon." Bradley nodded at me.

"What about Ms. Dixon?" my mother asked without turning her head to acknowledge Bradley.

Bradley's eyes flickered to mine. He knew my mother almost as well as I did. She was the one to hire him five years ago. It was to keep me safe, as she put it. I don't know why I would need a bodyguard since I rarely went outside.

I think my mom only hired Bradley to keep an eye on me.

"Ms. Dixon went into the security room when she arrived today, Mrs. Hawthorne. When I confronted her about it, she appeared nervous. I wanted Alex to know that."

"Mom, I think she just got lost." I felt the need to defend Aria even though I didn't know why she walked into the security room.

"How could she have gotten into that room? Isn't it locked, Bradley?" My mother turned to face him. Her dark wool blazer, tailored to her form, wrinkled as she crossed her arms.

"I must have left it open when I went to the bathroom. I didn't think anyone would walk in," Bradley said as he wiped his head over his brow. He knew what was coming.

What happened was a mistake and Bradley knew it. My mother detested mistakes.

Her gray eyes locked onto Bradley. He seemed to straighten the closer she moved. But when she reached him, my mother did something she rarely does—she touched him.

Her hand gently tapped his chest. "Thank you for letting us know, Bradley. I'm sure you weren't expecting her to be here and didn't think to close the door behind you. But now you know, don't you? You know to keep a watchful eye," my mother's head turned toward me, "on people who don't know us. Strangers only ever want to take from us. We need to keep our guard up."

Her mouth curved, and it reminded me of how she used to smile at me, before my father died. Back when she loved me.

ELEVEN

Aria

"I wish I was going to London on Sunday," I said just before I took a bite of my sausage.

Morgana wasn't kidding when she said Chuck's Sausage Shack had the best sausages in Chicago. I laughed when she mentioned going there for her lunch break with me and Tiffany, but I admitted I was wrong. How I admitted it was through moans of satisfaction that had several people in the place turning to gaze at our table.

"You're not. Evaleen and I are so you can suck on that," Morgana said with a smirk while pointing to my sausage.

"Don't rub the fact you get to jet off to London for your job in my face, Morgana. That's rude." I glanced over at Tiffany for backup but she was too engrossed in her sausage to care about us anymore.

"No, I'm not. Seriously, suck on it. It brings out the juices," Morgana said just before she brought the sausage to her lips and sucked on the tip.

Most of the people in the restaurant turned to stare at us.

"Why isn't Evaleen joining us for lunch?" Tiffany asked as she put her food back on her plate. A smile of satisfaction spread across her lips.

"She has a meeting with Edgar, the head of IT at Mimir. They are in the process of trying to hire someone in his department," Morgana said.

"We should have a SWIM Meet before you leave. How about tomorrow night? A special Saturday night SWIM Meet," I suggested.

My eyes roamed the restaurant. I kept expecting to find someone, but I didn't know who. Ever since meeting Alex all those weeks ago, I haven't felt comfortable in my own skin.

I was frustrated and knew what I needed. Reaching up to my neck absently, I realized my good luck charm necklace wasn't there. I never understood how often I fidgeted with the necklace until it was gone. I haven't seen it in weeks and wondered if it fell off in a certain art collector's bedroom.

"I can't. I'm having dinner with my parents Saturday night," Morgana said.

"I'll go. David is much stronger since he's been home from the hospital, and he's making tremendous progress. I can ask Henrik to hang out with him. David will love that," Tiffany said.

I smiled at Tiffany's happiness. She has worked so hard for that boy and he's worked harder to walk than all of us combined. But, as happy as I was that Tiffany would be coming out tomorrow, I wanted a wing-woman. Someone who would help me find a guy to ease this frustration.

"I'll call Evaleen later, see if she might be interested."

I don't know how much better Evaleen would be than Tiffany. Whereas Tiffany would probably okay any guy that showed me attention, as she has been out of the dating world far too long, Evaleen would also scare off all who showed interest.

That's why Morgana was perfect. I had known her since we were roommates in college. She had the ability to relax a guy into showing his true colors. Even the guys who had mastered the game would let down their guard around her.

"Can you at least bring home some pictures of the guys in London? I need to live vicariously through you for a while, Morgana," I said as I reached over to pat her hand.

"I don't know if I will be having any bangers and mash in London." Morgana gave an exaggerated wink before continuing, "I have a coffee date on Sunday before my trip. If everything goes as I think it will with my date, it will be all business across the pond next week."

"Can you take pictures of your date then? Preferably naked," I said and then bit into my pickle.

"What about Alex? You told me you were working hard to . . . how did you put it? 'Climb that mountain so you could reach his peak,'" Tiffany said before tossing a potato chip into her mouth.

"What? Aria, you are working for a man's affection?" Morgana's asked.

"No. Maybe. It doesn't matter, anyway. He thinks I'm trash. I know he's attracted to me but I'm just the *hired help*," I said before I rolled my eyes.

Morgana's mouth dropped open as she stared at me.

"What?" I said.

"You said once that if you ever have to try to get a man to sleep with you that he wasn't worth the effort and your vagina must have fallen out, so I should get you to a hospital right away."

Tiffany snorted and blushed.

"Maybe that's the problem. Alex's sex superpowers are tingling, letting him know that my lady parts have withered away."

"Oh, Aria. Don't talk like that. I'm sure your vagina is still young and vibrant and ready for a hundred Alex's." Tiffany reached over to rub my back.

I know Tiffany meant well but having her say all that had me feeling like I was going to throw up.

"Okay, since I'm not hungry anymore, let me go wash up in the bathroom. Thanks for the pep talk." I stood and nodded at Tiffany.

She smiled and took a sip of her water.

After I left the table, I made my way to the back down a small hallway. Pushing open the door I was shocked at who I found standing at the sink putting on lipstick.

Mrs. Hawthorne.

"Hello, Aria."

"Mrs. Hawthorne. I had no idea you were here." My eyes swept over the small room with one sink and a toilet in the corner. "I'll step outside to give you some privacy." I turned to open the door and leave.

"Aria, please wait. I wish to speak with you." Her rich voice halted my progress.

I took a deep breath and prepared for the assault. I knew she wasn't going to be happy with me helping Alex discover he owned that building. Seeing how she responded to something so insignificant like a mural on a wall, I can only imagine how she reacted when she found out that Alex owned the building.

"Look, Mrs. Hawthorne, I felt that Alex needed to know that he owned that building. If the lawyers were lying to you, then you should be outraged at them, not me." I turned and held up my hands in peace.

Twisting the lipstick case and replacing the cap, she dropped it into her black leather purse before turning toward me. "You are so right, Aria. I am shocked that my family's lawyer, a person who has worked for us since Alexander was a child, could lie to us. I'm here to thank you."

Alex has said many times that his mother was controlling and cold, but she has yet to treat me like that. Sure, she overreacted about the mural and got on my nerves with how picky she was, but she has taste. Any person with an eye for art should know what they want.

"Thank you. I have to say it's a relief to hear you say that. I thought you were here to tell me off." I laughed as I placed my hand on my chest.

Mrs. Hawthorne took her purse off the counter and walked to me. "I know what Alex says about me . . . and some of it is true. But you have to understand that, as a single mother, I am protective of my son. Maybe I shielded him too much. Having as much money as we do you don't understand the amount of people who would say or do anything to get at that money."

"I guess that makes sense. Trust me, Mrs. Hawthorne, I have seen how money can hurt people, especially the people you love. I would never do that to your son."

The corner of her mouth twitched. "I know, Aria, that's why I am coming to you with my problem. Something I haven't told anyone. The way you helped Alexander with discovering the truth about his inheritance; you have proven that you care for his well-being."

I nodded.

She stepped closer. Lifting her hand, she hesitated a moment before clasping my hand and holding it in hers. "My son, he isn't like the average man you would meet. This may be odd coming from his mother, but I love him too much to let him go through life alone."

Was this why Alexander avoided any talk about us sexually? I thought he was a snob but maybe it's much more than that.

"It's my fault, really. I shielded him from the world, protected him from people that would hurt him, but it also stopped him from understanding how to be, socially, with a woman. Please, tell me that what I say to you won't leave this room." Her eyes widened in what I could only assume was worry.

"Of course, Mrs. Hawthorne. I would never hurt your son, I told you that," I said and gave a small smile to reassure her.

"My son has never been with a woman before. Sexually."

I could tell when every muscle in my face registered what she had said. They loosened and slacked in shock, one by one.

"But, I don't understand. You're his mother. I am sure he's not going to tell you who he has been intimate with."

Alex can't be a virgin. He's gorgeous, rich, and seemed like a nice, if not somewhat naïve, guy. He may not have a lot of experience but I was sure at some gala or party he's attended some women threw themselves at him.

"I know he doesn't tell me everything, but I do have my sources. That's why I am coming to you."

My eyes widened as I shook my head backing out of her grasp. "Oh, no. Look, Mrs. Hawthorne, as I said to Alex yesterday, I will not be paid to be his friend. I will also not spy on your son."

My father may have easily been bribed but that gene wasn't passed on to me.

She laughed and waved her hand in the air. "Oh no, Aria, you misunderstood me. I would never ask that of you. You are better than that, I can tell."

That was a relief. For a second there I wondered if Mrs. Hawthorne was the monster Alex painted her out to be.

"Aria, I know Alex cares for you so I think you would be the perfect person to take his virginity."

TWELVE

Alexander

18 Years Ago, December 25th

I smiled.

Excited at all the gold wrapped presents stacked under the tree. But I did as my mother commanded and sat still on the couch.

We were waiting for my father. He arrived home last night while I was asleep. *I wonder if he saw Santa*. I covered my mouth with my hands to stop a gasp.

I bet he did. This was going to be the best Christmas ever. I couldn't wait to tell my best friend, Bradley, who lived on the twelfth floor of my building. He's going to be jealous at how cool my dad was compared to his dad.

Bradley was a year older than me and my cousin. He was always bragging about how his father took him places. One time he took him on a trip to Washington, DC to the Air and Space Museum to see all the spaceships. My dad doesn't take me anywhere . . . I really only see him once a month and for a few days at Christmas.

But, meeting Santa, that's bigger than any spaceship or trip.

"Alexander, what do you want more than anything this Christmas?" My mother smiled at me as she sipped her morning tea.

I love my mom. She was pretty. Her long black hair was shiny, and she smelled like flowers. I liked it when she wore earrings. After my bath, I would always ask her to put on her red dangly earrings before she put me to bed. I wanted to fall asleep knowing I had the most beautiful mom in the world.

She gave the best hugs, and she let me stay up late on the weekends to watch cartoons. Sometimes, she'd watch them with me. But I don't think she liked them that much because she always ended up crying and leaving the room before the shows were over.

"I hope Santa got my letter and saw that I really, super-duper, want an art set."

That would be *so cool*.

My mom was the one that took me places but she always made sure the places were empty when we went. Like this past summer, she took me to The Art Institute of Chicago. There were paintings and drawing and statues and all sorts of awesome things.

I told my mom that when I grew up I wanted to do that. She smiled and said, "Why do it when you can just pay people to do it for you?"

I think she wanted me to grow up to buy the paintings, which I would do. After all, they were awesome.

"I think Santa got your letter."

I nodded and was about to ask about Father when he stumbled into the room. My mom sat up straight and stared ahead as she always did when he came near her. I kept my eyes down and sat on my hands. It's best not to do anything that might upset my dad.

"Where is the fucking coffee?" he said as he tripped over a few presents getting to the couch. I heard a crunching sound as he stepped on one of the gifts.

"Maria has the day off. It's Christmas. I didn't make any because I don't drink coffee. If you want some coffee, make it yourself," my mom said.

I closed my eyes tightly. My mom didn't like my dad. I may only be eight years old, but even I could see that.

She wasn't nice to him. But, he was mean to her, too. Meaner than mean. My dad was mean to everyone.

My father fell on the couch near me and I bounced, almost falling off. He smelled bad and I frowned, but I didn't let him see that. My mom may be strong enough to stand up to my dad but I wasn't.

I felt something on my head. He was pushing my hair around.

"Hey there, kiddo. I got a surprise for you."

My eyes widened and I wondered. Did my father actually meet Santa? Did Santa help him be nicer? My dad never talked to me and he certainly never got me anything.

"Did you meet Santa?" I whispered.

I couldn't help it. I knew not to speak to my father, my mother told me not to so many times, but I had to know.

He crinkled his brow and snapped his head back. "What? No, damn it. Just shut up and let me tell you."

"Zachery, language," my mom said as she raised an eyebrow at him.

His eyes widened and he waved his hand around me, and I flinched.

"I'm trying to be a good father figure and got the boy something he might like, but he keeps going on about Santa. I'm really trying here, Emma."

There was silence for what felt like a minute. I was sad he didn't meet Santa but maybe what he got me would be just as cool.

My mother nodded. "Fine. Then tell him."

He sat up and turned toward me. "Alex, how would you like to come to a tropical island with me?"

That definitely beat a trip to Washington, DC.

"Yeah!" I jumped up and clapped my hands even though I knew I should stay seated.

"We leave tomorrow, and there is a pool and coconuts on the trees. You can even wear shorts because it's so warm this time of year.

Not like cold-ass Chicago." He frowned and shook his head as he mentioned the city.

I jumped some more. "I can get my swim shorts and take them. This will be awesome. Bradley will be so jealous."

"Why does that name sound familiar? Who the fuck is Bradley?" My father stared at my mom.

"My sister's son. He lives in the building, Zachery. He's friends with Alexander," my mom said but she seemed worried. She was bouncing her foot the same way she did when my father was about to come home for a visit.

"Oh, that's fine. I thought he was your man-whore." My father lifted the corner of his mouth and let out a puff of a laugh.

My mother's foot stopped bouncing. "I don't think it's a good idea for Alexander to go with you on this trip. He should stay with me."

"Are you kidding me? He's my blood." My father stood as his face turned red. "I may not be that close to him but like I said, Emma, I am trying here."

"He would need a passport and he doesn't have one. He might need some shots. Maybe a little more notice next time for something so big as an international trip."

My mother stood and moved toward me. She knew what was coming and so did I. My mom grabbed my hand and led me to the tree. She reached down and picked up one of the gifts my father tripped over and then handed it to me.

"Don't do that, Emma. Don't shelter him. He should know what a controlling bitch you are."

My mom straightened and turned, pushing me behind her back. "Am I? There is a lot of control in this family but I don't think it's me pulling the strings, Zachery."

"Why do you think I am never around, Emma? Do you think it's easy for me to look at you and him?" My father was pointing to me as I peeked out from my mom's hip.

"I never asked you to—"

"No, you didn't. I asked *you*. I loved you. As hard as that is to believe, I loved you. But you never loved me. Not once."

My mother turned toward me. "Alexander, why don't you take this gift to your room. I know Santa picked it out special. Play there for a while. I'll come and get you later and we can open the other gifts."

Bending down, she kissed my cheek and I smelled flowers and tea. I didn't want to leave her. He was going to hurt her again. I should be stronger and stand up to him. Push him off of her. I wanted to be bigger. So big that no one could hurt her.

I shook my head. "No. Come with me, Mommy. Please."

I grabbed her arm, but she lifted my hand and kissed it.

"I'll be there later, I promise." She walked me to the hallway and watched me go.

I didn't go very far. After I saw her turn back toward my father, I hid next to the table.

"Why would I love someone like you?" I heard my mom say.

"You're just a jaded bitch. You thought your beauty would get you money and power, and look at you. Keeping your own son in some gilded prison because you're weak. So afraid of everything."

I glanced around my home. It's not a prison. It's not at all like the prisons they show on TV. Besides, even if my mother only takes me out at night, I still get to go outside to visit places close by. Prisoners don't get to do that.

My eyes fell to the golden present in my hand. I tried to tear a piece of the paper but my mom heard me.

"Alexander! I told you to go to your room."

I scurried off and turned down the smaller hallway that led to my room. Once inside, I climbed up the dragon ladder next to my soft bed. The colorful checkered covers still unmade from when I hopped out earlier this morning, excited to see what Santa had brought.

Not even waiting to sit up, I started to rip at the paper. Gold flew around me and pieces of the present fell in my face. They were sharp so I grabbed one. It was a colored pencil. Taking a closer look, I saw Santa had given me a drawing kit. But some of the pencils were broken from my dad stepping on it earlier.

That didn't stop me from smiling. I had my very first art kit. That made me an artist. Now I could draw anything I wanted.

Taking the pencils and packet of chalk called pastels, I hopped from my bed and ran to my desk. It didn't take me long to have a clean sheet of paper in front of me. I knew exactly what to draw.

Time seemed to pass quickly and before I realized it, my mom had come into my room.

"What's that, Alexander?"

I turned to her with the biggest smile. She would be so happy when I told her what I drew.

"It's me and you." I pointed to the small people in the corner of the page. "We are pointing at a plane. Daddy's on the plane. It's his trip. Because I want to stay with you."

My mom ran her fingers through my hair as she stared at the picture. Her eyes seemed to glaze over and I noticed her cheek was swollen and red.

He hit her again. I hated when he did that. Now I was glad I drew what I did.

"It looks like Daddy's plane is flying into the sun."

THIRTEEN

Present Day

"Naked bodies everywhere," Alex said with a smile that was wide, wonderful, and caused me to blush.

Me. Aria Dixon. Blushing because a man said naked bodies. Not just that, but what he wore could burn the inside of a glacier. How was I to concentrate when Alex Hawthorne, the man full of sculpted muscle and corruptible sexuality, wore a pasted on black T-shirt, jeans, and bare feet?

"What do you mean naked bodies? There are two, maybe three if you count the cherub." I turned to him, my face serious. "I understand if you want to scrap this whole thing."

His amazing, sexy gray eyes widened and for that moment, I wondered what his O-face looked like.

Ever since Mrs. Hawthorne asked me to pop her son's cherry a week and a half ago, I couldn't stop thinking about sex when it came to Alex. Everything turned sexual and it's creeping me out.

Don't get me wrong, I like sex but when I work, I focus on the art. Now I can't concentrate. Not when he's standing next to me, heat rolling off his body as my sex-starved skin gobbled it all up.

Now I'm thinking about his skin. Not any skin, but a certain part of his skin wrapped about something that grows long and hard.

"Why would I want to scrap the mural? Aria, you're talking nonsense. It's even better than I imagined." His hand landed on my shoulder and it burned. "You are unbelievably talented."

I told Mrs. Hawthorne that I wasn't the one to take Alex's virginity. It's one thing for it to happen naturally between a man and a woman. But to be told to do it, by his mother, well, there was something terribly wrong with that.

"That's very kind of you, Alex, but I think the real point here is that this wall doesn't need a mural. Maybe just some new wallpaper. Or a splash of paint. I think the painting you bought of mine, joking aside, would look wonderful in the center of a deep blue wall," I said and nodded encouragingly.

Alex kept calling me but I ignored him until I accidentally answered his call last Thursday. I told him I needed time to work with Tiffany to create the print outs, which was mostly true. I had needed time but by Thursday I was done.

I stalled coming up with a way to get out of the mural mess. Get away from his screwed-up family. I ran away long ago from one crazy family, and I wasn't about to be wrapped up in another.

Yesterday I came up with the perfect idea. Alex needed to fire me.

These were the reasons why having one-night stands were much better than getting into a relationship with a man. Because you never just date the man, you also have to deal with the man's family. After what I had seen and heard about this family, I don't want to be near any of it, no matter how incredibly sexy and sweet Alex was to me.

"You mean the clown painting?" Alex threw his head back as his eyes widened.

"Yeah."

"Aria, I love your work and I bought the clown painting because it belonged with the collection. But waking up, or worse, falling asleep to a clown staring at me is not something that will make me happy."

I threw my arms in the air. "I'm just spit-balling here. Maybe my painting titled Beauty."

"The guy has a gun to his head in that one."

I never realized how dark my paintings were.

"Then don't use my paintings. You have a Warhol I presume, as you seem to have every other famous artist."

He nodded. "Yes, I own one Warhol."

"His paintings are colorful and have a brightness to them. Nothing about them should make you scared or sad. Use this wall for a Warhol." I waved my arm in the direction of the mural I traced out in pencil using Tiffany's printouts.

He grabbed my arms, bringing me close to him. "But I don't want a Warhol or even one of your paintings I already bought. I want something unique." Alex shook his head and dipped it closer to my neck. "I want something exceptional. Something never seen before. I want the only thing you can give me."

I turned my head, brushing his cheek with mine. It sizzled and the sparks scattered down my arm and through my chest. Alex was making this difficult. Maybe if he hated me then he would fire me.

I pushed him back. "Only a rich snob would want something no one else has."

I was pushing it but he needed to hate me.

"What?"

"You heard me. Don't think I don't remember what you said to me over a week ago, Alex. I'm just the hired help. Is that why you want me to stay and work on this mural? Because you get some sick kick out of watching people slave away at your every desire."

Even I was having a hard time believing the words coming out of my mouth. But something I said hit a spark. He narrowed his eyes as a vein on his neck pulsated.

He was mad. I needed to keep this up, really make him never want to see me again.

"I don't get a sick kick out of—"

"Don't lie to me, Alex." I pushed my hands onto my hip and flared my nose. "That's why you don't have any real friends, isn't it? You get giddy knowing people have to do what you say because they want your money."

My stomach churned with what I was saying to him. Alex was the nicest guy I had ever met. He genuinely wanted to get to know me, and when he complimented my work it was honest, not to flatter but because he felt it.

I hated saying these things to him but I knew if I stayed there would be a point where I would try something with him. He deserved a woman who wanted him for more than just one night. He deserved better than me.

He deserved better than someone his mother set him up with.

"That's not true," he said as he ran his fingers through his hair.

It was time to end this. Time I left. But first, I needed to land the final blow. A lump formed in my throat and I wondered if I would be able to get the words out.

"More lies, Alex. I talked to your mother over a week ago and she had some interesting things to say about you," I said and fought against the bile rising in my throat.

Alex moved quickly and was in front of me, breathing hard. His jaw set and his eyes wild as he grabbed the top of my arm. With a firm grip that told me to watch my tongue but refused to cause pain, he dipped his head to my ear. "Never believe anything my mother says, Aria. She will use you to get what she wants, even if it means telling you lies."

I tried to step back out of his hold but the back of my legs hit the bed.

"Then she lied about you being a virgin?" I regretted my words as quickly as they fell out of my mouth.

None of this was my business. Alex was right, I was hired help. His personal life had nothing to do with me.

"I'm sorry, Alex. I didn't mean any of the stuff I just said. This is none of my business—"

"She didn't lie about me being a virgin."

I stood there staring at the floor and when I finally gathered the courage to glance at him, he was watching the floor too.

A part of me thought Alex's mom was lying and when Alex said not to believe what she said I felt relief. No more awkwardness of pretending I didn't know. No more wondering what it would be like to give him his first orgasm while being inside of me. No more realizing that I couldn't be with him because he deserved a woman who wasn't going to run.

But, as he admitted that he was a virgin, I realized what I worried about when I came here this Monday morning ready to work on what he hired me for was ignorant. So what if he's a virgin? I was a virgin once. Did I want some sweet guy that was gentle with me to take my virginity? Yes, I did but that's not always what we get.

"That clears that up," I said unable to think of anything good.

I closed my eyes, embarrassed at how I handled this whole situation. A stronger woman would have got on with her work, setting personal feelings aside.

The last thing I was, was strong.

"Did she offer you money?"

My eyes snapped up to his in surprise. "What? No, she didn't offer me money."

He laughed and walked around me to go sit on the edge of the bed. "That's what she does, you know. My mother has to control everything, even my sex life."

I frowned and went to sit next to him. "That's terrible. Why would she go that far? When I talked to her, she mentioned about keeping you safe from people who wanted to take advantage of you. But she can't keep everyone out."

"She can, Aria. She has. My entire life has been orchestrated by her hands. Do you know that what the press said about me being with prostitutes was real?"

My hand went to my mouth. How could that be? He's a virgin. The more information I get about Alex, the more confused I became.

"But you're a virgin . . ."

"Anytime I socialized in public at an art event or gallery opening there would be a beautiful woman there, someone I was attracted to, that showed interest in me. They would talk to me and say just the right thing to make me want to get to know them even more. Until one night I got enough nerve to ask one of these women to come home with me."

FOURTEEN

Alexander

Aria was disgusted.

And who could blame her? I'm a pathetic twenty-six-year-old man who couldn't even have sex with a woman paid to get it on with him.

"They were prostitutes. I found out when I took the first woman home. She kept trying to push things with me. All I wanted to do was get to know her. Maybe kiss her," I said and gave a side glance to Aria to find out how she was taking it.

Her color was better. She didn't appear like she was about puke anymore.

"What do you mean she pushed things?"

I turned toward her, propping my knee on the bed. "She kept touching me. Trying to unbutton my shirt and move in to kiss me. At one point, I gave in to kissing her, but it wasn't long before her hand started to wander. So, I stopped it . . . stopped her."

That was embarrassing. I never wanted to tell Aria any of what happened but my mother hadn't given me much of a choice. Either explain things to Aria or completely lose her forever. At least if she left now, she would know the truth and not the lies my mother had said to paint me as the pathetic loser.

Maybe they weren't lies.

She reached over and placed her hand on mine as it rested on my knee. Her touch sincere, soothing, and I kept thinking if Aria's hand began to wander I don't think I would stop her.

"But how did you realize she was a prostitute?" Aria asked, her thumb brushing back and forth over my hand.

"She let it slip. When I stopped her before she could, you know, grab me," I pointed to the zipper in my jeans, "she mentioned how my mother paid good money for her time. When I told her to get out, the woman broke down, afraid she wouldn't get the rest of her money. She cried that she had a baby at home she needed to take care of."

"Oh no, that's terrible," Aria said moving her other hand to my shoulder. Every place she touched radiated, sending electricity straight to my crotch.

I was having trouble keeping my attention focused on her eyes. They kept falling to her lips, to her tits.

"It made me realize she was just another victim of my mother. I wanted to help her. I wanted to help them all. So, I let my mother continue her little game of controlling my life, but when I would take these women home, I would help them. Give them money, better housing, and found them good jobs that wouldn't require them to do what they had been doing. Until my mother found out."

I didn't realize what I was doing until it was too late. My hand lifted and I let my fingers drift across Aria's cheek until one finger trailed to her bottom lip. She was soft and that lip felt plump. My mouth watered to taste it.

"Do you want to kiss me, Alex?" Aria asked, her voice a whisper but rough around the edge.

In my head, I had answered her question a thousand times. But in that moment, I couldn't utter a word.

I moved toward her, scooting as close as I could before I dipped my nose to her cheek. Aria was the world and I inhaled. Instead of the satisfaction I thought I would find from her scent, I desired more. I brushed my lips over her temple and it was like kissing silk.

"God, you're sweet. So sweet," I mumbled.

"You haven't even tasted me yet," Aria said causing something to snap inside me.

Perhaps it was the years of frustration or how long I had wanted her, but I didn't want to stop. I didn't want to be the good guy anymore.

My fingers moved from my knee to the back of her head and within seconds, she was moaning as I curled my fingers into her hair, forcing her head back. I lifted my head and found her darkening brown eyes, opening wide for me. Her face was all lust, pain, and fear bound together into a few perfect features.

"Do you want me to taste you, Aria? Is that why you're here . . . for my tongue?"

Her fingernails curled into my shoulders as she held onto me. Fuck, it hurt but felt so incredible.

She wanted sweet Alex but didn't realize a monster would come out. I tried to pretend I could be normal. Hoped if I met the right woman I would be so attracted to her that I wouldn't want to act this way. I wouldn't be so fucking aroused by all this.

"No," she said and I loosened my grip on her hair.

I knew I would frighten her. How I desire a woman, it's not normal. After today, I would probably never see Aria again.

Sitting back, I studied the grooves of the dark wood on the floor. There was something soothing about the natural grain as it meandered lazily. I needed to focus on something to bring me back from that high of tasting Aria.

"Alex, what are you doing?"

She deserved an explanation. Forcing her like that, I didn't want her to leave scared of me. Even if she didn't like how I was, the last thing I wanted to do was frighten Aria.

"I'm sorry, Aria. I got carried away. Please don't think I wanted to hurt you." I finally got the courage to lift my head and face her.

Her brow wrinkled. "You didn't hurt me, Alex. I admit I was surprised at what happened but nothing you did hurt."

That was a relief.

"Good. I know what I did was wrong. I understand if you never want to see me again."

Everything happened so quickly. Her touch and how she softened as I talked about those past women, it felt almost unreal. I never thought she would understand why I helped those women. The way my mom put it, I was crazy for wanting to help people who could never change.

She believed that, always had, but I never did. I knew there were choices people made in life, tough choices that they didn't necessarily want to make, but life forced them to do it.

The way Aria looked at me, for the first time in my life I felt understood. In my mother's eyes, I'm still a sad, foolish little boy. But, for that moment, I was seen as a good person. As a man.

And then I had to ruin it by extinguishing the light and turning everything black.

Her hand moved to my chin, turning it so she could gaze into my eyes. They shone, big and brown, crinkling at the edge with a smile. "Now why would I never want to see you again, Alex? That was the hottest non-kiss I have ever had. For a virgin, you seem to know what you are doing."

What?

"I didn't scare you?"

Her hand slipped down. Her fingers trailed down my neck until she placed her palm on my chest. It was warm and I ached for that heat.

"No. I was hoping for more." Aria bit her bottom lip as she tilted her head.

"What do you want?" I had to ask.

This was all so much. It was better than any fantasy I had.

Her eyes dipped to where her hand rested on my chest. "I should be asking you that. You're the virgin."

My mind raced with every thought I had ever had about this woman for the past three years. But one stood tall. It was the worst one because it was never a fantasy but cold reality.

"I may not know exactly what my mother has told you but I have a pretty good idea. If she's paying you to help me, don't bother." I lifted her wrist, removing her hand from my heart.

I wanted Aria but not like that.

She stood and placed her hands on her hips. "Seriously? I know we may not have known each other for a long time, Alex. But I believe I made it clear at several points in our short time knowing each other that my friendship, or anything more, can't be bought."

Shaking her head, she turned and glanced around the room. Aria went over to pick up her purse and sketch pad while mumbling, "And here I was trying to get you to fire me."

"I'm sorry. I didn't mean to upset you, Aria." I got up and went to grab her arm so she would look at me. "It's just, every woman who has tried anything with me has been paid by my mother. You told me you talked to her. That she told you I was a virgin. I just assumed—"

"What? That trying to get you to hate me is my seduction technique?" Aria asked, her eyes wide.

"I don't know. Why did you want me to hate you?"

I frowned because deep down I knew why. There was only one reason. and it wasn't that I was a virgin, it was my mother. Who would want to be anywhere near a man with a controlling, crazy mother like mine? Sometimes I wish she had been the one to die in that plane crash, along with my father, and left me an orphan.

I hated myself when those thoughts went through my head.

"Because, Alex, look at your life. Look at your family. You have all the money in the world yet you don't live. That woman controls you and you let her. My father tried to control me. I understand what you are going through but I made a choice. I chose to leave and never look back." She pushed out of my grasp and walked to the doorway.

Just as she was about to turn the corner she said, "You could make that choice too but instead, you put up a mural."

FIFTEEN

Aria

"That was delicious." I smiled as I wiped my mouth with a napkin.

"Yeah, I've been craving sausage lately. It's too bad Drake is in New York missing all the good sausage," Evaleen said leaning back in her wooden chair.

"Maybe Morgana isn't." I wiggled my eyebrows.

We both laughed.

"I miss Drake but being in the office for the past two weeks has been a dream come true since Payne isn't there." Evaleen's smile widened so far that I wondered if her cheeks would crack.

I wish I could be that happy. Since my fight two weeks ago with Alex, the joy had seemed to disappear from my life. I even went back to my job at the bar and picked up a couple of shifts just to keep busy. But that didn't last long. Word had gotten out that A. Hawthorne bought my paintings. It seemed everyone who ordered a drink from me at the bar happened to own a gallery that would love to show my work.

Eventually, Sally, the manager, had to sneak me out the back to avoid the art groupies.

"I'm sorry, Dixon, I didn't mean to rub my delight of a Payne-less life in your face. You seem down," Evaleen said.

"It's times like these I wish I had Morgana to talk to. Her parents are going to visit her in New York next week, maybe I'll tag along."

"You can always talk to me. I'm your friend, too." She reached over and placed her hand over mine.

Would Evaleen even understand? It's not like she's the one-night stand type. But, maybe she could understand Alex's point of view.

"It involves sex with a wealthy man, Evaleen. Are you sure you want to discuss that?"

She rolled her eyes. "I told you I was a—"

I waved my hand at her. "Yeah, yeah, so you say. Okay, let's pretend this is a book. The hero is locked away in a tower on top of a high mountain by his evil mother."

"Stepmother," Evaleen said.

"No, his mother. Why does it have to be a stepmother?"

"That's usually how it goes in books; I don't know why. Especially in fairy tales—like Cinderella or Snow White—it is always the evil stepmother."

I groaned. "Okay, fine, stepmother. So, the heroine of the story makes it up the mountain and into the tower. But when she gets there to kiss the hero and save him, he insults her. Oh, he knew that she would never take money for sex but he assumed it anyway."

Evaleen's blue eyes wandered around the room before she narrowed them at me. "I'm a little lost. Are we still talking about the fairy tale or something else? Why would the heroine take money for sex?"

I slammed my hand on the square wooden table. "My point exactly!"

Evaleen stared at me for a moment in silence before she said, "Maybe you do need to speak with Drake about this. I'm so lost."

Why was I so angry? It made sense that Alex would assume his mother had paid me based on his entire history with women. Yet, I was so angry that he would think that of me.

Because you care for him more than you should, Aria.

It wasn't Alex I was angry at, it was me. More importantly, my heart. My silly heart and its need to have feelings for a big, sexy man who was born into a crazy family.

"I see him," Evaleen said through gritted teeth.

"What?"

"That hoodie guy from a month and a half ago. He's doing a piss poor job of trying to hide behind a plant. What's he like, six foot three and that plant is five foot at best?"

I turned to see what she was staring at. Evaleen was right. Alex was huddling behind a green potted plant that stood near the hallway to the restrooms.

He looked ridiculous—like a bear trying to hide behind a folding chair. I couldn't help but laugh.

"Alex, is that you?" I called.

His breathtaking gray eyes popped up, widening in surprise. He shook his head.

Evaleen and I stood. We walked over to him, cornering him.

"Yes, it is you. Why are you here?"

My smile faded as he stretched to his full height. Warmth bloomed between my legs and I couldn't remember anything about our fight. It was something about sex. Why would I fight him on sex?

His eyes flipped between me and Evaleen. "You were right, Aria. I need to stand up to my mother."

Memories were coming back to me as he spoke.

"I'm glad. But that doesn't explain why you are spying on me at Chuck's Sausage Shack."

His eyes landed on Evaleen before turning back toward me. "Can we talk . . . privately?"

I glanced around the small restaurant and the only private rooms were the bathrooms and a broom closet. I wasn't about to go back into a broom closet with him, and a bathroom at lunch hour wasn't private.

Turning to Evaleen I leaned into her. "Do you think we could use your office or an empty room at Mimir to talk?"

Her eyes widened. "With Hoodie? Are you sure that's safe?"

"His name is Alex. Alexander Hawthorne." I took a breath before continuing, "He's the guy trapped in the tower on top of a mountain."

Evaleen's lips thinned. "I know who he is, I just like calling him Hoodie." She bit her lip and eyed Alexander for a moment before she said, "Okay. You can use Payne's old office since he isn't there."

I waved Alex to follow us toward the front of the restaurant. However, he stopped just before we pushed through the door to the sidewalk.

"What's wrong?" I asked.

He seemed tense and pushed his hands into his navy hoodie. "Um, it's the outside. I don't do well in the daylight."

Evaleen snorted. "What are you a vampire?"

He shook his head and I placed my hand on his arm. "It's okay, we're here. Are you allergic to the sun?"

Based on his tan, I didn't think that could be a problem.

"No, it's my mother. She never took me out during the day. I'm sure it was more of her lies, but she warned me of bad people waiting to find me and kidnap me for money. So, I never went out during the day."

"But you're here now. How did you get here?" Evaleen said.

"That's one of the things I wanted to discuss with you, Aria. I knew you wouldn't take my call so I forced myself to come out and find you."

He's right, I had been ignoring all of his phone calls.

I nodded. "Okay, let's get you inside the Mimir building. Evaleen, can you take his arm and I'll grab his other arm. We'll be on either side of you. That might help put you at ease." I smiled up at him.

Luckily, the Mimir building was right next door and we were outside for less than a minute.

Once we were inside, I could feel Alex melt in my grip. I hadn't realized how tense he was until we walked through the turnabout glass door.

When the elevator opened, there was only one person inside and she stared at Alex with wide, doe-eyes.

"Hello, Jenson," Evaleen said to the woman.

"Oh, hi, Ms. Bechmann." She walked back to the corner of the elevator as we walked in.

"Don't you have to get out of the elevator?" Evaleen asked the woman.

"I just realized I forgot something at my desk," she said with a ghost of a smile before her eyes snapped up to Alex.

"You're Grace, right?" Alex said pointing to her.

Her tan cheeks turned pink as she nodded.

"I remember you from when I was here a few weeks ago. I'm Alex." He pushed his hand to her as she stared at him.

She reached for his hand to shake. "Hi, Alex. It's nice to finally meet you."

The elevator stopped and once the doors opened, Grace dashed out.

"That woman is weird. She's like that with every guy she meets. She seemed especially odd with you, Mr. Hawthorne. I'm sorry," Evaleen said as we left the elevator and moved down the hall.

Alex shrugged as we entered a large, empty office. It was bare bones with only a desk, a few chairs, and a black leather couch against the wall.

"I don't think so. She's just shy. There's nothing wrong with being shy," he said.

I don't know why, but my heart jumped at his words. I figured I would be a little jealous of Grace. It's obvious she was enamored of Alex, but she appeared to have a delicate nature. I think Alex's heart goes out to fragile creatures.

"Well, you don't need to worry about her. She has a boyfriend now. Hopefully, she'll gain some confidence with that. I'll leave you two alone. I have a meeting with Edgar Mimir so it might be a while," Evaleen said as she moved to leave and shut the office door behind her.

I turned to Alex. He sank into one of the black leather office chairs.

"Are you ready to tell me why you braved your fear of daylight to hide behind a plant in a sausage shack? I asked.

SIXTEEN

Alexander

"I'm running away," I said lifting my head in hesitation to watch as Aria came and sat next to me.

"Running away? What are you, ten?"

"I mean, I'm leaving Chicago. I wanted to get out during the daytime, see if I could do it, and I did."

My heart was pounding with excitement and fear, but most of all, I tackled something my mother tried to destroy in me. I was always curious why she told me to never be seen outside, keeping me almost completely locked away, knowing I would develop this fear of ever venturing outside during the day?

I had to wonder why? She told me it was because other people might hurt me to get to my money, but that always felt like a lie.

Something passed over Aria's eyes and she twisted her head away. After a moment, she turned back to me. "I don't understand. Why are you telling me? Just go if you want."

Her voice deepened with each word. She was angry. It surprised me. I thought Aria, with her free spirit, would be happy for me.

"Because it's what you said two weeks ago that made me realize that I needed to get away from my mother."

Aria leaned back. "I'm proud of you, Alex. If what you say about your mother is true, then it's a good thing you are leaving. I wish you the best of luck."

She smiled though it didn't seem sincere. Her gaze focused on her twisting fingers.

My mind filled with a thousand words, jumbling together for all that I wanted to explain, but I knew it would be too much. So, I started with one thing.

The seed she planted when she walked into my bedroom the very first time.

"Come with me," I said, taking her hand in mine.

She gasped and in that second her eyes gave me her answer. It was stark and surprising, but I smiled anyway. Her truth was the answer I longed for and something she wasn't ready to accept.

"No. I can't leave. No." Aria shook her head and pulled her hand from mine.

The more she fought, the deeper I dug in.

"Why? What's stopping you? You don't have a job to get to. And I would make sure you were provided for."

Aria stood and pushed the chair back in the process, causing it to tip back.

"I'm not a pet, Alex. I don't need a sugar daddy."

"Aren't sugar daddies supposed to be older? How old are you, Aria?"

I knew her age. There was a lot I knew about Aria. When you're attracted to someone from afar for three years, you spend a lot of time Googling them.

Just thinking that made me realize I sounded like a stalker. Maybe she doesn't need to know I've been lusting after her for all those years.

"I'm twenty-nine. Why? How old are you?"

"I'm twenty-six," I said and stood from the chair to face her.

"You're younger than me. Does that make me a cougar?"

She crinkled her nose, warming my chest. I wanted to wrap her in my arms and kiss her everywhere.

"I think you would have to be much older than me. At least ten years older. Not three years."

"Four years. I'm four years older than you."

"I may be a recluse, Aria, but I know simple math and twenty-nine minus twenty-six is three."

"I turn thirty in June. I will be four years older than you in a little over a month."

"Who's to say I don't have a birthday later this year?" I said knowing I didn't.

But she didn't need to know that.

She waved her hands at me. "Three years, four years, that doesn't matter. I'm still not coming with you, Alex. I have a life here. Chicago may not be a paradise island where we can sip mai tai's on the beach and make love in a room with the sounds of waves crashing in the distance, but . . . wait, what was I arguing about?"

The more time I spent with Aria, the more I learned what she liked. That's something you can't Google. As much as she complained about not wanting to be bought, she sure liked nice things and good food.

"I can make that happen," I said as the corner of my mouth tipped up. "And just think, I could feed you shrimp caught fresh from the ocean and grilled before us on the beach."

Her eyes were like saucers as she stared up at me. "I do like shrimp."

I took a step closer, placing my hand on her shoulder before dipping my head to the side of hers. "You know what I like, Aria? Pie. They make a great key lime pie in the Keys. I like other flavors, too. But when I find that perfect pie—as if it was created just for my tongue—mmm, it makes me want to lick the whole thing."

"Yes. That does sound good," she said, her voice but a breath.

I lifted my hand to her neck. My nose dipped, tickling under her ear and it took every ounce of my restraint not to bite her. But I didn't. I held firm until her chest pushed against mine. Her breathing picked up the more I inhaled.

"I'd love to have pie with you, Aria."

"So much yes right now." Her fingers gripped my shoulders trying to pull me closer.

But, again, I held firm. I wanted to give in and let her do what she wanted to me, but I needed something more from Aria. A promise.

I straightened my back and stood to my full height. It surprised her but she refused to let me go.

"Then come with me. Let's find that perfect island together. No more cold Chicago winters."

That's when she gave in. Her eyes widened and her lips—they were the key—spread into a breathtaking smile. Full of as much hope as I felt.

But then one person ruined everything. As she had for most of my life, my mother walked in to take control.

"What on earth?" Aria said as her head turned toward the door my mother walked through moments ago.

She was surprised by mother's appearance but I wasn't. My mother had spies everywhere. This wasn't the first time I tried to leave my home during the day. I once talked an old friend, someone I thought was a friend, into coming to a gallery showing by a new artist with me.

Turned out that friend was one of my mom's spies. My mother showed up there too. But not before the true beauty of the night captured my heart.

My mom's gray eyes narrowed on Aria. "Alexander. What are you doing here?"

My instinct was to push Aria behind me, protect her from the woman who used my love like candy. When she had a sweet tooth, my mother would visit me only to chew me up.

I wanted to lie to my mom and never tell her what I was planning, but it was time to face her. Despite my promises long ago to my mother, I needed to do this for me. Even if it meant breaking those promises. She broke enough promises over the years.

"I'm leaving. I won't marry whoever you picked out for me. This isn't the middle ages, Mother." I turned my eyes to find Aria's mouth wide in surprise. "I'm only here to tell Aria that I won't need her to paint the mural anymore. In fact, she might be coming with me," I said before I looked at Aria.

Not wanting to overstep my bounds I asked, "If you're interested?"

She chewed on her bottom lip. And after what felt like forever, Aria grabbed my hand and smiled up at me. "Yes. I'll come with you, Alex."

There was an ache in my chest and a burn that prickled and twisted throughout my body. It was almost too good to be true. This beautiful, amazing woman wanted to be with me.

Noise disrupted my joy and I turned to see my mother clapping her hands.

"Aww, that is sweet, but I'm afraid you can't run off with your little love, Alex."

All I cared about was that Aria wanted to be with me. My mother could make fun of me or spread lies about me or Aria, and it wouldn't matter. The only important thing was that we were going to be happy together.

"Don't even start, Mom. I told you I'm not marrying Alexa Dorton," I said feeling emboldened with Aria at my side.

My mother told me when I was a kid that I am destined to marry into a powerful, politically connected family. I met Alexa when I was a kid. She was sweet and as nervous as me. We planned to run away together, not so we could be together, but to get away from our controlling parents.

My mother rolled her eyes and waved her diamond-cluttered fingers at me. "You can't run away from your destiny, Alexander."

I stood there and stared at my mother. What sort of fantasy world did she live in?

"It's done. None of that matters anymore because we're leaving." I tried to make my way past my mother, pulling Aria along with me.

"You can walk out and break my heart like that, Alexander? After all I protected you from. I'm the one that gave you everything. If it weren't for me, you would be lost out there in the world with the worst life. Maybe no life at all."

I stopped and looked over at my mother.

"What are you even talking about, Mom? You think sheltering me, making me scared to step outside in the daylight was protecting me? The most it ever protected me from was mosquitoes. Bravo," I used the slow clap on her, "you saved me from malaria."

"And West Nile virus. Oh, and also the Zika virus," Aria said.

We both turned toward Aria. She shook her head. "But you aren't a pregnant woman so you don't really need to worry about Zika." Aria's eyes lowered to the floor and she frowned.

"You are right, Ms. Dixon. He doesn't need to worry about that or you, for that matter. Since you are already married."

Another one of my mother's lies. She really thought I was that naïve, that stupid, that I would believe Aria was married just because my mother said it.

I shook my head. "How can you lie like that and then look at yourself in a mirror?"

There was a tug on my sleeve and I glanced down at Aria.

"Alex, she's not lying."

SEVENTEEN

Aria

*"**Aria, you're married?**"* Alex said as his voice cracked.

No one knew about it and I had hoped no one ever would. Even Morgana didn't know about my marriage.

"Yes."

"Alex, you should come home with me. I can tell you everything. Never believe a woman who is only after your money. Besides, you already know that she's not the woman meant for you." Alex's mom sneered at me.

Just a few weeks ago she was practically begging me to be with her son and now, it's as if I turned into a lost beggar child from a Dickens' novel.

"No. This doesn't involve you," Alex said to his mom.

I thought he was going to storm off when he pushed past her, leave me behind for good. It's what I wanted, right? Be free of this family and all its crazy. But now I didn't want to leave Alex. Something about running away with him to some far-off locale sounded exciting.

That's what I wanted. Excitement. Part of why I missed working was the stimulation. When things were busy, I came home from work exhausted but happy. Now there was no exhaustion, only boredom.

Maybe adventure was the key.

It surprised me when Alex grabbed my wrist and tugged me along. We kept walking until we were inside the elevator moving down. That's when the silence took over. I kept glancing at him but his head was down, his brow wrinkled.

Some may see him and think he was deep in concentration, but I knew better. Alex was angry. And as much as I wanted that irritation directed toward his mother, I knew it wasn't. It was because of me.

I was about to speak, to explain, but the doors opened and he pulled me with him. His fingers tightened around my hand as we went through the turning doors and stepped into the cool, windy May sidewalk. A black car with tinted windows sat out front and Alex walked over to open the door.

He waved for me to get inside but I stood my ground.

"Aria, I need to speak with you. Please, get inside."

I folded my arms refusing to go anywhere until I got answers. "Where are you taking me?"

He's mad at me, fine. He has every right but that doesn't mean he can pull me around like a rag doll. Expecting me to do go wherever he wants as if I have no say.

"Somewhere safe. Somewhere to talk."

My shoulders shook with laughter. "And where would that be, Alex? I am coming to notice that no matter where we go, your mother seems to show up." I waved my hand back at the large, metal and glass Mimir building. "Just take me home."

I was getting tired of this crazy world he inhabited. As much as I sought the adventure with him, I also wanted it to be carefree, not full of worry and confusion.

I moved to the car and stepped inside. Once we were buckled in the car took off.

"To garage number one, Ben," Alex said to the man driving the car.

"That's not taking me home." I turned toward Alex, his eyes still set on the front of the vehicle.

"No, it's not. But there is something there that not even my mother knows about."

Or maybe there was nothing there. Maybe he could get rid of me and no one would know about it.

I may have known Alex for a month and a half, but what did I really understand about him? Maybe this was all a way to lure me into believing him. What if there's a reason no one knows what A. Hawthorne looks like? What if he plans to hurt me, or worse.

Gazing over at him, I noticed the curves in his arms as he flexed his muscles. To say the man was built was an understatement. He could break me in half easily.

"Don't worry. Where we're going, my mother won't be able to find us." Alex finally turned to look at me. His eyes narrowed as if they were measuring me. Probably for my grave.

I was surprised when he still wanted to talk to me even after finding out that I was married. No guy would do that unless they wanted something from me. Something that I might not want to give, like my life.

"It's not your mom I'm worried about," I mumbled as I twisted my head to figure out where we were.

He placed his hand on my shoulder and I tensed.

"Why would you be afraid of me? I would never hurt you. Since I first laid eyes on you all those years ago, all I ever wanted to do was make you happy."

I whipped my head around. "What? Years ago. You mean . . . weeks ago, right?"

"Shit." Alex pulled back. "I didn't mean to say that. It doesn't matter," he said waving his hands at me.

"Mr. Hawthorne, we're here," the driver said as the car came to a stop.

I glanced out the window and noticed we were in the Roger's Park neighborhood, near the northern Chicago border. I recognized a restaurant I had been to before. At least, if I had to escape, I knew where I was.

The driver took us to a garage and dropped us off. Alex took me to another car—a yellow Volkswagen Karmann Ghia. Before we got inside, Alex looked under the car. When I asked him what he was doing, he only told me it was to make sure we were absolutely alone. That answer didn't help my anxiety. I glanced around to find an escape. Before I could get away, he put his hand on my arm, opening the car door, blocking my escape.

I thought that was where he wanted to talk but we ended up going north, out of the city and to a motel. My eyes took in every road sign and turn we made. When I got away, I'd knew where to run.

I tried to think of an excuse to not go into the motel room, but Alex pulled me inside. Not much had changed in this room for a few decades. It smelled of mildew and everything was either brown or dark green.

If he thought I was compliant he would be more likely to leave me alone, and then I could escape. I sat on the bed and tucked my hands under my thighs.

"Is this where you plan to kill me? I have to say, Alex, I thought if you were going to off me it would be in a classier place."

I, obviously, wasn't very good at being compliant when it came to possibly being killed.

"Why do you think I want to kill you?" Alex asked as he sat on his knees in front of me.

"Because I'm married." I crossed my arms around myself feeling my old life creep back in.

That life would be right at home in a room like this.

"I'm not going to kill you because of that. I'm not going to hurt you at all, ever. I only want to find out the truth and knowing my mother, she would find a way to listen in on what we say. I don't want what you tell me to be twisted later into something unrecognizable from her."

My shoulders slumped as I decided to stop making excuses to run from Alex. He wasn't going to kill me. If he had wanted to harm me, he had plenty of times in the weeks I have known him to do it. I think I was only worried that he would see the real me.

Maybe, like my parents, he wouldn't like what he saw.

As much as I didn't want him to see, it was time to own up. Out of everyone I knew, I guess Alex would be the one that would most understand.

"My father, he's a lawyer. Not the type of lawyer you think of, but the one who works for the scum of the Earth—you know, the mob, criminals, even a few terrorist organizations last I heard." I felt sick talking about him.

Alex moved up to the bed and sat next to me, placing his arm around me. Until he pulled me close, I hadn't realized I was shaking.

"When I was a teenager, my father went to work for a group in California. They called themselves the Freedom for Oppressed Peoples. I was so happy he was finally working with a good organization. He took me and my sister to a party they had. I was excited because I wanted to find out more about helping people. I had a dream since I was young to use my art to help others."

I shook my head but continued, "But the name of the organization was a front. It was another criminal organization. But this one wanted to infiltrate the government. They were Russian. They wanted to work to destroy various governments around the world, giving them the power. And my father offered me and my sister up to two of their high-ranking officials so they could get citizenship."

"Oh my God. I'm so sorry, Aria."

Alex's fingers began to rub my back and it felt good. It helped to settle my nerves.

"We were left at the party and locked in a room together. My sister told me at the first chance I got, I should run. So, that's what I did. The next day I was forced to sign some paperwork. They left me alone in the room with the man they had told me I married. Most of the things the people said was in Russian, which I didn't understand. But the worst part wasn't the fact that I was married . . . it was what the man did to me after. He took a part of me that I can never get back."

I felt tired. Scooting toward the pillows, I lay back on the bed. Alex gave me some space but moved to lie near me.

"When I used the bathroom after it was over and the man was asleep I noticed a small window. I climbed out and ran. I didn't know where I was but somehow, I found a woman on a bicycle and told her what happened. She called the police. Later, when the police raided the house—"

I stopped. Turning to my side as I curled up in a ball, the tears flowed and I didn't know if I could ever get the words out. I miss her so much.

"It's okay, Aria. You don't have to tell me anymore," Alex said as he eased closer.

He curled up behind me and hugged my body to his. I needed that. Every time I thought about that time in my life, about my sister, I was alone. Only able to cry into my pillow. I never realized how much it helped to have that touch, to have someone to talk to, until now.

"It was abandoned. The house. Things were torn up as if they were trying to get out in a hurry. Only they left one thing behind. My sister."

"Was she safe?" Alex asked, his hot breath tickled my neck.

"No, she was dead. The coroner said they found heroin in her system. She never did drugs, never. I was the wild one. Ava was the straight-laced one. She did everything right. I called her a parent's wet dream." I laughed at the memory.

"She was the one who talked me into going with my parents to that supposed party. She said she wanted to help Mom and Dad. That she had heard them fighting about money problems. Ava believed that if we supported them, looked like the happy family, then these people would give my dad money. Instead, they destroyed her."

I gritted my teeth and bit out, "I knew they filled her with those drugs. They killed her. My father basically sold us and caused my sister's death. And all I could think about was the fact that I left her there. She was scared and alone, and I ran away. She had just turned eighteen. About to start a life as an adult, instead everyone she loved left her to die. I may have only been seventeen, but I was old enough to find a way out for her."

A sob rattled my body. It was deep and long and still not enough. Despite how much time has passed, I don't know if I can ever forgive myself for leaving my sister to die.

EIGHTEEN

Alexander

She brought pain wherever she went. My mother. Her words, her actions, only rotted away lives that were happy before she entered them.

I used to feel bad for my mother. I used to think she was the victim in this world. But youth had a habit of making any parent seem perfect.

I watched Aria sleep after her confession. Lying next to her as thoughts about my life, my mother, and this stunning artist swirled in my head. My heart ached knowing my mother tried to twist Aria's life into one of the pieces on her board game. It was coming together. All of it.

Of course, my mother knew of Aria. She probably planted her to begin with. Maybe even three years ago when I first saw her in that gallery.

What I feared was that she might have known Aria far longer than three years.

Nothing was an accident with Emma Hawthorne, despite what she may say. The only thing that I haven't been able to figure out was why?

Why use so many people? Why control your son's life to the point that he won't go outside in the daytime? My mother may be evil but she wasn't crazy.

"What time is it?" Aria's head lifted from the pillow, her hair stuck to her cheek. My chest rolled with an intense twinge. I wanted to see that silly, sexy, sweet look every day.

"It's about six in the evening. I'm getting hungry. Do you want to get something to eat?" I asked as I turned to my side to face her in bed.

I wanted to kiss her. Pull her close to me, but I knew now wasn't the time. She needed to relax after opening up.

"Yes. That's sounds great. What's good to eat around here?"

I shrugged my shoulders. "I have no idea. Why don't we take a walk and find out?"

She smiled and when her hand lifted to my cheek, I felt my heart stumble. Now I really wanted to touch her and never leave this bed.

But we did leave and after a few minutes, we were walking down the street. I had been to this place many times but never came out for a walk. Mainly strip malls and gas stations.

"Not very scenic," Aria said.

"I don't know about that. I like it here. Everything is what it is. It doesn't pretend to be something it's not. Like over there," I pointed to a sign at a strip mall, "it just says laundromat. Nothing fancy. If you need to do laundry, you know exactly where to go."

Aria laughed and slipped her fingers into mine sending prickles up my arm. "You're right. I never thought of it that way. How about that place? Sausage, Chicken, & Fries. I have a pretty good idea what I'm going to get in there."

"I think we found where to get food, and we didn't even need the Internet," I said.

We walked over and ordered our food. There wasn't any place to sit and eat so we took it back to the motel.

I ordered most of their menu and realized, after we ate half of it, not to order food when I was ravenously hungry.

I leaned back in the small chair in our room. "I think my stomach might explode."

"But what about dessert? We haven't even gotten to that yet. You're a lightweight," Aria said before taking another bite of her fried chicken breast.

"My God, woman, how can you eat so much? You're so tiny."

"Pacing. Any true food connoisseur knows to spread out the meal. Take lots of small bites and never fill up on water. Water is for losers."

I threw my head back and laughed. I don't know when I had enjoyed myself that much. It was nice talking about nothing with someone and knowing they weren't going to run off and tell my mother everything I said.

"You can have the dessert. I'm going to lie down on the bed and let that food work its way through me."

"Unbutton your jeans," Aria said after she wiped a napkin across her mouth.

"What?"

"I do that all the time when I stuff myself with food. It helps. And since you are a newbie at gorging, I thought it might help," she said pointing to my zipper.

"Oh, uh, okay."

I unsnapped the top button of my jeans and she was right.

"This is what it must feel like to take off a girdle," I said and then burped, which felt incredible.

"Now you're getting it. Let everything go. But if you have to fart, please release that in the bathroom. No need to call in a hazmat team to air out the place." She laughed as she stood and walked over to the bed.

"What about your farts, Aria? Maybe you're the one who wants to kill me. Death by suffocation due to too many farts." I fell back on the bed kicking up my legs.

Her eyes widened. "You have no idea what my farts smell like. My ass burps could smell like honeysuckles and baby powder."

I lifted my shirt and rubbed my belly hoping that would help.

"You know what would really help with that? Sex," she said standing over me next to the bed with a straight face.

"Does that ever work? With guys. Just saying it like that?" I tried to sit up but I farted.

Aria covered her nose with her hand. "Eww. Oh no. Now I have to call the fumigators."

Her shoulders shook. That was it. It was time to teach this woman a lesson.

I grabbed her wrist and pulled her onto the bed. Her giggles grew louder, deeper as she fell.

"No! Someone help me. He's trying to murder me with his gas. Fartocation!" she said in between fits of laughter.

I climbed on top of Aria and pulled her arms away, pinning her down.

"Looks like you're trapped. This was my plan all along, Aria. To get you in this small room so I could fart you to death," I said.

That's when I realized how close her lips were to my cock. It grew warm and hardened at the thought. My laughter slowly died as did hers. She must have been thinking the same thing as her eyes drifted to the jean-clad bulge growing on top of her chest.

"Do you not want me, Alex? Is that it?" Aria's eyes lifted to mine. There was something different in the way she looked at me. A sadness or vulnerability that I hadn't seen before.

"Of course, I want you, Aria," I said as I climbed off her and lay on my side next to her. Folding my arm, I propped up my head with my hand. "I keep waiting for this to feel right or natural. And every time I want to kiss you or pull you close something in my head stops me. I talk myself out of it because I'm afraid you won't like what you find in me."

She smiled and with her hand, she pushed me so my back was flush against the mattress.

"We are going to play a little game, Alex. It's called, what do you really want."

"All right." Willing to say yes to anything she said.

My brain began to feed me doubts so I shook my head, trying to stop them. Aria was here with me in a motel room. Nothing about the night screamed lavish. All the times I told myself women only cared about my bank account, I couldn't say that here.

This place was shoddy. Our dinner was cheap. Aria wasn't getting turned on because expensive things surrounded her, she was getting turned on because I was with her.

And that thought made me hard.

"What do you really want, right now, Alex?" She tucked her legs under her, hovering over me.

Her body. I wanted to see her body.

"For you to take off your top."

Her lips curved into a sexy smile and she reached up, unbuttoning the three buttons at the top of her black- and white-striped blouse. Her creamy skin stretched as she pulled the top from her skin, throwing it onto the floor.

What was left was a smooth stomach, petite but perky breasts hidden under violet lace, and long, lean arms. Those were the facts, but what did I care of facts at that moment.

I loved color and texture. Tone and movement. My eye was attracted to line and contrast. I looked for that in every painting and I couldn't help but notice it on Aria.

But she was no painting. She wasn't even a masterpiece. Aria was real and something no painter, no matter how talented, could ever capture the extent of her beauty.

"You are more beautiful than air."

"Air? You can't see air, Alex." Aria laughed but there was hesitation behind her eyes.

Her arm lifted to cover herself and without thought, I stopped her. "No, but I can feel it. It feeds me. Without it I couldn't live."

"Oh, well, when you put it that way. It's not bad." She lifted her hand, drifting her fingers across my arm. "Now it's my turn," Aria said as she lifted her deep brown eyes to mine.

My heart picked up in my chest and I wondered if she could hear it. I both feared and desired what she wanted. For three years, I imagined her telling me how she wanted me to fuck her. And then I would imagine doing it.

But now that the time had come for her to answer that question, I was afraid of what the answer might be.

"Aria, what do you want?"

NINETEEN

Aria

"I want everything," I said because I did.

But I needed more from him. We came here today to talk but he hasn't explained anything to me yet. I have come clean about my life, my marriage, but he's not said a word to me.

"We have to start somewhere. What would you like first?" Alex said as his eyes stayed locked to my chest.

I moved across him and swung my legs on either side of his stomach, pinning him to the bed. His chest felt firm as I drifted my fingers over him.

"With a question," I said, wanting to ask more than just one. "You said earlier that you first laid eyes on me years ago. Since you were a recluse, how could that have happened?"

His eyelids slid down my body. Alex made a sound, telling me that wasn't the question he expected. Resolve settled over his gaze when he finally looked up at me.

"I wanted to go to an art show in a new gallery that opened up. The one that showed your paintings where I bought your work. That gallery was brand new three years ago."

"I remember. I asked the owner for a job, hoping to get her to show my work eventually. She did, but it took years of working for her in addition to my job as a bartender."

His eyes dipped to my chest for a moment before he smirked and turned his head to stare at the light peeking through the old curtain.

"I talked Bradley in to coming with me. When we got there, it was an interactive showing. One area had a white ball pit that people could play in and another area had the white balls hanging from the ceiling—"

"With strings hanging from the balls and you could turn them on and off with the string. I remember. You were there?" I asked as my mind raced through the crowd of that night trying to find his face.

"Yes. And I saw you. I remember worrying if you were one of the prostitutes my mother had hired. In a way I wanted that, because then it meant I could get close to you but in a way, I didn't want that for you. My heart began to ache thinking that you could be part of that life. But you weren't."

I was surprised he remembered me so vividly and I don't remember him at all. "And you remembered me from that long ago?"

Alex reached up placing his hand on my stomach as it curved toward my back. His hand was warm and when his thumb rubbed at my skin, I wondered how long I would last with these questions.

"How could I forget the woman I fell in love with that night?"

Something crawled up my neck, both inside and out. For a moment, I thought he was touching me there, but I realized it was my imagination. I felt intensely attracted to Alex, and I cared about him . . . but love? As I stared into his heart-stopping eyes, I wondered if I was capable of feeling love for a man, even one as wonderful as Alex?

"But you never talked to me that night. Trust me, Alex, I would've remember if someone who looked like you came up to me. How can you fall in love with someone you never met?" My throat tightened at my last question, making it a whisper.

I shifted back as he lifted up onto his elbow. "How can music touch your soul with one note? How can slabs of different colored oils spread across a canvas move you to tears? These are all inanimate objects, yet people spend their lives desiring them. Perhaps I don't know enough about relationships, or maybe my mother screwed me up so much that even my idea of love is sick. But I can't help how I feel, Aria. And being here with you, it has only deepened."

Something about tonight was twisting my mind and clawed at my heart. Shaking my head to clear things, I hugged my knees to my chest. I trusted Alex and knew he would never hurt me, yet I felt like that young girl trying to break free from her captors through a bathroom window again. My heart was racing, and I was on the verge of tears all because Alex told me he loved me.

I hated how fucked-up I was.

"I didn't say that to scare you off, Aria. I wanted to be honest. And I know you couldn't possibly feel the same for me. There are things you are used to men giving you that I couldn't."

Alex tried to reach for my hand but when I pulled away he looked as defeated as I was scared. "What can't you give me, Alex? Why do you say these things to me? To confuse me? Am I some game to you that you play at my emotions like sculpting clay?"

A tear finally broke free and I pushed it away with the palm of my hand. Alex frowned and crawled over the bed to me. "No. Aria, no. I am not playing at anything. I never told you because I was afraid." He released a breath, sinking further into the bed. "Afraid I would lose you when I finally had a chance with you."

"What is it you can't give me? A life with you? I'm wondering if I am even capable of that." I paused, releasing a stuttered laugh. "I have never spent this much time with a man I was attracted to and not had sex with them. And here we are. I have no shirt on. We are lying in bed in a crappy motel room and you still haven't kissed me. Is that what you can't give me, Alex? A kiss."

"I guess we are both new to this," he said as he brushed his fingers over my lips.

Despite the war inside my body his touch was more than soothing, it was wanted. That confused me even more. As much as I feared his love, I craved his touch.

"But what can't you give me?" I asked and feared what the answer would be.

"Sex. I can't . . ." he said and pulled away.

When I sought out Alex's eyes, I saw the same war raging there.

"You can't, or you won't?"

"Neither. Both. I don't know anymore." He shook his head.

I reached my hand for his and he smiled. "Then tell me. What are you afraid of?"

Maybe we were both fucked-up. And in our crazy, messed up minds, perhaps our hearts could find peace together.

"Of hurting you," he whispered as his shoulders slumped as if he just released the biggest secret and the weight of that burden was no longer his to carry.

"What? Is your penis the size of a broomstick with the girth of a can of pop?" I had to make a joke. It was becoming too intense in here, and not in a good way.

"No, of course not. It's not about the size. I'm afraid I'll hurt you by doing what turns me on." Alex's face reddened and as I tried to lift his chin he turned away, refusing to see me.

"What turns you on, Alex? Please tell me it's not having sex with dead bodies because I'm pretty adventurous, but I will draw the line with that." I held up my hands but hoped my words would ease his heartache.

He smirked. It was the best half smile I had ever seen. The man was a virgin. He probably thought doggy style was depraved.

"No, I don't want to have sex with dead bodies or animals or anything like that."

"Oh, thank God. For a moment I was worried." I winked.

"A few weeks ago, when we almost kissed. That's how I am. I pulled your hair and forced myself on you. I am sorry."

I was silent as I thought back to that moment. How he took control and the usual shy, uncertain Alex turned into someone with confidence and restrained power. Even the memories warmed my thighs and I squirmed at the wetness that grew.

"Are you kidding me right now? That was so hot, Alex," I said as I shook my head, smiling and running my fingers through my hair as if he was pulling it right now. "We didn't even kiss but I went home and used my vibrator a few times replaying our scene in my head."

"You did?" His eyes widened in surprise.

"Yes. I would imagine that you finally kissed me. Shoving your tongue into my mouth. Not gently but pushing it inside and later . . ." I drifted off overcome by my imagination.

"What about later?" Alex scooted closer.

I sucked on my lower lip as I noticed his cock thickening between his legs. "Later you replaced your tongue with your cock."

His nose flared as he closed his eyes. I had a feeling, a warm, nipple-hardening feelings, that Alex had the same thoughts about me.

"What if I hurt you?" he whispered.

He inched closer despite his question. I watched with dripping anticipation as his cock grew beneath his jeans. He had unbuttoned them earlier from the meal and now the zipper was lowering due to the pressure building behind. I licked my lips at the show.

"If my mouth is full of thick cock than I'll pinch you just above your belly button. And you'll stop," I said as I drifted my finger over his lower stomach. "If I can speak then I will say the word you least want to hear."

"What word would that be?" His thick lips were only an inch from mine.

"Mom."

Alex groaned and winced. "Yes, that would stop me instantly. But what if your mouth is full and your hands are restrained?"

My back arched, pushing against his chest. I had played at being tied up by a man before, but this was the first time I craved it. Anything Alex wanted to do to me suddenly became my deepest desire.

"Then I will wink at you."

He removed his gray shirt without a word from me. My fingers itched to slide along his hard chest.

"How do you want to start all this?"

"We start with a kiss, Aria."

TWENTY

Alexander

"Kiss me where?" Aria asked.

I furrowed my brow. "Now. In this room."

Her lips curved. "I mean here," Aria pointed to her mouth, "or here?" She sat back spreading her legs, letting me know which kiss she preferred.

I didn't know if I would be alive when this was all over because I might die of bliss. She was perfect. My cock twitched and I had to cup myself to ease the tension.

"Why don't you lie back and find out."

Aria shifted to the middle of the bed and did as I said. It didn't take her long to remove her clothes. The purple lace she wore under her jeans instantly became my favorite color.

Curiosity took over. I slid my fingers over the tender skin of her inner thigh until I reached the lace edge. Aria's expression was a cross between longing and impatience.

I should kiss her first. Do all the things I had seen in movies, but my hand wouldn't stop. My fingers discovered even softer skin. Slick and hot and tempting me further.

She sighed. That was it. I closed my eyes and pushed my fingers inside her.

Aria shifted and I heard her moan. I opened my eyes to watch her as my fingers sank inside. She was exquisite. I could barely think as my hand moved in and out of her body.

"Oh, Alex," she said biting that plump lip of hers that I wanted to fuck later.

My thumb moved over her folds and she whimpered. The more I gave her the more her hips moved up and down and the wetter she became.

I stopped and lifted my hand. My fingers glistened and my nose flared at the scent—her scent. I wanted more of her and I licked my fingers.

It was different than I had expected—not that I had any idea how a woman would taste—but it caused my mouth to water. I had a feeling this was uniquely Aria and that made me crave more.

"Do you want to continue?" Aria asked her greedy fingers dipping under her panties.

"You want more?" I said watching her play with herself.

She nodded, her back arching as she pushed both hands down and began to fuck herself. She was incredible. I knew I wasn't going to last much longer, so I pushed off my jeans and navy boxer briefs so I could work my cock.

"I'm going to watch you, Aria. And when I come, I want you to lick it off me," I said to see if she would agree to something I so desperately wanted. These fantasies filled me with shame for so long, and I wondered if Aria would want them too.

"Yeah. God, Alex. You are so hot," Aria said, and I could hear the slapping wet noise as she rode her hands.

She wanted more, from me, so I gave it to her. I reached over and added two of my fingers to her pussy so she was taking me with her own.

She arched her back. "Oh yeah, Alex."

"You like that, Aria? You want to be filled?" I said as I moved with the motion of her hands.

"Yes, make me come, Alex. Please."

It was the begging that really did it. To watch her squirm and plead for release made me rock hard.

"What do you want?" I said watching her brown eyes turn almost black from desire. Her body was flush and all I wanted to do was climb her, pin her to the bed, and go wild.

But if I did that, I wouldn't last.

"I want to see you. I want to watch you touch yourself."

Until that point I was only lightly touching myself, just enough to ease the tension. My focus was on her. I never realized that she would be as turned on by me as I was by her.

Once the high of all this wore off, would she even want to look at me? I hesitated for a moment before I gave Aria what she needed.

Spreading my legs out, I sat back with a perfect view of what she was doing to herself. Slowly but with a tight grip, I used her slickness to rub over my cock. When I got to the base of my cock, I squeezed trying to make this last but I knew I only had a few more strokes in me.

Aria sat up on her elbow using one hand now to play with herself. I reached over and pulled down her panties, removing them. When I glanced back, it was too late. I lost it seeing her like that—so wet and playing out my fantasy.

One stroke and I was coming. I moaned her name and even a few curse words. Hot cum sprayed across my stomach as my head fell back. Before my orgasm was finished, Aria's hot breath was on my skin.

She was doing what I asked, licking everything up.

I pulled Aria up to me and consumed her. My lips crashed onto hers and she tasted like heaven. Her tongue pushed its way into mine and I let it. We kissed for what seemed like forever before I eased up, nipping at her lip as I pulled away.

"Did you come?" I asked realizing that I came so hard I had no idea if she had too.

"Oh yeah I did. Watching you orgasm was like watching a unicorn shoot a rainbow out of its butt. Un-fucking-believable."

I felt more relaxed than I ever had. Laughing, I tucked my hand under my head and pulled her toward me with the other. She curled into my side and everything felt right. As if her body was made to be next to mine.

"What's your obsession with butts. First you worry about dying from farts and then you compare me to something coming out of a butt," I said before I kissed the top of her head. She smelled of the sea and sex.

"What can I say? I like butts. Speaking of butts, I never got a good look at yours. Turn over," Aria said as she propped herself up on her elbow.

"Am I being inspected?"

"No. Just shamelessly ogled."

Rolling over, I tried to glance back to see what she was doing but I only caught glimpses of fluttering, flaxen hair. I suddenly felt what she was doing. There was a slap followed by something sharp digging into my ass cheek.

"Ow. What was that?"

"Just my teeth. I had to take a bite. I can now officially say that I am the first woman to tap that ass."

"You're a butt woman, huh?" I said as I rolled over causing her to frown.

I grabbed her and pulled her on top of me, nuzzling my head into her neck. Even after all we did I couldn't get enough of her.

"You know my one true weakness."

Pulling my head back I stared up at her. "You have more than one weakness, Aria. I would say you have two."

"Mmm. And what are they?" Aria asked as she peppered kisses across my chest.

"Sex and food."

Her kisses came to a stop and she looked up at me. "I think you're right. I once had a dream where I was having sex and eating a three-course meal at a fancy restaurant. When I woke up I was angry because the dream ended. That was the best dream ever."

I combed my fingers through her hair. I wondered if the satisfied smile on her face was from what we did together or memories of her dream.

"I know your weaknesses, Alex."

"Okay, what are they?" I said.

"You have many."

I shook my head. "No, I don't. I only have one."

Her eyes widened and she sat up. "Based on what just happened on this bed, I would disagree. If you do only have one, what is it?"

Lifting myself up I cupped the back of her head with my hand. "It's you." I leaned in to kiss her. She sighed as my tongue found hers.

The kiss was light as we soon drifted off to sleep still wrapped in each other's arms.

A buzzing sound woke me and I glanced over at the clock. It was ten thirty in the morning.

"That's my phone," Aria said with a groggy voice as she scooted to the edge of the bed. She grabbed her purse from the bedside table and dug inside until she got her phone. "Hello?"

Relaxing back, I made a mental note of all the smooth curves of her body.

"Oh no. How bad is it?" she said before pausing. "Of course, I can be there. I'll meet you there in a half hour."

My heart sank as she pushed the phone back into her purse. Our time together had to end. I knew it did. I just didn't think it would end so soon.

"Alex, I have to go. Tiffany's son is in the hospital. She needs me right now."

TWENTY-ONE

Aria

"He fell down," Tiffany said, her eyes red and swollen.

It hurt to watch my friend upset, so I wrapped her in my arms and brought her to a chair. Memories of my sister comforting me the last time I saw her added to the pain.

We sat in two of the three black leather chairs in the doctor's office. Alex hovered in the corner. While I comforted, he appeared uneasy. His eyes scanned the room for something.

I wondered if he had a problem with hospitals. I knew some people didn't like them and given Alex's unusual life, I wouldn't be surprised if his mother caused him to fear hospitals too.

"Tell me what happened," I said cradling Tiffany as her tears streamed down her cheeks. I took a tissue for her, from a box that sat next to a plush unicorn, off the large wooden desk in front of us.

Tiffany and I had grown closer over the last month. As she helped me with the mural, I spent more time with her and her son, David. She was the kind of friend who would never bother you with her problems unless it was an absolute emergency.

I knew when she asked me to meet her at the hospital with David it had to be serious. How could I run off to some paradise with Alex, knowing I left my friend behind in her time of need?

She's everything to that boy and that boy was everything to her. Tiffany was the example of how a mother should be. Alex's mom and my mom should have taken lessons from her.

"The physical therapist tried to get him to climb up steps in the stairwell of the building. Usually, he does the steps in the physical therapy room, which has three wide steps and a lot of room for someone to work with him. But the stairwell is four floors and the steps are cement."

She took a breath as her voice began to waver before continuing, "I don't know what happened exactly but I think the therapist looked away for a moment and David slipped. He was making such good progress. A million thoughts are running through my head. Did he break something? Will this cause him to regress? Why wasn't the therapist focused on him? Grrr. I want to hit that therapist so hard."

Tiffany shook her fist in the air. I was about to say something about finding some guys to beat up the therapist when Alex came over and sat on the other side of Tiffany.

He placed his hand on her shoulder. "Tiffany, remember what I told you when I first met you?"

She sniffled, shaking her head. "No. I'm sorry. I don't."

"You are a good mother. Accidents. They happen. It can't be helped. But you took him straight here and are fighting to find out what went wrong. That's what counts. Maybe this therapist was in the wrong, maybe he wasn't. But, since you are a wonderful mom, you will find out and do what is best for David."

Tiffany took a deep breath and relaxed back into the seat. Her tears had stopped. "You're right, Alex. I know sometimes I doubt myself. Especially when something like this happens. Our old physical therapist moved away so we have this new one. He's okay, but sometimes I get the feeling he isn't one hundred percent present."

She took another breath. "Anyway, I keep thinking that if I got him a different therapist this wouldn't have happened. I blame myself. I'll do what needs to be done for David. Thanks, Alex." She gazed up at him and he smiled.

The door opened and there was a woman standing there. "Ms. Blackburn?"

"Yes?" Tiffany stood.

"Dr. Gerald wishes to speak with you. Your friends can stay here, it shouldn't take long."

Tiffany walked off with the woman and I turned to Alex when the door closed. "You are like the mother-whisperer."

"What is a mother-whisperer?" Alex said before chuckling.

"You have the power to calm a distraught mother. It's a gift, Alex," I said and realized that his mom didn't deserve him.

Maybe I didn't deserve him either?

"I was just pointing out the obvious. She seems nice and she cares very much for her son. It's something I have rarely witnessed."

Now I wanted to find some guys to beat up Alex's mom. This giant of a man had the heart of the sweetest child. So much kind innocence flowed through his veins that it made me want to do anything to keep his mother away from him.

"Thank you for coming with me, Alex." I got up and sat in the seat Tiffany vacated.

I took Alex's hands in mine and gazed into his wonderful gray eyes. "I know you want to run away to paradise with me but I don't think I can leave."

He frowned and his fingers intertwined with mine. "Why not? I've told you everything about me. You've shared things with me. I feel closer to you than I have to anyone."

"Yes, I haven't told any guy I've been with as much as I've told you about my life. Even Morgana doesn't know some of the things I told you, and I've known her since I was a freshman in college."

"Then what's the problem?" he asked and my heart ached as I watched the pain in his eyes.

"This is the problem." I waved my hand around. "I have people here I care about. You don't. My friends are my family and I love them. Before my roommate, Morgana, left for New York I stayed up with her as I helped her get over a broken heart."

I got up and picked up the unicorn. It was worn and a little dirty, but I could tell it was loved.

"And my friend Evaleen. She doesn't open up much but when she does, I want to be there for her. These are women who I'm not blood related to but it doesn't make me love them any less. I can't just run away from them. It would break my heart."

I heard him sigh and we stayed there like that, in silence, as the sharp sting of reality tore at our happy dream.

"Maybe we don't run away together," Alex said.

I nodded. "Yeah, that's what I said."

"No, I know that. Hear me out. What if my mother thinks she won?" Alex said as he stood with a grin curling his lips.

"I don't understand. I'm sure she will think she won. Wow, that woman's control issues run deep." I chuckled, shaking my head.

My breath caught as Alex stood and placed his hands on my arms.

"Yes, she has control issues. Bigger issues than you realize. But what I'm talking about is tricking her. Making her think she's won."

"But what would be the point of that? She did win, Alex. We aren't running away together."

Alex pulled away, taking the unicorn out of my hand and walking over to the window.

"This unicorn is the key."

Oh God, he's gone mental. At least we are in a hospital. It may be a children's hospital, but they have medical staff that can help him.

"And what does the unicorn say to you, Alex?" I said in a very calm, unemotional voice as I crept backward toward the door.

"What? It doesn't speak to me, Aria," Alex said as he turned around. "Where are you going?"

"Nowhere." My eyes widened from being caught.

"Anyway, it has been eating away at me that my mom seems to show up right when something is about to happen. When I planned to run away with you or when I decided to paint a mural."

"Okay." I was beginning to realize that maybe I decided too quickly that he was losing his mind.

I felt bad that I kept doing that with him. Like earlier when we left the Mimir building I kept thinking he was going to take me somewhere to kill me and now, that he was losing his mind. I seemed to jump to extreme conclusions with him.

Maybe I was just making an excuse to run away from him.

"When I started to take down the wallpaper for the mural, I found a small piece of black plastic near the ceiling. It blended into the pattern of the wallpaper. At first, I thought it belonged to something that was hanging before, like an old picture or shelving that had been removed. But the more I looked at it and now, with my mother always showing up at certain times, I believe she is bugging me. Spying on me."

I gasped. Based on what I had witnessed from his mom I knew she was bad, but to spy on her son, in his bedroom, that was pure evil. Not to mention disgusting.

"Oh God. She's crazy." And I thought Alex was the crazy one. Now I really felt terrible.

"You have no idea," Alex said as he shook his head.

"Then what should we do?"

I glanced around the room and wondered, how many places had she bugged? Did she spy on me too?

"That's why I took you to that cheap motel. I paid cash for our room knowing she would never find me there. I didn't want anyone to know where we were going. I wanted to talk you into running away despite what happened at Mimir. But the more I think about it, the more I think we should let my mom think she won."

"Okay, I'm in. What's the plan?"

TWENTY-TWO

Alexander

"Is he mangled?" Aria asked with worry surrounding her words.

She sounded faint. Like her words were being muffled. I opened my eyes and had no idea where I was. This wasn't my bedroom but the smell of coffee had me smiling.

"Just a sprain then? Oh, that's good. I was worried when you came back and said he would have to stay in the hospital. But everything is fine now." Aria's voice was coming from the bathroom.

I sat up and realized I was naked. In Aria's bed. In her room.

We came back here last night after Tiffany told us she would stay the night in the hospital with her son. From what I gathered, her son, David, had an operation a few months ago to help him walk. The doctors wanted to make sure the fall didn't have any negative effects on what the operation helped.

I got up from the bed and went over to the bathroom. The door was open enough that a sliver of light shone through. Aria was sitting on the sink speaking on her cell phone wearing a long yellow T-shirt.

"I've got to go, Tiffany. Alex is spying on me." Aria lifted her middle finger toward the door as she curled the corner of her mouth.

She tapped at her phone and put it down on the counter. Pushing open the door I let my full-on erection guide me toward her.

"Can't a woman have a private conversation in her bathroom without a Hawthorne spying on her?" she said as I pushed myself between her legs and wrapped my arms around her waist.

"No. You know us Hawthornes. Besides, there's lots of work to be done," I said as I leaned in and kissed her neck.

"Work in bed or on the mural?" Her words full of questions but her hands full of temptation as she dug her nails into my back.

When we came back here, I was worried her place might be bugged too, so we wrote down our plan. Handing the paper back and forth like children passing notes in class.

Growing tired and horny, we came to bed and fooled around.

"The mural," I said and I could see the disappointment in her face. "I know it seems weird but when we do have sex, I want it to be right. If that makes sense. I don't want to be worried that we're bugged or hiding from my mom."

"I get it. But when will that be, Alex? I feel like your mom will always be watching us."

Maybe it had nothing to do with my mom. Maybe it's because I was worried that I wouldn't be good enough for Aria.

"How about after the mural is complete? Can you wait that long?" I said.

I fought my body every day when I was around Aria. Part of me wanted to sink so deep inside her I might never come out. And the other part, well, it was rotted. It had been controlled by an evil woman for so long that it would make any excuse to keep me hidden.

She reached down to tug at the T-shirt she wore. "Yeah, I can wait."

Tilting her head, she peered up at me with a sly grin. We kissed for a while. Aria had already showered before I woke up so I took one while she went to the kitchen and made us breakfast.

After the shower and a belly full of scrambled eggs, toast, and coffee, we made our way to the L train. We decided taking the train was another way for us to discuss our plan without my mother hearing about it.

Having never ridden the L before, Aria showed me the ropes and I loved the feel of the rumbling wooden platform and being surrounded by all the people going about their day.

For a moment, I felt real. Like I was an average person, and not some weird man sheltered by his crazy mother. It was now mid-May and an unusually nice day. Warm enough to be without a jacket, even in the early morning. Aria looked beautiful as the warm breeze rippled her lavender blouse across her skin. I loved watching the contrast of her. The fire in her eyes and soft warmth of her skin.

Aria glanced down the tracks looking for a train. "When we get to your place I'll start to sweep the place for bugs so you can take care of your thing. When I got up this morning, I Googled what we should be looking for."

"And I know my part," I said, shoving my hands in my pockets trying to prepare myself for the worst.

The train arrived, almost knocking me back with a gust of sound and air. Once we were inside and seated Aria turned to me, placing her hand on my shoulder. "It's not going to be easy, Alex. I understand if you don't want to do this."

I didn't. That rotten part of me wanted to go home, crawl into bed, and never come out. But having met Aria and gotten to know her, that sick part of me was shrinking every day.

"No. It has to be done. And when it is," I said as I glanced around and pulled Aria closer, "I'm going to lick you. I'm going to eat you. And I'm going to worship every part of you."

My finger outlined the blush that swept across her cheeks. When we came to our stop I followed Aria out. It took a few minutes and many blocks, but we finally got to Michigan Avenue and to Haute Tower.

When we walked through my condo door Bradley was standing there. I wondered if my doorman tipped him off that we were on our way up.

His dark, brown eyes flipped between me and Aria. "Alex, glad you're home. There's an urgent matter I need to discuss with you . . . in private."

That was the excuse I needed. I nodded to Aria as she nodded back. Waiting for her to move down the hall, knowing she was heading toward my bathroom as I told her to start there first, I turned to Bradley. "Of course, Bradley. There's something I need to discuss with you, too."

He waved for me to follow him. When we got to the security room, he shut the door behind him.

"I mentioned two months ago that I saw Aria in the security room." Bradley waved his hand toward the monitors. "Since that day, every time she has been here I have kept my eye on her."

I held up my hands. "Bradley, that isn't really necessary. I know Aria. She would never steal from me or try to deceive me."

"Are you so sure, Alex? Because what was she placing under your bed all those weeks ago when she first started that project in your bedroom while you stepped out?"

Bradley leaned over the desk and typed away at a keyboard. The screen of the monitor closest to me was nothing but static before it flickered and finally a video of my bedroom appeared.

"This is from the day Aria first came to work on the mural about a month ago," Bradley said pointing to the monitor of my bedroom.

Anger surged through me as I stared at the screen.

Aria was looking at the wall. Her hand touched her chest. After a moment, her head swiveled as if looking for something. She glanced around the room and lifted some things from my end table next to my bed. At one point, I could see her bending down and reaching back behind the table.

"There. Right there. I think she placed something right there. Also, a minute later, you see her do the same thing but under your bed."

I didn't care that he was right. My heart sank as I watched Bradley's words come to life. My fists tightened as I turned to face my cousin.

"You were filming my bedroom?" I said through gritted teeth.

His eyes grew wide. That wasn't the reaction he expected.

"I'm your security Alex. It's my job to keep you safe."

"Are there cameras in the bathroom too? Or am I allowed to take a shit by myself?" I asked as I took a step closer. He stood a little straighter but he wouldn't lift his gaze.

That was my answer.

"I'll take care of this, Bradley. You don't need to worry about Aria anymore."

He nodded and just before I turned to leave I said, "But we do need to discuss your job later."

That sickening feeling, the one that came over me whenever my mother said she had to speak with me, erupted and sank to the bottom of my stomach. There were so many people in my life that were using me and I had no idea who to believe anymore.

As I maneuvered down the hall I went straight to my bathroom. Aria was still there. She was lying on the floor with half her body inside the cabinet.

My eyes softened when I watched her smooth legs flex and twist. But then the images of her digging through my things, probably tapping my room like my mother, caused every muscle in my body to harden.

"Aria, let's move into the bedroom. I want to get started in there," I said.

She pulled out, her cheeks flush with a beautiful smile on her face. As unhappy as I was with what she had done to me, I would be lying if I said I wouldn't miss that breathtaking smile.

"Okay, but I haven't completely finished in here."

Once we were in my bedroom, I pointed to my bed. "I'll start here and you can start in my closet."

I watched her eyes closely to see if she was worried. Waiting for her to protest or make an excuse for her to work on the bed, but nothing came.

Aria nodded and gave me a thumb up before turning to the closet. Perhaps she believed I would mistake it for one of my mother's bugs so she wasn't worried.

I immediately pulled back the side table to check where I saw her reach back on the video. There was nothing there but some dust. I removed the lamp and pulled out the drawer but everything was fine.

That's when I turned to under the bed. I got on my back and scooted as far under the bed as possible. I tried to find anything unusual but only felt the wood frame and box spring. Twisting my head, something metal caught my eye.

I reached over and pulled it toward me. Scooting out I stood to get a better look at it in the light. Holding it up I knew immediately what it was.

"My lucky charm necklace. You found it. I was wondering if I lost it here," Aria said as she walked over to take the simple gold heart charm.

"You did?"

She nodded studying the gold jewelry. "Yeah, I even searched your room about a month ago to see if I could find it but couldn't."

Aria threw her arms around me. "Thank you, Alex. This may not look like much but the necklace is very important to me."

I stroked her head as I gazed out my door. "Then it's a good thing I found it."

Or I would have let the wrong person go.

TWENTY-THREE

Aria

"I hate cleaning," I said to the dust bunnies.

With a broom in one hand and a dust pan in the other, I sniffled as I swept up the dirt and dust from my wooden floor.

It had been a few weeks since getting rid of the listening devices and working on the mural. Today I decided to take a break from painting and stay home to clean. Alex and I had found twenty bugs in his place before we came to my apartment where I found fifteen.

We destroyed most of them, except for the ones that were in our bedrooms. Those we kept and planted them near the animal exhibits at the Lincoln Park Zoo.

If Mrs. Hawthorne wants to listen in on what her son does in bed . . . well, she will now get her fill of crazy monkey sex.

Morgana comes home next week from New York and I wanted the place to be clean for her return. I went to visit her two weeks ago with her parents. She looked good but wasn't as happy as I was hoping she would be.

Maybe coming home to a clean apartment and some of her mom's cake that her mom was planning to make for a welcome home party would cheer Morgana up.

As for me, I've never been happier. Alex and I have yet to do the deed and I'm surprised that it doesn't bother me.

A little too surprised. Something kept nudging at my chest every time I thought about having sex with Alex. And that scared me. I don't mind him being my first boyfriend. I've been with him longer than I have been with any man, but eventually things will have to come to an end.

It's not like we will be together forever. Just a summer fling, right?

Besides, Alex's mom mentioned this woman Alexa. Perhaps she's an old love. Some friend of the family that his mom would be overjoyed for Alex to be with.

My chest began to hurt again.

There was a knock at the door pulling me from my thoughts. I dropped the broom and dust pan like they were terrible because they were and went over to the door.

I glanced out my peephole expecting to find one of my neighbors since someone from outside would have to be buzzed into the building.

I gasped when I saw who it was. My hand shook as I reached for the doorknob and opened the door.

"Mom, what are you doing here?" I asked in shock to see the woman I hadn't laid eyes on in over five years.

"Aria, it's nice to see you," she said as she tried to smile.

She was lying. Someone made her come here. My mom never wanted me and made it obvious with her actions, and even if she didn't say the words, she believed the wrong sister died.

"Are you going to invite me inside?" She lifted her jaw the same way she did when she was unhappy.

"Yes, please come inside." I stood back, opening the door to let her through.

I wasn't surprised when her lips pursed as her eyes scanned my apartment. My mother was used to high-priced, upscale, and anything that was made of gold, platinum, and silk.

"It's quaint."

"You can stop pretending now," I said as I frowned and waved toward the living area. "Come sit on the couch and tell me why you're here. Is it Dad? Did he send you?"

I moved to the overstuffed chair next to the old, brown couch. Our hodgepodge of furniture was not up to my mother's standards as she leaned down to sit like she was about to take a shit.

"Your father wants you to come to California," she said as her eyes wandered around the room.

"Why?"

I wasn't about to up and leave my friends and especially Alex, just because my father snapped his fingers.

"He's having his fiftieth birthday. I am planning a big celebration." My mother finally brought her attention back to me and not my second-hand furniture.

"You both live in California now?"

Last I knew they lived in Winnetka, just north of Chicago.

"Yes, we moved two years ago. Your father took on a client that is quite powerful. Has a lot of connections. You know how your father is, always trying to move up in the world."

I rolled my eyes knowing what connections she was talking about. Where they saw money and power, every normal person saw crime and danger.

"I see you have moved on from Ava's killing," I said and watched my mother's brown eyes for any hope of sorrow.

I was disappointed in what I found.

She scooted toward the end of the couch and reached over, placing her hand on mine. "Now, Aria, you know your sister wasn't killed. She died of an overdose. The doctors confirmed it. I suspected she had a problem and hoped the clinic would've helped but we were just too late."

I drew my hand back as if my mother's touch was full of venom. "Clinic. Is that what you two have told yourself? You think if you say it enough you'll believe it." I laughed because if I didn't I would sob. "Dad sold us to those people. Those disgusting criminals. His *children*. They drugged her and they would have drugged me but I escaped."

I was the lucky one. Ava should have escaped. She was smart and brave and she deserved all the things. She could have found the cure for cancer or ended world hunger or done something that would go down in history. What could I do? I could paint. That doesn't save lives. And even if I filled a million canvases with every color known to man, it would never bring her back.

My mother gazed down at her fingers and I noticed for the first time how worn they were. There were calluses and wrinkles and spots that I would expect to see on an eighty-year-old's hands, not a fifty-five-year-old's.

I leaned in as my mother started to speak with her head down as I could barely hear her.

"We were young when we had your sister. Your father had just started law school. It was hard in the beginning. The bills, the cost of college, and having a baby . . . we struggled. And then when you came your father had just started with a good law firm. We made a pact. He would take any job they gave him, even the cases none of the other lawyers would take, if it meant we would have enough money for you two."

"That was then, Mom. And that's no excuse for what happened to Ava."

She gazed up at me, tears streaming down her face. "You're right, Aria. But by then everything was out of control. And your father, he changed. It changed him. He became like them."

The moment had come. My mother was finally admitting the truth. I fell to the floor, kneeled at her feet as I clasped her hands in her lap, my words pleading, "Then come with me. Get away from him. I can make sure you never see him again."

Her eyes traveled my face as only a mother's could. It had been so long since I had seen her look at me like that—full of love and pride.

"I'm so proud of you, Aria. No matter what's happened, please know that I love you. That there hasn't been a moment that's gone by that I haven't thought about you."

That's when tears fell from my face. I knew what she was doing. For so long I told myself I never wanted to see her again, but now that she's here I never wanted her to leave.

I hated her and my father for so long, but now, I felt nothing but pity. My sister and I needed their help that day and they turned their backs, leaving us in hell. But I refused to make the same mistakes as them.

"Mom, please, I promise I'll help you."

Her smile grew soft as she waved me up to sit next to her. She drew me into an embrace. It felt good and long overdue.

When she pulled back I had hope. "I do miss Chicago; it's so nice this time of year."

She pushed a few tendrils from my brow.

I nodded. "Yes, it is. We can visit the Tower Road beach and take walks like we used to."

She laughed. "Remember when Ava was so excited that we had a warm day in May that she ran into the lake, not realizing how cold the water still was."

I threw my head back with a deep belly laugh at the memory.

"I remember. She shivered so much and I was worried when her lips turned blue. I hugged her the whole walk back to keep her warm."

"We were so happy then," my mom said and then sighed.

"We can be that happy again."

She squeezed my hand and was about to say something when something in her purse buzzed. I had no idea what was in her purse but deep in my bones I felt it related to me. My stomach twisted as my mother reached for her purse to pull out her cell phone.

She tapped at it, reading whatever caught her attention.

"It's your father. I have to go, Aria," my mother said refusing to look at me.

"But you'll come back, right?"

I got up as she made her way to the door. She opened the door and turned to me.

"It was wonderful to see you again. I meant it, I'm so very proud of you. Can I have one more hug before I go?"

I'd lost her. Just one word from my father, whatever he sent her, and she was lost once again.

"Of course, Mom. I miss you. I'll always be there for you."

She pulled me close. Her arms tightened around me. I felt the tears begin to fall as I tried to hold them back. Just before she let go she whispered into my ear, "Run as far as you can and don't ever look back."

TWENTY-FOUR

Alexander

*"**This drink's hot,** like your body,"* the kid said as he pushed Aria's coffee order toward her. The final blow, he winked at her.

My eyes narrowed trying to saw him in half with my stare.

"How old are you?" Aria asked trying to hold back her laughter.

"How old do you want me to be?" he countered as he made a kissy face.

"Where's a manager?" I demanded, glancing around the shop. The only things I noticed were the small wooden tables, a couple of customers, and brown painted walls, but no one who might be another employee.

"My uncle owns Wake Up Joe's and he's in the back. I suggest you don't disturb him."

"Come on, Aria, let's go find a seat." I placed my hand on her back to guide her away from the sleazy kid.

As we sat in a brown leather booth back in the corner, I gazed around the place to make sure I wasn't followed. I only saw an old man with a golf umbrella despite the cloudless sky outside and a guy in a leather jacket reading a book while enjoying some coffee. He appeared too scruffy to be anyone my mother would hire.

"I did it," I said.

"Great. So, he hasn't been back?"

"I changed the locks and codes to the doors on Monday and since then, I haven't seen Bradley," I said.

I tried to fire Bradley weeks ago when he attempted to make me believe Aria was using me. He flat out told me no. Reminding me that my mother employed him, not me. He told me my mother had brought up Alexa Dorton again. I worried how far my mother would go to separate Aria from me.

It was difficult for me to be alone with Aria. Especially when we wanted to be intimate with each other as Bradley made it a habit of showing up. Even when Aria came over to work on the mural.

We considered having me stay at her place but every time we would come back to her apartment, we found a new bug. There was no winning with my mother.

She had the power and the money to gain access to anything she wanted. I was unhappy but not that surprised when I discovered my place bugged, but when we found them at Aria's place too, I wanted to destroy her world piece by piece. Never, would I believe a single word that exited my mother's mouth again. She's twisted me and everyone I cared about without a care of how much it hurt.

Aria tried to get me to go to the police, but I knew my mother. She was smart enough to have enough cops in her pocket. A detective Cindy Hardy's card, from the Chicago Police, fell out of my mother's coat pocket a few months ago. I knew she had that card for a reason and it wasn't to report a crime.

"Good. At least we got one person taken care of," Aria said before she took a sip of her black coffee.

For years I dreamed of being with Aria. Never believing she would want me and now that I could have her, my mother made it almost impossible to be everything I wanted to be with Aria.

I twisted a discarded plastic stirrer in an attempt to delay having to tell Aria what I knew.

A warm hand, soft in its touch halted my finger's progress with the object. I glanced up to find Aria, her eyes wide with concern.

"He called me," I finally said unable to hold back when she gazed at me like that.

"Who?"

"Bradley. Just before I texted you this morning. He told me that I can't even begin to understand how high this goes. That it's not about me. It is so much bigger than that. When I tried to fire him, and had to change the locks, he brought up Alexa again—" I hesitated as I watched Aria's expression turn fearful.

But she had to know. Maybe if I told her everything she would agree to leave Chicago and go to that tropical island we talked about. "He said I'm just a tool in my mother's arsenal. He admitted he was a part of her arsenal too, and the only difference was he knew about it and was paid for it. I was to marry as part of the plan."

"But why, if he is being paid to help your mom, why would he tell you all of this?" Aria asked.

"Bradly said he meant it all those times he said he was my friend. He saw how my mother poisoned everyone around her with her lies and he saw what it did to me. But he always respected me because I was the one person who refused to believe her. Who wouldn't let her control me."

I had no idea how Bradley thought my mom never controlled me. That woman had been manipulating me since birth. It's only now, that Aria was finally in my life, that I was even attempting to leave my mother's grip.

"Who is this Alexa? And why does your mom want you to marry her so badly?" Aria asked.

I shook my head. "Her family is powerful in politics. Her uncle is a senator and her grandfather was a former vice president. Her parents have a lot of money and a lot of sway in Washington DC. I met her once when I was ten. She's as controlled by her parents also."

She took a sip of her coffee and let my words sink in. "Do you want to marry her?"

I didn't hesitate as I shook my head. "No, Aria. I want to be with you. I want to be free to marry who I want and do what I want." I hoped my smile, as I reached for her hand, conveyed that I meant everything I said.

Aria nodded but I could see the doubt in her eyes. She glanced around the café and took a moment to stare at the man reading the book. I looked over, noticing the book was gone and he was using his phone. I couldn't quite make out his face as he had his phone up with the back facing us. I wondered if he was filming us. Even if he was, he wouldn't know what we were saying.

Aria leaned in to me, turning her head from the guy with the phone. "My mother showed up at my place last week."

I squeezed her hand. "What did she want?"

She let out a small puff of air and gave a grin that didn't convey happiness. "She gave me the excuse of wanting me to come to California for my father's birthday party. I didn't believe her. That's when she finally told me the truth."

Aria had mentioned what happened to her and her sister due to her parent's abandonment. It broke my heart to hear that anyone would treat their children as objects to be bought or sold. But then I knew my mother, and realized there were some people in this world who didn't deserve to be parents at all.

"I kept thinking, why now? Why did my mother show up at this moment? That's why I wanted to tell you. I wouldn't be surprised if my parents were being used by your mom. If that is true, your mom doesn't want me with you. And wants me gone so much she's willing to have my parents drag me off to California."

I took her other hand in mine and brought both of her hands to my chest. "That's why we need to get out of here. After what Bradley said, I'm wondering if we should just ditch the idea of trying to fool my mother and leave tonight."

Aria took her hands from me and I knew that she was about to say something I wouldn't want to hear.

"But my friends? Morgana comes home in a few days, on Saturday, and I want to be here for her."

"But you saw her three weeks ago when you went with her parents and grandmother to visit in New York." I knew I was being selfish but this was my mother I was trying to get away from. If Bradley was right, which I suspected he was, then Aria could be in danger.

"Can't we at least wait a week. Then I can go. I am going to Morgana's welcome home party at her parents' house on Saturday night. I'll tell her we are going away. How about you come with me? Meet her."

"I already met her, remember?"

She laughed, her eyes crinkling and it made me want to lean over and trace the lines on her face. Imprint them in my muscle memory so I can feel them forever.

"I mean really meet her. Outside of a basement garage." She smirked.

I didn't want my mother's people to follow me to Morgana's parents' home, put her family in danger. As much as I wanted to get to know Aria's friends, I felt it was safer to stay away. I was about to tell her when the back of my neck prickled. Someone was watching me.

"Is that Grace?" Aria said leaning to the side to stare at something behind me.

I turned and found a pair of brown eyes focused on me. A chill ran down my body. It was the way she was staring. As if she knew me even though I had barely met her twice. Once when she brought in coffee when I was speaking with the Mimir lawyer, and the second time in the elevator at Mimir.

"What is she doing this far north? It's Thursday, shouldn't she be at Mimir?" Aria whispered to me.

As Grace began to move toward our table, I turned back to face Aria. Something about this felt off. Evaleen had mentioned Grace was weird and now I was beginning to believe her.

"Hi, Aria. Funny running into you here. Oh, hello, Mr. Hawthorne." Grace stood at the entrance of our booth so neither of us could escape.

Was it strange that I had the urge to run?

"Hello, Grace? Yeah, it is funny. I figured you would be downtown."

The corner of Grace's lip ticked up as she turned her gaze from Aria to me. "I had to run an errand for Mr. Mimir." She held up a manila envelope before continuing, "Some photographer's studio around the corner. Figured I'd pick up lunch on my way back. I hear Morgana's coming back this weekend."

The more Grace watched me the more I squirmed in my seat. I noticed Aria's eyes narrowed at Grace. "Yeah, I'm going to see her Saturday."

Grace finally took her eyes off me but only for a second. "I assume her mom's going to make some cake."

"Yes, her parents are throwing a welcome home party. Aria is taking me." For some reason, I felt the need to make it obvious to Grace that I was with Aria. Get her to stop taking an interest in me.

"That should be fun. Is Mr. Payne going to be there?" Grace's eyes fell from us and glanced around the room, focusing on the scruffy man with the phone. The man was tapping at it, his face turned down.

"I don't think so, Grace. Why would Morgana want that piece of garbage there? You want him? He's all yours." Aria waved her hand at Grace.

Grace's eyes cut to Aria and by the way she looked at Aria, I would think Aria had said Grace smelled of roadkill on a summer's day.

"Why would I want someone who would lie like that? He's a fool. Anyway, I have to be ordering my food so I can get back. It was nice to see you both."

And just like that, Grace's expression turned from pure hatred to polite friendliness as she waved goodbye.

I leaned toward Aria. "Let's get out of here."

She nodded in agreement. We walked out the door and made our way down the street before Aria saw another Mimir employee.

"Edgar?" Aria called out.

I looked up to find a tall, blond man with a dark gray suit looking over at Aria and waving.

TWENTY-FIVE

Aria

"I'll make tea," Evaleen's mom said as she scurried off farther into Edgar's townhouse.

When we mentioned we had run into Grace at Wake Up Joe's, Edgar told us to come home with him as he lived a few blocks away. We explained as much as we could about Alex's mom and everything that's been going on as we made our way through the zigzag streets to his place.

He was surprised but mentioned there was someone from his past, a man that took advantage of his family, that suddenly reappeared. He wanted to show us this guy's picture to see if he looked familiar. Based on what we told him about Alex's mom, he wondered if she was involved.

Now we sat on his blue velvet couch being catered to by Evaleen's mom.

"Doesn't Evaleen have her own place?" I asked because why would her mom be here in the middle of the day without Evaleen.

Edgar walked to the other side of his silver and glass coffee table and sat on the cream leather chair. His posture told me relaxed but there was uncertainty in his voice. "They are in the process of finding another apartment. I told them I had plenty of room and they could stay with me until they found something."

But everything changed once he added a wink. It was funny the way that wink seemed to reassure me more than his explanation.

"About that picture of . . . what was his name?" I asked.

"His real name is Damien but he has gone by the name Shane, too. Here, I have it behind this picture." Edgar got up and removed a folded piece of paper from behind a silver framed photograph of an older woman who I assumed was his mother and a slightly older version of Edgar, which was probably his brother.

Unfolding the paper, I realized it was a different picture. He placed it in my open palm. Something cold and clammy broke out over my skin as I gestured to it. "Is that Damien?" I pointed to one of the three men in the picture.

"No. That's one of his thugs. I don't know who that is. This is Damien." He indicated one of the men staring straight into the camera. It was creepy. I knew criminals—even well-paid ones—and he looked like a criminal.

Alex glanced at the picture but shrugged his shoulder, "I don't recognize anyone."

"That's the guy who was reading a book at the coffee shop. The one Grace was staring at," I said and pointed to one of the thugs in the picture, the one that wasn't Damien.

Alex leaned toward the picture to get a better look but Edgar took back the photograph and studied it.

"What would he want with you? I know why he would be interested in Eva—" Edgar said but stopped himself. His eyes flared for a moment before his usual laid-back expression surfaced.

"What?" Alex asked.

"Nothing. Obviously, your mom is involved in all this. But why?" Edgar said before folding the picture back up and tucking it behind the frame on the mantle. His fingers gently grazed the edge of the frame as he stared at the people surrounded by silver before turning back to us.

"She must have hired him to watch me. Watch us." Alex turned to me and grabbed my hand, giving me a weak smile. No matter what was happening, his touch did something to me. A peaceful, happy calm came over me.

Evaleen's mom came back with a tray filled with a white porcelain teapot and matching teacups on saucers.

"Wow, you go all out for tea," I said as I admired the simple beauty on the tray.

"It's Evaleen's. We took a trip to Scotland once a few years ago. She bought it while she was there," Mrs. Bechmann said as she tucked some blond hair kissed with silver behind her ear after placing the tray on the table.

As she poured out the tea into several cups, I couldn't help but be captivated by her warm expression. She was strikingly beautiful—like her daughter—with those sharp, high-class features. But where Evaleen tried to mask her beauty with restrictive chignons and no makeup, her mother's loose hair and soft expression made her seem approachable, almost inviting.

At that moment, I was jealous of Evaleen. She had always been strong and I wished I had her breathtaking good looks, and it was obvious that her mother loved her. I don't think I would ever know what that felt like.

"If that's true, you two aren't safe," Edgar said as he took the filled teacup Mrs. Bechmann offered before sitting back on the leather chair. He was comfortable but from what I had seen of Edgar, he was comfortable everywhere.

I glanced over at Alex. I knew that look. He wasn't comfortable. When I first met him, I thought that meant he was trying to be intimidating with his clenched jaw and fists. But now that I had gotten to know him, that posture said more to me than any of his words could. His bright, startling gray eyes lifted to mine and I knew there was no going back.

Alex's plan to trick his mom into thinking we were only working on the mural together and nothing more wasn't working. To the point she was hiring strange thugs to follow us. We had made the decision to stop trying to find the bugs we knew would be replanted in both our places. I thought when we had a pretend fight while I was painting his mural a few weeks back, she would think I was only in his life to complete the painting and that would be it.

But now I was getting scared. How can I fight a woman who has all the money in the world to make me go away? Perhaps even leave me to die in a dark room, alone, like my sister. The more I got to know Mrs. Hawthorne, the more I knew she was capable of the absolute worst. Heat traveled up my neck and burned my ears as the reality of the situation settled in.

"That's why I want to leave, Aria. Go far away from here," Alex said and took a sip of the tea he got from Evaleen's mom.

Maybe Alex was right. We should run away. I couldn't think of a way we could fight his mother. I glanced at Evaleen's mom and grinned. Maybe if I were Evaleen I could fight his mom. That woman was smart, in a good way. Unfortunately, Mrs. Hawthorne was smart in an extremely bad way.

"Here you go, Aria. Evaleen was so right about you." Mrs. Bechmann handed over the tea to me. She looked up in my eyes as she smiled.

"Right about what?"

"She said there weren't many people in this world who she trusted. She counted me and Edgar." Evaleen's mom pointed at Edgar who blushed and tried to hide it behind a teacup to his lips. "But she said if something happened, as long as she had you by her side she would feel safe. She called you kick-ass."

"You got all that just from only knowing me for a few minutes?" That was nice of her mom to say but she didn't know me.

"I see the wall behind your eyes, dear. It's the same wall I see behind my daughter's eyes. I wish it wasn't there, but I know that wall served a purpose. I have a feeling that wall has made you strong in the past but maybe now," she glanced over at Alex before turning her attention back to me, "now is the time to tear it down. It takes strength to rip it apart. And I know you have that power inside you or my daughter never would have mentioned it to me."

My faced burned from her words. I tried to smile but I knew it was achingly desolate. Therefore, I turned my attention to the warm tea, seeking comfort in the murky waters.

"What about here, Edgar? You have that spare bedroom . . ." Mrs. Bechmann offered.

"What about here?" Edgar asked and I glanced up at him to find his usual expression consumed in confusion.

"You said she isn't safe and I know this has something to do with Damien, so why not here?" Mrs. Bechmann said as she inched closer to me gently placing her hand on my shoulder.

As Evaleen's mom's words hit Edgar, his usual calm and temporary confusion changed drastically. I snorted and tried my best to cover it up with a cough.

"Oh, I couldn't do that. You already have two people staying with you. I really don't want to be the odd woman out." I tried to give Edgar a way out.

It was clear he didn't mind Evaleen's mom staying with him, and knowing what I knew about Evaleen's feelings and Edgar's history with women, I knew he really didn't mind Evaleen staying with him, either. But me? I might be a little more than he could handle.

"I don't think that's a good idea," both men said at the same time.

"It's just with, uh . . ." Edgar's eyes searched the room in desperate need for an excuse.

Alex's eyes, on the other hand, were laser focused on Edgar, narrowing with each word Edgar said. It was strange watching this quiet, artistic man turn protective of me. As he kept his eyes on Edgar, Alex scooted toward me on the couch, placing his hand possessively on my knee.

Was it wrong that my thighs and heart warmed at the gesture? I think, from any other man, I would have rolled my eyes and maybe even been insulted. But Alex had consistently been beaten back and controlled by his mother. I believed he finally gained his confidence to stand up for what he wanted and desired.

Edgar snapped his fingers. "Henrik's place."

"This Henrik is a man?" Alex said through gritted teeth.

"Yes." Edgar smiled widely at Alex.

Evaleen told me many things about Edgar and having spent the last half hour with him, I see that everything she said was true. A smile from him could melt dried up, frigid panties. But it seemed to be having the opposite effect on Alex.

"She wouldn't be staying with him. Henrik is selling his condo. Maybe he would let her stay there until someone buys it. I could ask."

The grip on my knee loosened.

"No need. I'll buy it. Aria can live there," Alex said as my mouth, and every mouth that wasn't Alex's, dropped open.

TWENTY-SIX

Alexander

"Alexander, let's talk." My mother leaned against my desk as I entered my office.

I swallowed, unsure if she'd found out. When we left Edgar's place yesterday, I made Edgar and Mrs. Bechmann swear they wouldn't say a word about me buying Henrik Payne's condo for Aria, not even to Evaleen. They had promised but I didn't know them like I knew Aria. I had to believe if Aria trusted them, then I could, too.

"What is this about, Mother? I have somewhere I need to be." I walked past her as if my mother's presence wasn't causing my blood pressure to skyrocket.

When I changed the locks and security access for Bradley, I was tempted to exclude my mother from accessing my home. But Aria mentioned that it would be too obvious if I did that. That it might cause my mother to do anything necessary to get to me, and possibly get rid of Aria.

"Has Ms. Dixon finished her masterpiece yet?" My mother's lips curled and yet through sheer medical intervention, no wrinkles appeared on her face.

I turned over some papers on my desk, feigning a search for something to gaze at other than my mother's bitter eyes.

"No." My blunt answer was anything but satisfying to her as I knew it would be.

She sighed tempting me enough to look up. My mother's eyes bore into mine but something in her stare altered. If I wasn't mistaken, it appeared to be uncertainty. Of course, knowing my mother, she might pretend to be unsure to trick me. That seemed like a more plausible excuse.

"She sure is taking her time. How long has it been now? A month and a half? I know artists that would take half that time to paint an entire room, not just one wall," she said as she gracefully lowered herself into the chair opposite me.

I was used to my mother's cutting comments. She prided herself on slicing people to their core just by a few calculated words. But today, something about them rankled me the wrong way. I knew she was feeding me crumbs of doubt for Aria until I was so full I would be too tired to challenge the words that left her mouth.

But that was the old me. Before I knew the achingly beautiful, highly talented, and strongest woman in my life, both past and present. Aria made me realize my mother's vile anger disguised as critiques were only words, as sharp as a puff of air.

"I guess that's what makes Aria so much better than your artist friends. Talent takes time. Only a hack would rush it."

Her eyes flared and for a moment I thought she would stand, challenge me with her body, but I was wrong. My mother, even with as many spies as she had in her pocket and rooms she had bugged, still didn't realize that the couple of months I had known Aria changed me. Even if my mother made sure my worst nightmare happened—that she would be right and Aria would only be using me for my money—I could never go back to her control.

I needed to make my mother see that she held no power over me anymore.

She believed me weak and easily manipulated. At one time I was, but not anymore.

"I do admit the woman does have talent. That's why I went back over the rental agreement and was surprised, as were you, to find out the building was in your name. I wanted Ms. Dixon to paint for you." Her syrupy smile appeared more tart than sweet.

I rolled my eyes. "Do you honestly expect me to believe you anymore, Mother? You have lied to me since I was a child. Sheltered me for years to the point I had anxiety when I went outside in public during the day—"

My mother cut me off, finally standing to beat back my words. "I did that to protect you, Alexander."

I leaned forward, pressing my fingers into the wood of my desk until I couldn't feel them anymore. "From what? What exactly were you . . . are you protecting me from? From the paparazzi or some gold diggers? Why don't you let me worry about that now? I'm a grown man."

"You don't understand, Alexander. There is so much more to all this than money. Fine. You want money, take it. Take everything, but understand I did this because you are my son and I won't let anyone take my offspring from me. Even a fair-haired artist."

I stared at the woman who gave birth to me. She finally told me something that remotely felt like love. In her sick mind, what she did was for affection, for her family. I hadn't felt her tenderness for twenty years. Perhaps by standing up to her she finally admitted to having any feeling for me.

But it's too late.

"Unfortunately, Mom, I will always be your son. Not even Aria can break that link," I said as I straightened my back and flexed my fingers, running them through my hair.

"This is all your father's fault. If he hadn't gotten himself killed, we would be so happy." My mother turned her head as she wrapped her arms around herself.

To my surprise her hand lifted and swiped a tear from her cheek. How could she be upset by my father's death? She never cried over his plane going down. I even caught her smiling on the phone with the police as they discussed the details of his death. She pretended she was yawning but I knew a smile when I saw one.

"You hated Father."

Her head turned back to me as a whisper of a grin curled her lips. "If you only knew, Alexander. Then maybe you would understand. Which is why I came to visit you today."

Frustration, and pain so old it felt like a dull knife lazily sawing at my skin, boiled as I shook my head to try to fling it away. "Why did you come then? Just tell me so I can make my meeting."

I hadn't lied to her about that. I was about to leave with Aria—who was hiding out in my bedroom working on the mural. We were meeting Henrik Payne to pick up the keycard to his old condo. He had agreed to a quick closing and Henrik agreed to let Aria stay there until the sale was finalized in a few weeks.

"The man you know as your father, Zachery Hawthorne. The one that died in the plane crash twenty years ago was not your actual father. Your real father was his brother, August Hawthorne. He died in a car crash six months before you were born."

Whatever bitterness I had for my mother drained away to something much worse—emptiness. I felt hollow and my throat tightened as I tried to speak, to cry out, but nothing came. I stood, watching as my mother's tears dried and she composed herself.

"He was the man I loved, Alexander, you have to believe me. Yes, I may have lied to you over the years, but I am telling you the truth now. Even today, I still miss August. He was everything Zachery wasn't. He was charismatic," she explained as she stepped closer to me, "and intelligent, and so talented. Do you know you get your love of art from him?"

She reached over and placed her hand on my arm. It felt strange and normally I stiffened or pulled away from her touch, but my soul needed to feel her. And I suspected she needed my warmth, too.

I struggled to control my emotions, to process what she told me as I asked her what I needed to know, "Why haven't you told me before? I deserved to know."

"There were so many times I wanted to tell you everything. Your father, your *real* father, discovered something. Something that very powerful men in this country would never want the public to know." She sighed and gestured to the chairs for us to sit.

Once we were seated she continued, "One of the powerful men was his father and later, his brother. Their hands were dipping into political pockets, criminal elements, and terrorist organizations. They took their power as a free pass to do anything they wanted. They were nothing more than white-collar criminals but more elite. A powerful CEO may go to jail, take the fall once caught after years of debauchery, rape, and stealing, but twenty others would continue in his place."

Her jaw tightened as her face flushed. "August threatened to go to the CIA and the press. To expose their criminal activity. You know what his father, your grandfather, did?"

"No." My voice quiet as the heavy weight of her words sunk in.

"He had August killed. The police said it was an accident. A drunk driver that drove away from the scene but that drunk driver managed to get out of his car, moved with perfect gait, and reached into your father's car to make sure he was dead."

I shook my head. "But how would you know that?"

"Because my sister, Bradley's mother, was out for an early evening walk with Bradley who was only a year old at the time. She saw the crash and started to run off to get help but looked back just as she turned the corner to see what that driver did. I promised her, as she feared for her safety and the safety of her son, that I would keep it a secret."

I rubbed my forehead and sat back in my chair. "My God, was that why you hired Bradley?"

She nodded. "His mother told him a long time ago. He wanted to make sure you were safe. Especially after he heard what happened to your sister."

My eyes widened. "Sister? I don't have a sister."

For the first time in almost twenty years, my mother's eyes softened. Her whole body relaxed as a tear trailed down her cheek. She reached up and cupped my face with her hands. "You do. They took her from me after your birth. I thought she died during birth but she lived. It was your grandfather's way of threatening me. That he had the power to take everyone I loved away whenever he wanted. Why do you think I kept you hidden for so long?"

"We were twins?"

The slight nod from my mother had my world spinning. The only thing I could think of doing was leaving. So, I did. I left my mother and went to get Aria. I needed time to process everything. But more importantly, I needed time to find out if what my mother said was true or just another evil trick.

I feared that this time it was no trick.

TWENTY-SEVEN

Aria

"And the view." Henrik Payne waved his hands at the wall of windows overlooking Lake Michigan.

I pasted my body to the wall and didn't care if I was leaving a body shaped smear mark.

"My God, why on Earth would you sell this place?" I asked turning my head to find the usual dark and brooding Henrik leaning his shoulder against the glass with a smile on his face as he gazed out to the water.

"Can't afford it anymore. Besides, I need the money for other things."

I nodded and turned back to the view. When Edgar mentioned staying at Henrik's place I thought there was no way Henrik would let me do that. It's not as if Henrik and I are on friendly terms. The last time I saw him I screamed into a full restaurant that he was a pervert and had him thrown out.

But, if he needs money, I guess he can't be choosy. Especially since Alex is paying full price and requesting a very quick closing on the property.

That surprised me. Alex buying his place so I would be safe. I know that man is a billionaire but this is a multimillion-dollar condo. That's not throwaway money, even for a billionaire.

"What do you think, Alex? Is this a wise investment?" I reluctantly left the glass and made my way toward him. He stood at the entrance to the living room, his eyes glued to the floor.

I was worried about him. I knew his mother showed up to talk to him. After she left he came back to the bedroom to get me for the meeting with Henrik, but when I asked what she said he only shook his head.

He was quiet. Too quiet. Alex wasn't acting his usual sweet and sometimes, silly self. I feared what his mother had said to him. Was it about Alexa again?

I needed to remember that we weren't going to be together forever. But that's becoming harder and harder to believe.

"Huh?" Alex gazed at me, bewilderment filling his features as I wrapped my arms around him.

"The place?" I waved my hand around the room. "You are the one buying it. Do you like the condo?"

"Oh, right. Yeah, it's nice. When do we sign the papers?" He glanced over at Henrik. His lips a thin line and if it weren't for the soft circle he was drawing on my back with his fingers, I would have thought he changed his mind about all of this, including me.

"I believe my lawyer told me closing is on June seventeenth. But you both are welcome to stay here for as long as you need." Henrik walked over and handed Alex an envelope. "These are the keycards for the entrance to the building and your personal elevator. I'll say goodbye now. Got a dinner meeting to get to."

Henrik turned and made his way toward the elevator, as the entire top floor of the building was the condo. Before he pushed the elevator button he turned, his usual stoic features softened with melancholy.

"How is Morgana?" he asked.

"I talked to her on the phone a few days ago. She's excited to come home. Though, I think she is more excited to have some of her mom's cake," I said to lighten his mood.

As much as Henrik had been a jerk to Morgana, I was beginning to feel sorry for him. He could have been spiteful with me, especially after what I did to him, but he's being more than kind.

Henrik smiled as he gazed at nothing. Slowly that grin faded before he sighed. He turned to the elevators. "It was nice to see you again, Aria. And a pleasure to meet you, Mr. Hawthorne. I hope you two find happiness here."

He mumbled something else. It sounded like 'I wish I had.' But before I could ask what he said, the elevator opened and closed after he stepped inside.

I pushed away from Alex, lifted my arms in the air, and twirled around like a kid. "We have this place to ourselves. Your mother and her spies don't know anything about this. Can you believe it?"

I was giddy and my cheeks began to hurt from my smile. Except, Alex wasn't grinning. He wasn't anything. He stared at me and fear crept up my neck.

Glancing around I saw there was still furniture in the place. Henrik explained some of it was his stuff that I could keep and a few pieces were show furniture he rented for when he had showings.

I had my back to Alex and decided to find out the truth, even if I didn't like what he had to say. I needed to know why he was acting this way. "Alex, if you have changed your mind about me . . . about us . . . I need to—"

My words were swallowed as he stepped in front of me and reached down to take a kiss. It was the way his lips curled over mine and his tongue begged for a taste that spoke more than any word I had asked of him. I clung to him as his mouth dashed my uncertainty away.

My back arched, reaching for more and pushing my chest into his hard stomach until he lifted me. I couldn't get my legs around him fast enough as I scrambled to curl them around his solid waist. I was wrong before when I said Alex wasn't acting like himself. I could feel his lips curl at my sigh as he tenderly cupped my face and dug his fingers into my ass.

There was something savage but controlled in his touch. My lips raw, my skin bruising under his fingers, but everything led to sweet reward. This was the true Alex. He gave me a slight taste all those weeks ago in that motel room, but now, whatever moderation he had was gone.

This was Alex unshackled.

We began to move and I tried to focus on where he was taking me, but his mouth made it very hard to see past the sexual kissing fog. My heart was pounding so hard I thought he could feel it. And maybe he had before he threw me.

I fell down and landed on something soft, bouncy, and covered in blue. A bedroom. He somehow, in our kissing, groping frenzy, found a bedroom. I laid on a bed with my knees bent and my lower legs and feet hanging off the side.

"Undress for me," Alex said with hooded eyes that were trained on the button at the top of my jeans. I wore a ratty T-shirt and old jeans when I came to his place today—my usual outfit for painting. But, with how Alex's eyes heated and sank into me, you'd think I was wearing the skimpiest, laciest lingerie.

I bit my lip to hold back the groan. His words did things to me. The Alex standing in front of the bed was demanding, confident, and ready to take what he wanted. He had been afraid to show me this side of him but he never realized how I would have given anything to experience him taking control.

My jeans and shirt flew across the room. Sweat broke across my skin as I raced to remove everything for him—to give him what he desired. I had no bra on which he appreciated. His lips ticked up for a moment, just a second of time, before disappearing. That slight movement flooded my core with heat.

I moaned and twisted at his stillness. The more skin I revealed to him the further controlled he became. Once my red lace underwear slid down my legs and dropped to the floor, he grew. I don't know how but he became taller, his eyes almost slits as he peered down at me.

"When I'm done with you, I want you to stay naked. You dress when I tell you," he said.

Did he know how that request almost brought me to the edge?

"Yes," I said and wondered if he understood me as it was more of a moan.

The past several weeks had been frustrating trying to steal seconds together knowing we were always being watched. Even when we went back to the motel, Alex thought a few faces seemed familiar and noticed that his Volkswagen was being followed. There was nowhere we could lay low.

Now we didn't need to hide. We could do what we wanted and I coveted this. I drank in the dark Alex and couldn't wait to reach my tongue out for the last drop. He was ready to pin me down like a predator and fuck me like a wild animal.

"Spread your legs," he demanded, his deep voice a rumble.

I didn't have time to respond as he grabbed the back of my knees and lifted them, pushing my thighs back. My skin burned as his fingers traced a path up my legs to my hips before finding my spiked nipples. He pinched hard, and I gasped at the prick of pain before it melted down to an addictive ache between my thighs.

"You get everything, Aria. I want to give you the breath from my mouth, the strength from my fingers, and the heart of my soul. Right now, the only way I know how to do that is to give you what I have never given anyone."

I reached for his arm wanting to give him something too, even if it was the lightest touch, but he took my hand and placed it back on the bed. It was that small movement, not his words, that caused my throat to tighten strangling my voice.

It was soft, so achingly gentle, in the throes of his dark and wild act. Something to tell me that the everyday Alex, the sweet Alex, is still there ready to hold me when the heat is spent and the pleasure has turned into a sleepy smile.

One of his hands stayed on my breast while the other one, the one that moved my arm, reached lower until I gasped as his fingers plunged inside of me. No warning, no light touches beforehand. Alex worked me until my legs widened more, my hips rolling to chase his thumb as it rubbed my clit.

I shouldn't have watched him. That's what did it. That's what sent me over the edge. How his eyes feasted on his wet fingers, glistening as he pulled them out of me. But the worst was when Alex tightened his jaw before pushing them back inside. As if all this thwarted what he was truly after.

Yet his hard cock—that looked painful as it pushed against his dark jeans—and the groan that unfurled from the far reaches of his throat spoke volumes of intense pleasure and awe.

And when I came, his mouth slacked and I wondered if he could feel the luxurious bliss that erupted from his hands and crashed across my body. Did Alex know that no one else would ever make me as happy, as satisfied, as grateful, as him?

TWENTY-EIGHT

Alexander

I could stop.

Part of me wanted to stop. Just watch Aria writhe from my lack of touch. Hear her beg for me to fuck her. Feel her greedy hands try to grapple my jeans to get at my aching cock.

I slid my fingers in my mouth as I stared down at the most beautiful creature in the world. My tongue eagerly lapped at her sweet, almost creamy flavor. She smelled of sweet wine with a hint of the beach and tasted like nirvana.

"Alex," Aria said with a raw voice, shredded from ecstasy.

This was the moment. Everything I had been waiting for with the woman of my dreams. I should be tripping over myself to tear off my pants and fumble with a condom. But I stood, struck by the moment and emblazoned by her. My heart thumped loudly in my ears and all I could think was building this captivating misery until it could only, naturally, tumble into euphoria.

Aria's hands, agitated, moved to her tits, pulling at her tight rosy nipples. I watched with no plan but to savor the moment. It's torturous for her, for me, and it's glorious with that agony.

"I want you, Alex. Please, fuck me," Aria said as she moved her hands to her thighs, pulling them back to show me her dripping pussy. And that gave me some satisfaction. I made her weep for me.

My eyes flickered up from watching her lips drip onto her fingers. She was flush, begging me still with her eyes. "You just want me to shove my cock," I cupped my hand over the hard bulge in my jeans, "into that sweet, greedy pussy? Is that what you're used to, Aria?"

She didn't know what to say. Her eyes drifted down my body and off to the corner as she contemplated my words. If she said yes, then that meant she accepted the bare minimum from a man. The basic act of sex was something most adults could do. And Aria was worth more than that.

If she answered no, then that meant her mouth didn't water and pussy didn't clench at the thought of me deep inside her.

"Anything you give me, Alex, will be better than what I have ever had. It already has been."

I slipped. My eyes fell shut as I reached into my pants and stroked myself. She was to blame. I wanted to stay focused, not touch myself until I had to. Until it was time to put on a condom. But she always knew how to catch me off guard with her words.

"I could paint you," I said as my eyes opened, falling on the rise of her chest down to the smooth skin that surrounded her belly button.

She nodded and a slight breeze swirled in the air as she sat up moving to my pants. I couldn't imagine anything better than this. Her fingers trembled and groped as they tried to break me free. I touched her head and curled her silky hair in my hands. My thumb and forefinger rubbed a few strands and I thought how delicate, how beautiful, and how easily pulled apart.

What was I doing? Aria deserved better than me shoving my dick in her mouth, as luscious as that would feel. When she did accept my cock, it would be after I made her earn it.

"I think it's time to stop, Aria."

Her hands halted and those beautiful chocolate eyes stared up at me in surprise.

"But, Alex, I thought you wanted to fuck me? I don't understand."

I put my finger under her chin and pulled her up. My breath hitched as she easily did what my body commanded, sitting up on her knees. My lips crashed onto hers. If my lips were deep and searching, then Aria's were maddening.

My control was crumbling with every lick of her tongue. My arm wrapped around her, pulling her close. There was no premeditated, slow, mind-fucking plan to drag this out until she screamed for release. Her lips, with their plump debauchery, had me groaning and thrusting and finally, pushing her on the bed.

I didn't think, I acted. I reached in my front pocket and pulled out a condom. That was the one thing about this day that was well thought out. Since I met Aria, I made sure I had at least three in my pockets at all times.

My black T-shirt, jeans, and navy boxer briefs were on the floor in seconds before I began to rip the wrapper. Having practiced many times at home, for fear I would embarrass myself when the day finally came, I rolled on the condom in very little time. Then I crawled until I was on top of Aria.

She tried to reach up and kiss me but I shook my head. "No, I want to watch how you take my cock as I enter you."

Her legs widened at my words and I could feel the tip of my cock press against something warm and so very soft. I rocked my hips and realized I was slowly entering her. It felt incredible but better than that, I saw as it all played out on her face.

Aria groaned the deeper I moved inside her and when she finally fit tightly around me, it was me who had to stop.

"Fuck, you feel better than I thought," I said as I closed my eyes and dropped my head to her chest.

I needed a minute or this would end before it even began.

"Alex, please, don't stop. You feel so good," she moaned, making it worse.

Now I really couldn't move. I lifted my head and sank into those molten eyes. "Give me a moment, dream girl. You feel too good to rush."

Her lips curled. "Dream girl?"

"Yes, you are the woman of my dreams. Therefore, you are my dream girl."

"I like that."

I did too, and slowly, I began to move. The heat from between her thighs and how she gripped me…. I didn't expect to last long.

And the way she squirmed made my impending release turn from a crawl to a race. I had to grab Aria's hands and pin them down with my own. After a moment, I decided to change our position and pulled her back to the edge of the bed so I stood between her thighs. I lifted her legs so they shot up and over my shoulders.

That was better. I could watch her, feel her, and make her come anytime I wanted. Moving my thumb to her clit, I slowed my thrusts. Even though I really wanted to speed them up because her pussy was so nice to slip and slide in and out of.

"I'm going to have you come all over my cock," I said and felt her pussy spasm.

That was my answer because Aria's words were nonsensical groans now.

It didn't take much from playing with her until I could feel her tighten around me.

"Come for me, dream girl," I told her and she obeyed like the breathtaking woman that she was.

"Oh, yeah, Alex. Fuck me," Aria said through gritted teeth as her head flung to the side and she arched her back.

This was irresistible. Watching her submit and tighten around me was too much. My balls tensed and I had to drop her legs as I bent over letting my orgasm take me.

The rush was intense and better than any orgasm I had ever had. I jerked my hips twice more, pushing into Aria a few more times before the fantasy ended.

I tried to support my body above hers as my muscles gave way. My chest tightened as I felt her arms and legs circle around me.

Aria was more than a dream; she was that first intake of air on a warm spring morning. She was the moment when I first walked up to The Starry Night by Vincent van Gogh and noticed the tiny strokes of oil, astonished that it created such beauty. Aria was that most powerful experience that had me chancing the feeling again, despite knowing it couldn't be duplicated. She's that sensation, only I get to hold it, touch it, and revel in it anytime I want.

"Now I know why people seem to like sex so much," I mumbled into her neck as her throat rumbled with laughter.

I wanted to bury myself in the soft skin right below her ear but she moved and I rolled away to give her the space she required.

"That was epic," she said and my smile was so wide I didn't even care how goofy I looked.

"It was. Fully agree." I nodded staring at the ceiling before turning my head to her. "So, when do we do it again?"

I was being honest. What happened, just now between us, was mind blowing and I only wanted to stay in this bed so I could fuck her until we both passed out from exhaustion.

"Hold up, cowboy. We need to rest in between. Besides, it's going to take you a bit of time to get hard again."

I turned on my side and traced her body with my fingers. When I got to her nipples she gasped. But it was when my fingers drifted down and sunk into her still swollen folds between her thighs that I realized she didn't need time to get back in the mood.

"How did I get so lucky to have you in my life," I said and never meant it as a question. Despite her answer in the form of another orgasm on my fingers.

TWENTY-NINE

Aria

"It's Hypno-eyes." Morgana's eyes widened as they stared up at Alex.

I laughed as I wrapped an arm around the man that seduced me with his eyes.

"Yeah. His name is Alex. This is A. Hawthorne," I said as Alex's fingers traced circles on my back, inching lower and lower until he had a handful of ass cheek.

Morgana leapt at his extended hand. She shook it to the point I thought it might fall off.

"So, you sent me that cake two months ago. Thank you. It was delicious," Morgana said.

Confused, I was about to ask Alex about it but he answered before I had time to speak.

"Aria said you loved cake, and I felt bad for making you think we, me and my security guard, were going to harm you. It was his idea to detain you."

"Well, it was the best apology I have ever had. You are forgiven. Anything can be cleared up with cake," Morgana said with a smile before a car passed by. Her head turned to watch but she frowned as it went further up the street.

"What are you doing hanging out on your parents' front lawn? I thought for sure you would be waiting inside to be as close to your mom's cake as possible," I said.

She shrugged. "Just waiting outside for guests."

I didn't say anything because I knew who she wanted to see. A few weeks ago, I would have warned her that it's best he not show up, but after witnessing Henrik's pain earlier today, I kept my mouth shut. I might have been wrong about him. But it's up to her to figure out if she was wrong about him too.

"Anyway . . . did you see each other again after we dropped off the painting?" Morgana's eyes flicked between me and Alex.

"Something like that," I said and glanced down at the grass beneath our feet. "I'll tell you later. Maybe meet for lunch tomorrow?"

I wanted to tell Morgana everything. She's my best friend and it's been hard keeping this from her. One more thing I had to keep from telling her.

Evaleen found out, but she always seemed to know everything. Morgana's my best friend, so it hurts when I can't tell her things about my life. Like the fact that I am living in Henrik Payne's old condo. She told me tales of his condo a few months ago when she first went there but I thought she was exaggerating. I was wrong, very, very wrong.

"Oh my God, you're pregnant!" Morgana jumped up and down clapping her hands.

"What?" both Alex and I exclaimed at the same time.

"Is that true? So fast like that?" Alex said with confusion wrinkling his brow.

"No and no." I groaned. "Morgana, you are too much like your mom, jumping to wild conclusions. And you," I pointed to Alex, "you are coming with me so I can explain the birds and the bees to you."

I pulled the sexiest, most oblivious man toward the front door. As we stood there I turned to Alex. "Did you really think I was already pregnant from four hours ago?"

I couldn't help but laugh as his hypnotic eyes widened as he hitched his shoulder. "I don't know how that stuff works. I never studied up on the technical side of sex, only the physical."

"I guess that makes sense. But I should warn you first before we head inside, about Morgana's grandmother. She's—" I didn't have time to finish as the woman herself opened the door without us having to knock. She either had a sixth sense or was listening at the door.

"Aria! So good to see you again." Morgana's grandma, Ms. Austin, threw her arms wide and pulled me in for a hug.

The hug was short and sweet, unlike her grandma. I loved Morgana's grandmother but she lived in a very different reality than the rest of us. One where she swore Morgana and I were lesbian lovers, and that she had her pick of men, including one's young enough to be her grandson.

"Oh my, well didn't you just fall from the sky." Her hazel eyes zeroed in on Alex as she perused his body.

Poor Alex, I knew Morgana's grandma would take an instant liking to him.

"I didn't fall from anywhere. I'm Alex. I'm friends with Aria."

Completely ignoring me, she took Alex's arm and guided him inside the house. He turned his head back to me with a look of fear, confusion, and muffled laughter.

I followed into the small two-level home with a very lived in feel. And by lived in, I mean not updated in thirty years.

Ms. Austin brought Alex into the kitchen, completely bypassing Morgana's father, brother Daniel, and Daniel's date in the living room watching baseball.

A slightly aged version of Morgana with graying red hair stood over a pot on the stove, stirring.

"Annette, Aria is here and she brought something very delectable," Ms. Austin said as she squeezed Alex's arm.

Morgana's mom turned, her smile was wide and loving and shone with affection.

"Oh, Aria, I'm so glad you came. And could this be a special someone?" She walked over and clasped Alex's hand. "Hi, I'm Annette, Morgana's mom."

"Special someone? Annette, you do know that Aria is gay." Ms. Austin paused for a moment before turning to me. "It is still gay, isn't it? I can still say that, right? It's not another name like non-straight or same-sexual or something?"

"Aria's isn't homosexual," Alex said and blew out a chuckle.

Morgana's grandmother narrowed her eyes and was about to explain her reality to Alex when Morgana's father walked in the kitchen.

"Are you Alex?" Morgana's father, with his tall, burly body filled the doorway and glared at Alex.

"Yes, I'm Alex." He stood a little straighter in the presence of Mr. Drake's intimidating stance.

"Your mom's here." Just as Morgana's dad said the words a hand, covered in jeweled rings, pressed on his arm causing him to turn.

"Thank you so much . . . uh, oh, I don't believe I caught your name?" Alex's mom appeared uncomfortably close to Mr. Drake, causing that big bear of a man to turn crimson.

"It's James."

"And I'm Annette, his *wife*," Morgana's mom said, her tone curt.

Alex's mom ignored her and moved into the kitchen. Her gray eyes scrutinized the room causing her lips to purse.

"Thank you for inviting me into your very humble home. I'm Emma Hawthorne, Alex's mom. Sorry to interrupt your fun, but I realized I forgot to tell my son something very important and since I am leaving in the morning, it just couldn't wait." She clasped her hands and refused to look anyone in the eye.

"There's a great invention called a cell phone," I mumbled.

"What was that, Aria?" Alex's mom said as she lowered her eyes to me.

I was about to tell her it was nothing when Morgana's grandma piped up.

"She said there's an invention called a cell phone. Unless cell phones are too bourgeoisie for you?" She arched her brow and in that moment, I never loved Ms. Austin more.

"Yes, well, this is something that needed to be told in person." Mrs. Hawthorne sneered at Morgana's grandmother before turning to face Alex.

"This couldn't have waited until later?" Alex said under his breath as his mom came up to him.

"No, it couldn't." She glanced over to Morgana's father who had been staring wide-eyed at her for the entire conversation. "James, I hate to be a bother but is there somewhere I could speak to my son in private?"

"Yes, of course, you can use Morgana's old room. It's now my weight room," he said as he flexed his arms.

Alex and his mom followed Mr. Drake out of the kitchen as I heard Mrs. Hawthorne say, "Oh, James, is that why your arms are so big?"

I nearly threw up in my mouth.

"What a manipulative bi—" Morgana's grandma said before she was cut off by Morgana's mom.

"I really don't like that woman. Come with me, ladies."

Morgana's mom took us up the stairs and into a room that was decorated for Christmas before shutting the door.

"Have you not taken down your Christmas decorations?" I asked because it was June, not December.

Mrs. Drake knitted her brow. "Of course not. This is my year-round Christmas room. It used to be Daniel's room but once he moved out, well . . . I love Christmas so much and this was always my dream."

Oh.

"Yes, yes, it's wonderful you have a room now to fulfill your delusional dreams, Annette, but why did you bring us here?" Grandma shied away from the animatronic Santa Claus and Mrs. Claus as if they might come to life and drag her back to the North Pole.

Morgana's mom ignored her mother-in-law and knelt before a vent in the wall. She brought a finger up to her mouth gesturing for us to be quiet.

We came close and knelt too, leaning close to the vent. That's when I realized we could hear into the weight room.

"I'll leave you two to it." I heard Morgana's dad's voice and the door creak shut. We heard footsteps in the hall and I figured it was Mr. Drake returning to his beloved chair and baseball game.

"Alexander, as you know I am leaving tomorrow for California," I heard his mom say.

"Yes, you already told me. Why did you do this? I'm meeting Aria's friends and people she is close to, and you purposely show up to cause trouble. Can't you let me live my life?" Alex said.

I was proud of him. My heart soared hearing him stand up for himself.

"If you wish to get to know them that's your business but know it will make it that much more painful when you have to leave."

Leave? What did his mom mean? Did she know about our plan?

"How did you find out about Aria and me leaving?"

I could hear Mrs. Hawthorne's bitter laugh through the slotted grate. "I don't think you will want to leave when I tell you what will be in Las Vegas next week."

My heart began to speed up. People could get married quickly in Las Vegas. Many a drunken night ended with a legally binding marriage the next day in that town.

Is Alexa there? Is that what all this was about?

"What could I possibly want in Vegas? I'm not a gambler or much of a drinker, Mother, so why would I want to go there?"

"She's going to be there for you, Alex. Who we spoke of earlier. She wants to see you. After my trip to California this week, I'm going to Vegas the following week, to be with her. I know it's been a long time, too long. But, I know deep in your heart you love her. It's time she's in your life forever, as it should be."

My jaw began to hurt as I gritted my teeth. I didn't like how this felt. It was all new. My heart felt like it was being ripped from my chest and thrown across the room. I wanted to race into that room and tell Mrs. Hawthorne that Alex was mine. That Alexa will never have him.

Perhaps I was wrong to think my feelings for Alex were fleeting. Maybe this was what it felt like to be in love.

A slight flutter tickled my chest at the realization but it didn't last long. My joy and happiness at finally wanting to give my heart freely to a man ended as that man stabbed it into a million pieces with his words.

"I do want her in my life. I have thought about what you said before and I keep imagining holding her in my arms for the first time and never letting her go," Alex said as tears fell from my eyes.

THIRTY

12 Years Ago, June 15ᵗʰ

Alexa was pretty.

Her violet eyes were wide as they moved over my body. I scratched my arm, suddenly feeling like a wiry stick figure in front of her slight, soft curves.

"Alex," my mom placed her hand firmly on my shoulder, "why don't you show Alexa your paintings?"

My mother had her happy mask on. That's the smile she gave when she wanted to endear herself to others. And, I had begun to learn, she used it to get something from them.

I sighed knowing my mother would ultimately use this pretty girl, and she had no idea.

"Of course." I glanced at her before my sight glided over to her parents.

Her father was tall, thin, and had thick, light brown hair. The corner of his mouth ticked up and I got the feeling he was impatient for me to leave.

Alexa's mother looked just like her. Average height, her curves more pronounced with long, dark brown hair. She didn't smile or look at me. Her focus was on the furniture, the walls, and everything that might have a dollar sign attached to it.

I waved for Alexa to follow me. She nodded, moving just behind me as I made my way down the hallway to my room.

Ever since my dad died in a plane crash the day after Christmas eight years ago, my mother has grown more distant, colder. A plane I was supposed to be on but my mother refused to let me go.

Now I wish I had been on it so I didn't have to live with her. She never lets me out and I'm not allowed to play with the boys in the building anymore. Occasionally, I got to hang out with Bradley, my cousin, but Alexa was the first kid my age I'd seen in a while.

"Wow, I love your room. Did you paint all these yourself?" Alexa finally spoke as she moved around my room.

"Yeah. I don't have much else to do, so art keeps me occupied. How about you? What do you love to do?"

She turned and her pale skin bloomed with a pretty pink, but it was her smile I liked the best. I wondered who else she smiled for.

"Don't tell my parents but I would love to be an actress. My parents are always making me take social lessons but when I have time to myself, I watch TV. I especially love the old comedy shows."

"I watch some TV, too. Do you watch *Get Smart*?" I asked since she said she liked old comedies.

"I love that show."

I grabbed my remote from my desk and pushed a button. A large monitor came down from the ceiling.

"That's cool," she said as she watched it descend.

I smirked, feeling proud of my latest tech feature. If I was stuck here in this building, I might as well have fun.

"Wow, it's *Get Smart*. What are the odds it would be on?" Alexa took a seat in my desk chair.

"I have a program that can get me any television show I want. Give me the name of some obscure television show and I can find it." I walked over to show her my remote which looked more like a keyboard to a computer.

"Hmm. Oh, I know, how about *Get A Life*. It was on in the early 90s."

Never heard of it but she was the couch potato so I typed it in. Episodes popped up on the screen of some balding guy on a bicycle.

"I can't believe you found it. This is fun. I have a more modern one. How about *Coupling*? It's a British TV show."

I typed it in and up it came. She kept naming shows, especially British shows.

"I bet you don't have *Spaced*."

After I typed it in a young Simon Pegg looking confused showed up on the screen.

"How about we go make some snacks in the kitchen and sit and watch some of these shows?" I said.

She jumped up and clapped her hands. I liked her. Alexa was cute and funny. I wondered if, after today, I would ever see her again. I hoped so.

We started back down the hall and as I turned the corner I heard my mother's voice. "But she *should* be a Hawthorne. She needs to be with me and Alexander."

I came to a stop and gazed over at Alexa who cocked her head. "Be with you?" she whispered to me.

Did my mother want to keep Alexa for some reason? I feared that my mother was hatching a plan that now involved Alexa. "Come here," I said in a low voice so my mother wouldn't hear as I waved Alexa to stand next to me behind the wall.

"I understand that, Emma. We want that, too. She is meant to be a part of your family. But now is just not the time," Alexa's father said.

"I know, Douglas, but I had hoped . . ." my mother said.

My mother wanted Alexa to live with us. But why would she think her parents would allow such a thing?

"We have spoken with her." I could tell instantly that it was Alexa's mother by her thick Russian accent.

"Did you tell her about me? About us? About what will happen?" my mother asked.

"She's too young. When she's older. Then you can have the perfect family. And Alexa will also play an important role. We are still agreed on that?" Her father's voice held uncertainty.

That's when I heard the slight inflection in my mother's voice. The smooth snake-like tone that told me these were selfish plans she made with the Dortons. Whether they were in on the plan or not, didn't matter. In the end, my mother would do anything to get what she wanted.

She's already killed, it wouldn't surprise me if she did it again.

"You can rest assured that Alexa is one of the most important pieces in the puzzle. Where will Alex be without his perfect bride? With the perfect political family at his side," my mother said.

I felt Alexa stiffen at my side and I glanced over at her. Her mouth dropped open and I moved my hand quickly to cover it. I knew she was about to gasp or scream or, more likely, cry.

Wrapping my arm around her side I ushered her back to my room. I let go of Alexa to hear her whimper as she fell back into my desk chair. I came to her side and bent down to gaze up at her tear-stained face.

"You can't say anything, Alexa. Please. You don't understand my mother. It will only make it worse if she thinks you know," I said understanding all too well what happens when someone found out one of my mom's secrets.

"Who am I going to tell? As you heard, my father wanted to make sure I would be married off to you. It feels like I'm living in the sixteenth century. Is this what wealthy families do? If so, I don't want any of my parents' money. They can keep it." She waved her hands in the air.

I moved over to my bed and flopped down on my back. "I don't know. It feels like it in my home. I've seen movies about that time period and royalty. There's always intrigue and manipulation and murder. Just like being a Hawthorne." I couldn't stop the bitter chuckle that escaped my lips.

"What? Oh my God, Alex, that's terrible. Do you think my parents are involved in all that?"

I rolled my head to the side and watched her. She's so pretty, so innocent, and a part of me wanted to protect her.

"If they weren't, then they are now. I used to feel lonely here, by myself. My mother never letting me out but now I think it was for the best. No one should ever get to know my mother. She used to be kind and loving, but that changed when my father died. Something snapped in her and she's been on a mission ever since. I don't know what that mission is but I have a feeling it's not good."

As terrified as I was for Alexa, I had grown used to what my mother did. A part of me was even happy. It felt good to confide in someone about my mother. I didn't feel so alone anymore.

"We should run away." Alexa stood and came to sit on the edge of the bed.

I sat up and scooted next to her. "Where? We won't even be eighteen for several years. How would we get anywhere?"

Alexa frowned. "I don't know."

We sat in silence for a moment before I thought of something.

"How about when we are adults, we run off to a tropical island. Somewhere that no one will find us," I said and smiled.

She turned her body toward me, excitement lighting her features. "Yeah, but we have to have money so we can leave without a trace. I've seen enough TV shows to know, you can only use cash to really disappear. You said your father died. Do you get an inheritance?"

"When I turn twenty-five I inherit my money. It should be more than enough to leave and live happily for a while."

She nodded. "If I know my family, I will get a check when I graduate school. I'll put it away and use it for when we leave. Maybe when they get us together for our wedding, we can sneak away and disappear." She stuck out her hand. "Let's shake on it."

I shook her hand and then got an idea. Walking over to my bookshelf, I pulled out two books and handed it to Alexa. Taking the paper cover off one and placing it on the other, I handed her the one with the fake cover.

"This is a book about the Native American code talkers from World War Two. I'll write to you. When I do, it will be a secret message. You can decode it. When you write me, you do the same. This way, no one, not even my mother, will be able to figure out what we are actually saying to each other."

She jumped up. "Yes! That's a great idea. But why did you put," she looked down at the cover, "*The Self-Taught Computer Programmer* cover on this?"

"If anyone sees the book, they won't know what it really is."

"Ahh!" She smiled and tapped the side of her head. "Smart thinking."

I gathered up the other book and cover and put it away on the shelf just as my bedroom door swung open. My mother stood there, her eyes on the hunt for anything out of place, like always.

"Alexa, I'm afraid it's time to go. Your parents made dinner reservations. Alex and I can't come, but we did invite you over for brunch tomorrow before you two head back to California."

Alexa nodded and the brightness of the girl I was talking to dimmed in my mother's presence.

"Bye, Alex. Thanks for the book. I have a lot to learn."

My mother watched her go before she turned back to me. I kept my eyes level with my mother's trying to find any sign that she knew what Alexa and I were up to. But there was nothing. Only the usual coldness I had come to expect from her.

THIRTY-ONE

Present Day

"I love you." I stared at the elevator wall.

It's silent. Which was what I expected as it's a wall.

Sighing, I shook out my hands. They're clammy and I feared I'd be too gross to kiss when I'm finished with my speech.

It's been a week and a half since Morgana's party. When Alex's mom left her parents' house, I asked Alex what she said and he explained he would tell me later.

He has yet to say anything. That's why I'm here, riding up the elevator to his place. I came to the decision last night. Sitting in the kitchen with Morgana, eating some cake from Morgana's favorite bakery, I realized that I needed to stop running. Since today is my birthday and I'm officially thirty years old, I figured there was no more using the 'I'm in my twenties, I'm too young to fall in love' excuse anymore.

I had to tell Alex I loved him.

It's not so much the telling him that had my hands feeling like giant slippery otters, it's his reaction. I knew, logically, he found me attractive and had a crush on me for years . . . But now that he knew me, had taken his time to witness all my flaws, would I hold a candle to the image he painted in his head of me so long ago?

Despite what his mother told him before and during the party, I couldn't help but believe that Alex was stronger than her words. Besides, we had sex every chance we got. If he didn't have feelings for me anymore then he would end things, not keep trying to bring me to orgasm.

The door opened and the sight of the paintings, the same masterpieces that captivated me all those months ago, gave me hope. They reminded me of Alex—so vibrant, almost magical, and could easily take my breath away with its power.

When I arrived at the front door it opened automatically. It still gave me the chills knowing no one was behind it. Once I started to paint Alex's mural he added me to his list of approved people that the door would open for.

The mural had yet to be finished. It's not that I'm a slow painter but in order to trick Alex's mom into thinking I was only coming over to paint, I took my time with the mural.

"Alex!" I raised my voice to let him know I was here.

Listening for a response I heard nothing. Perhaps he was in the shower. My lips curved at the thought of joining him.

As I made my way to the bedroom I found it empty, as well as his bathroom. I turned and was stopped by a hard wall covered in a white button-down shirt.

I pulled back and realized it was Bradley. His usual scrutinizing gaze was unusually soft as it fell on me.

"What are you doing here?" I asked, putting my hands on my hips.

"Alex asked me to watch his place while he's gone."

I sucked in a breath a little too fast and started to cough. It took a moment but I finally regained my composure. "You? Why would Alex ask you?"

My heart began pounding in my chest as none of this made sense. Where would he go? And why Bradley?

I thought back to when I saw him two days ago, the last time he stayed at my new place. Alex never mentioned going anywhere.

"He knew I could handle any security issues that came up. If you haven't noticed, he has millions of dollars' worth of art in his home."

That did make sense. Perhaps Alex just needed to travel for a short time. That's when a thought creeped into my head.

What if he's finding us somewhere to stay on some tropical island somewhere like we dreamed? I bet that's why he hasn't told me anything. It's a surprise.

Maybe he told his mother he was leaving before Morgana's party and that's why she showed up at the party to talk him out of it. He didn't tell me because it would ruin the surprise.

I turned my back to Bradley so he couldn't see my smile.

"I guess that makes sense. When will Alex be back?" I asked but my mind raced with images of tropical beaches and eating fresh fish in the warm breeze.

"I don't know. He left this note for you."

I turned to find Bradley holding a small white envelope. Taking the note, my finger traced the black ink on the back of the envelope spelling out my name. I tore it open and barely noticed Bradley turning his back, this time to give me privacy.

Dear Aria,

I know I promised to tell you everything my mother said but there are things I must do first before I can explain. I understand now why my mother locked me away for all those years and I never thought I would think this, but I don't blame her.

I paused and flip the paper over.

"Alex wrote this, Bradley? Are you sure about that?"

I didn't believe for one minute that Alex would ever understand anything that awful woman did to him.

"Yes. I stood next to him as he wrote it and saw him seal it in the envelope." He turned slightly until he could look me in the eye.

"Why don't I believe you?" I narrowed my eyes at him.

As Alex mentioned, Bradley was being paid by Alex's mom. He could easily lie to me. It's not like I would know Alex's handwriting. The most I ever saw was his signature on a few legal documents when I looked at the rental contract months ago.

Bradley turned fully to me and stepped closer. There was sorrow in his eyes. The normally tall and menacing Bradley slumped his shoulders with what I thought might be pity or perhaps, exhaustion.

"Aria, I know I haven't done much to earn your trust, but you have to believe me when I say I care about Alex. I grew up knowing about Alex and playing with him when we were young. When I became a teenager, my mother told me what had happened in his life. All the bad people that surrounded him. That's why I wanted to work for him. To make sure he was safe."

"But you never worked for him. You worked for his mother."

He rubbed his hand across his forehead looking conflicted. "I did, yeah. I did."

"Did?" I asked.

"I don't have a job at the moment. Alex said I could stay here while he was away, but his mother fired me when she found out I was locked out of her son's condo. And I was so relieved. Relieved and scared at the same time."

I waved my hands to stop him. "Wait. Wait. I don't understand. I thought you liked Mrs. Hawthorne?"

Bradley threw his head back, laughing heartily. I had always thought of him as a man out to get Alex. His usual steely glare and rigid posture made me want to be as far from him as possible. But as he loosened up with a smile, I suddenly noticed how attractive he was. I'm sure some woman would be thrilled to take him home with her. I wonder if Tiffany would be interested in him. She deserved a man who would fall at her feet and protect her and her son.

"Emma Hawthorne. I don't think it's humanly possible to like that woman. My mother did, a long time ago, but Mrs. Hawthorne has changed in the decades Alex's father's death. The only reason I let her employ me was so I could keep an eye on Alex. He needed someone, even if it was just me, to look out for him."

"I'm sorry. I always thought you wanted to hurt Alex, too," I said.

"Same here. When I first met you and your friends, I thought Mrs. Hawthorne planted you. I didn't trust you at all. But when you both removed the bugging devices from the room, I knew you weren't with Emma. You actually cared about Alex."

I opened my arms wide as a gesture of peace for Bradley. He took my offer and gave me a hug. When I pulled back, I realized I hadn't finished the letter.

Lifting the paper, I continued.

There are things about my family, about the world we live in, that are dangerous and I am finally starting to understand that. I have to be with my family for a while. It may be days or weeks but know that when I come back, there will be a woman I want you to meet. A woman, though I haven't seen her since I was too young to remember, I love no matter how much time has passed.

She will be a part of this family when I return. When you meet her, I know you will understand even if you may not right now.

Love,

Alexander

The paper turned translucent where it was pelted from my tears. He loved her? Was this about Alexa? He hadn't told me much about her, but by the way Alex talked about their past, he had only met her once and neither of them wanted to marry each other.

"Who is Alex talking about, Bradley?" I lifted the paper as it shook in my hands. "Who is this woman?"

His brow knitted as he took the letter. "I don't know. I was just in the room when he wrote it. I didn't see what he put in here."

Bradley began to read it. His eyes widened. He knew. Whoever Alex wrote about, Bradley understood who he mentioned.

"Who is she? You know, don't you."

He took a breath before lowering the letter to his side. "The only 'she' Alex could be writing about, that I know of, is Alexa Dorton. But I can't imagine . . . Oh no!"

I snatched the letter out of his hand and made a fist, crumpling it and letting it fall to the ground.

Happy fucking birthday, Aria!

"Oh no? What, oh no?"

"Emma had me intercept Alex's letters when I first started working here five years ago. He wrote to Alexa once or twice a year. Usually birthday or holiday cards. Nothing I thought was out of the ordinary. Except what he wrote on them. And not just that, but what she wrote back."

His eyes searched the floor as if looking for answers to Alex's letter on the hardwood.

"What did they write?" I asked.

"It was weird and made no sense. Like they were using a strange language. Nothing I had seen before. I thought maybe it was old Gaelic or German or Russian, but I couldn't figure it out," Bradley said and then held up a finger before disappearing out of the room.

My mind raced with two teenagers making up their own language to send secret messages of love to each other. Was I just something to trick Mrs. Hawthorne into thinking they weren't in love? It's not like his mom didn't want them to marry. So why use me like that?

Bradley ran back into the room out of breath. "Here." He handed a Christmas card to me. "Alexa sent that to him this past December."

I opened the card to find two paragraphs of words in a completely different language. The words brought a smile to my face. My heart taking refuge in my throat as I tried to speak.

"Oh my God, I know this. I know what it says," I said as tears ran down my cheeks.

THIRTY-TWO

Alexander

I waited nervously. My knee bounced up and down causing the bed to vibrate as I sat on the edge. I probably had pit stains the size of Nevada under each arm but I didn't care.

It had been a few days since I'd left Chicago and seen Aria. I wanted to tell her so many times that my mother was bringing me to Vegas to meet my sister for the first time. But every time I opened my mouth something stopped me.

That something was fear and a little bit of selfishness. I wanted to meet her first. To get to know my sister on my terms. I love Aria but this was my time to discover my family.

But more than those selfish needs, I feared if I told Aria, I would have to tell her why my sister disappeared. My grandfather, and the man I thought was my father, were dead, but that didn't mean there weren't others willing to silence us. The less Aria knew, the better.

There was a knock at the hotel door and my head shot up. I hesitated for a moment before I stood and made my way to the door.

This was it. The moment I got to meet my twin sister.

I stood in front of the door, refusing to look through the peephole. I wanted this to be the best surprise. Better than any birthday present.

Taking a breath, I opened the door. The woman on the other side was a surprise. My heart raced as I took in her petite form because I knew her.

"Tiffany?" I said staring at her as she nervously bit her bottom lip.

"Hi, uh, hi Alex," she said without meeting my eyes.

Tiffany fumbled with a cloth bag in her hands before standing on her tiptoes and reaching for my head. She couldn't seem to do whatever she was trying to do with that bag but that didn't stop her from trying.

"What are you doing?" I asked as I stepped back before she fell on me.

"I'm trying to get this bag over your head but you are too tall. We should have waited for Evaleen. She would have the height to do this."

"We? Did my sister send you?"

Is my sister in hiding? Maybe that's why my mother wanted me to meet her in a hotel and not bring her to Chicago.

"Sister? Aria never said you had a sister," Tiffany said before giving up on putting the bag over my head.

"Wait, I'm confused." I held up my hands. "Is Aria here?"

Tiffany groaned. "I'm not supposed to tell you that. Can you just put the bag on your head and come with me? I'm here to help you."

None of this made sense but the few times I met Tiffany when Aria started to work on the mural, she seemed like a caring and honest person. Maybe she had something to do with my sister. Maybe she was my sister and she needed to play dumb until she took me to a secure location.

I really hated how nothing about my life was normal.

Putting the bag over my head, I let Tiffany pull me out of my room and down the hall. The material was thin enough I could easily see where she was taking me.

"We are going to have so much fun at the bachelorette party tonight. Can't wait for you to strip for my friends, stripper man," Tiffany yelled.

"Stripper? What is happening?"

"Shh," Tiffany whispered. "If anyone sees us I need to make it seem like this is all part of some crazy bachelorette party. Just play along. I have to say, this is a lot of fun kidnapping you."

Before I could respond to the kidnapping part, a door flew open and Tiffany pushed me inside.

I glanced around and realized I was in a much smaller hotel room. There were only two double beds and a television on the wooden dresser. The golden curtains were drawn shut and the lights were on. Someone stood from the bed and I wondered if that was my sister?

"Take the bag off since I can't reach," I heard Tiffany say behind me.

I did as she instructed and gazed at the woman who came toward me from the bed.

Aria.

"Are you married?" Aria said with fear in her eyes.

"Married? Why would I be married?"

This whole thing became crazier by the second.

She threw her arms up in the air in frustration. "Because this is Vegas. That's what you do in Vegas."

I knitted my brow and looked around the room searching for any sense.

"Can someone please explain to me what is going on because I am totally lost."

"We're kidnapping you," Tiffany said at the same time Aria said, "I am trying to save you from your mother."

I went over and sat on the edge of the bed with a lavender bedspread. My eyes bounced between the two crazy women in the room.

"How can you kidnap me? You couldn't even get a bag over my head."

Tiffany folded her arms in front of herself. "Obviously, you would help us."

I pointed at my chest and glanced over each shoulder before turning back to face Tiffany. "You want me to help you kidnap me. Can you hear how crazy that sounds?"

There was silence as Tiffany twisted her lips thinking about what I told her. She finally blew out a breath, her lips flapping in the process and answering me, "I don't have time to explain the details. I need to pick up Morgana and Evaleen at the airport."

Tiffany grabbed a different bag from the dresser, what I assumed was her purse, and left the room.

"Is Tiffany my sister?" I stared at the door she left through.

"Sister? You never told me you had a sister. And if you do have a sister, I really don't think Tiffany is it. She's here because I asked her to help me save you," Aria said as she came to sit next to me on the bed.

"Then why are you kidnapping me?"

She placed her hand on my thigh. It felt warm, and I'd be lying if I said I hadn't missed her this past week.

"Because I love you, Alex. I have been an idiot for not seeing how wonderful you are. For not running away with you the moment you asked me. I was afraid you would leave me and when you did go to marry someone else, it woke me up. Your heart is too precious for some wild fling. I want more. I want the wild ride that never ends."

That's when I kissed her. My surroundings, why I was sitting here in this hotel room was a confusing mess. Even her explanation filled me with questions, but her heart was the one thing that gave me contented happiness and made total sense.

I clawed at her clothes and we tore into each other like savages. We moved so fast and I was thankful when Aria pushed a condom packet into my hand. I smirked at my hot lady as I ripped the packet and pushed the condom onto my cock. She was always prepared in case sex came up. Since I have known her I have discovered condoms hidden everywhere on her. Once she removed her bra and a condom fell out.

I didn't even bother to take off her shirt before I pushed my throbbing cock deep inside her. There was no restraint, no taking our time. I needed her as if I had a consuming sickness. Aria felt like the best drug as she straddled my hips and rode me.

I wanted to say she was like poetry as she swayed her hips and lifted her T-shirt to pinch her nipples. But she wasn't. She looked like love and sex and euphoria as her head flew back in orgasm.

As her climax continued, I pushed her body over so she was on her stomach and pulled up her hips. When I pushed back into Aria, she tightened around me again, her orgasm resurged. I watched her fingers curl into the bedspread as my hips jerked hard enough to hear her gasp for breath.

Knowing Aria was giving me everything—her body and soul— caused my climax to come down hard. I shuttered and groaned out her name. I fell on top of Aria, her skin slick with what I had done to her.

After a moment, I removed the condom and leaned over the edge of the bed, throwing it in the trash. Moving back, I pulled Aria close. "I'll never let you go now. But there's something I need to tell you," I whispered the words as I combed my fingers through her soft hair.

"Don't, please," she said and I felt her tremble in my arms.

Turning Aria to face me, her hands tried to cover the tears falling from her eyes. I grabbed her wrists and pulled them apart.

"Why are you crying?"

"You're going to marry her, aren't you?" Aria's words were slightly mumbled but I understood what she was saying.

I was back to being confused.

"Marry who?"

"Alexa. That girl you told me about. I guess she's a woman now. Alexa Dorton." Aria's beautiful face scrunched up in pain.

"No, oh, Aria. No. Is that what you thought? That my mother brought me here to marry her?" I brushed my thumb across her cheek to wipe away her tears.

"Yes, of course. I read her Christmas card to you. She mentioned that she heard her parents talking on the phone with your mom. That this was the year you two were to marry. That you had your inheritance and she would be getting her master's in education in June. You two would be free to marry."

I blinked for a moment as what she told me sunk in.

"You figured out our code?" I asked.

Aria nodded. "Yes. I took some Navajo in college. I knew enough to figure out a few words and looked up the rest."

"Wow, that's just . . . wow. And here I thought I was being so clever when I came up with the plan. Who knew I would one day meet a woman who could outsmart me."

She smiled and her eyes glittered with unshed tears and mischief. "And more beautiful and sexier. And more—"

"And more than I could hope to ask for."

We kissed for a few minutes before Aria pulled away with confusion etching her features. "So, if you aren't in Vegas to marry Alexa, then why are you here?"

"To meet my twin sister," I said just as the door opened and in walked three women.

"That's not how we kidnap someone, Aria," Tiffany said as she clasped her hands over her eyes. Evaleen covered her mouth and ran into the bathroom. Morgana winked at Aria before giggling and turning her back to us.

THIRTY-THREE

Aria

*"**Orgasm, to go**."* Morgana winked at Tiffany who sat next to her on the barstool.

"How many drinks have you had?" Tiffany asked as she turned to Morgana.

"None. When we left the dinner buffet and you went to your room, I met Aria in my room. I texted you that we were heading to the hotel bar but didn't get a response. How is Evaleen, by the way?" Morgana lifted her finger in the air to try to grab the bartender's attention.

Tiffany shook her head. "Not good. I ordered some chicken noodle soup from room service for her but she can't hold anything down. Maybe I should room with you two. Whatever she has, I don't want to catch it."

"Too late, you already have," I mumbled as I turned my head to find the bartender.

"What?" Tiffany asked.

"Nothing. I'm sure you won't catch it, Tiffany," I said already knowing what Evaleen had.

The tall, thin bartender finally came over and sat a drink in front of Tiffany.

"From the man across the bar." He pointed to a man as he turned in his barstool and got up. I didn't get a good look at him but the ladies did.

"Damn, Tiffany, that guy is hot!" Morgana raised her voice so most of the room turned and looked our way.

After kidnapping Alex yesterday, we spent the night together. I haven't seen him since breakfast as he wanted to meet with his sister. He finally told me everything. Now I was conflicted about his mother. If what she said was true, then what she did to Alex was to help him.

Maybe she wasn't the enemy. I was beginning to think the enemy was something or someone we had yet to fully understand. And that scared me. At least with Mrs. Hawthorne it was obvious what she was doing. But now, we had yet to uncover who was really pulling the strings.

I was becoming worried. I hadn't heard from him and it was nine o'clock at night. The ladies wanted to get a drink but I thought I might need my wits about me tonight.

"What would Evaleen do?" Tiffany closed her eyes and cupped the large amber colored drink in her hand.

"She wouldn't drink it. Evaleen would assume it was drugged," I said.

The bartender leaned over the bar at me. "Hey. Why would I drug you? I made the drink, not him."

I narrowed my eyes and leaned close to him, feeling like that was something Evaleen would do. She wasn't here with us and I needed her strength tonight.

"Don't worry, I have on that special nail polish. I can dip my finger in to see if it's been drugged. Henrik insisted I wear it as he didn't trust any man in Vegas." Morgana rolled her eyes as she held up her pointer finger and pushed the tip into the cup. When she brought it back out it was the same color.

"I told you I wouldn't do that." The bartender pushed away from the bar and walked off. I turned my head to try to find the man who bought Tiffany the drink. Not that I knew what he looked like, but there had to be a man walking toward us or looking our way. But what I found wasn't a man at all, but a woman. Two women to be precise.

Emma Hawthorne. She was just outside the bar in the lobby of the hotel speaking to a short woman. Mrs. Hawthorne blocked the woman so I could only make out the woman's dark hair. They began to walk away, so I got up with the intent to follow them.

Tiffany lifted the glass and took a sip. Her eyes widened. "Wow, that's pretty strong. I wonder what it is?"

"Hey, um, I'm going to go check on Evaleen. I'll see you guys later," I said and waved at the women.

I heard a male voice behind me as I left answering Tiffany's question.

"A whiskey sour," he said. I turned to get a look at him but all I could see was his back.

He was wearing a black suit, might have been a tuxedo. Obviously, some high roller. At least Tiffany attracted someone who could afford to show her a good time tonight and not some thug.

I followed Mrs. Hawthorne and the other woman until they went to the elevators. There was no way I could get on the elevator with Mrs. Hawthorne and not have her recognize me.

At that moment a group of loud, drunk women stumbled their way to the elevators. I could see Mrs. Hawthorne doing everything in her power to avoid them, but when the doors opened, they followed her inside and that was my chance to slip in unnoticed.

I pushed my way through and huddled near the back with my head down, pushing my hair in front of my face. When the elevator stopped, I saw Mrs. Hawthorne get off with the short woman. I still hadn't gotten a good look at her.

Just before the doors closed, I pushed through the drunken ladies and fell to the floor. Thankfully no one but the giggling drunks in the elevator saw.

When I got up and turned the corner I saw Mrs. Hawthorne at the end of the hall standing in front of a door. Again, she was blocking the woman who was with her. I wondered if she was Alex's sister.

The door opened and they both went inside. I went down the hall and got the room number: 708.

I turned around and went back to the elevators. Before I went to find Alex, I checked on Evaleen. She was sleeping and I put a fresh glass of water beside her bed.

Once I made it to Alex's room, I knocked on the door.

"Hey, how are you?" Alex's smile was wide when he opened the door and waved me inside.

"I saw your mom. She was with a short woman," I said, almost out of breath, as I quickly walked inside.

"Okay." He closed the door and came over to me.

"Have you met your sister yet?"

"No. I waited in here all day but nothing. I even called my mom but she wouldn't answer my calls. She wasn't in her room when I stopped by either," he said looking defeated.

"Is her room 708?"

"No, why?"

Something was going on. Something that reeked of Emma Hawthorne's deceit.

"I saw her go there with a dark-haired woman. Someone let them inside. I am starting to wonder if your mother hasn't made this whole thing up to get you to Vegas. Maybe I wasn't crazy for thinking she was going to try to marry you to Alexa."

Alex sat on the couch in his room. His room was larger—one of the suites with a separate bedroom—though the décor was the same gold, cream, and lavender as our room.

"I can't believe I fell for this. She has lied to me so many times that I stopped believing anything she said. But this, oh God, this I wanted to be true." His fist punched the couch cushion. "I wanted to believe that my mother actually cared about me. That somewhere out there, a sister was waiting for me. Someone untouched by all the awful things my mother put me through. Someone I could call family and not be ashamed by it."

His head dropped into his hands. I came over, placed my purse on the coffee table, and sat beside him. His body shook. Anger and heartache pumped through my veins as I tried to hold it inside to calm Alex down.

After a few minutes, he lifted his head and had an expression I had never seen before. It was as if all feeling, all thought, left him and I was frightened by what I saw.

"I'm going to go to room 708 to find out what's really going on," Alex said and stood.

"No, Alex. Maybe we should think about things first. Wait until your emotions are a little less raw and you can think clearly."

It was as if I never spoke. Alex grabbed his key card and walked out of the room. I grabbed my purse and ran after him. He ignored me as I pleaded with him.

Even when we took the elevator he stared straight ahead like I wasn't there. His fists clenched, his arm muscles twitched, and I dreaded what he was capable of doing. Alex had been caged up for so long by his mom that I wondered what would happen if she pushed him too far. I feared I was about to find out.

When the door opened, he moved like a robot even as I tugged at his arm. He finally stopped in front of room 708.

"You don't understand, Aria. It's not as if your mother dangled love in front of your face only to laugh as you reached for it before throwing it away," he said facing the door, refusing to look at me.

"Maybe not, but my parents still hurt me in the worst way. Why don't we just run away like we said we would? Right now. Forget your mother. Don't let her take anything else from you," I said and hoped he heard me.

I wished what I said sparked something and he would change his mind about confronting his mother.

I let out a breath I hadn't even known I held as he turned his head and stared into my eyes. My heart ached with the pain I saw on his face. Reaching up, I cupped his cheeks wanting him close. That maybe if I touched him, he would know how loved he was.

"But when will she stop, Aria? If I run away with you, it won't stop her. She will continue to use and hurt people for some sick gain. Tell them what they want to hear. Tell them that she understands and cares, when the only thing she cares about is power. If that power hurts people, it doesn't matter to her. Her actions are too horrible to let her continue."

I nodded. "You're right. Let's find a way to take that power away from her. You can't do that if you go to jail, Alex."

He let out a sigh and glanced back at the door. "At least in jail I would be away from her."

At that moment, the door flew open and a pair of familiar brown eyes stared back at me.

"Dad?" I said.

THIRTY-FOUR

Alexander

He was thin. Not at all what I thought Aria's dad would look like. The man was short, reedy, and had a mass of wispy gray hair. He had the appearance of an evildoer—like some villain in a Shakespearean play.

"Aria, it's wonderful to see you again. Please, both of you, come in." He smiled with a look that made me ponder if he rarely grinned.

I walked into the suite and placed my hand on Aria's back to guide her inside. She appeared too stunned to make the decision to move herself.

I gazed around the living area and noticed the sliding doors to the bedroom were closed. The room looked exactly like mine, only opposite. Aria, her dad, and I were the only ones in here.

"Is, uh, Mom here?" Aria asked.

"Yes, she went to get something from our room. This isn't our room," her father said as he walked over to the couch and took a seat.

"Whose room is this?" I asked looking around the space.

His lips curved in a similar way as Aria's. Only when Aria did it, it made her seem sexy. When her dad did it, I wanted to throw up in my mouth.

"It's the Dortons'. I believe you know them, Alex. Your mother has told me so much about you." He stayed seated as he watched me react to that bit of information.

"I never told you who I was. How do you know me?" I said to Aria's father, my jaw tensing.

"Of course I know you, Alex. I've been working with your mother for years. Since you were this high." He outstretched his arm so his hand hovered several feet from the ground.

"Have we met?" I asked and my mind raced with thoughts of when my mother brought home various business men to meet with when I was young.

Aria's father brought the hand that had been hovering to his chin, tapping his finger to it.

"Actually, we have. Once. This involves Aria. She was a teenager at the time. I think you were in elementary school. I brought my daughters to a home. Not your home, but a home of a client. Your mother came and brought you. It was at night." He sighed at the memory.

"I was making a complicated deal with some men from Russia. It didn't go well. I blame the translator as the men thought I was insulting them. Your mother was there because she had a deal with them, too. It was something different, but since they were in town that night, they wanted to meet with us then."

He turned his head to look out the window. "Anyway, I needed to offer them something valuable. Something that would make up for any implied insult. Aria knows the rest of the story."

"You monster! You sold us like cattle. Your own daughters. Made to marry criminals!" Aria sobbed as she lunged at him.

I managed to step between her and her father in time, holding her back.

Even though I had my back to her father, I could hear him stand.

"That's right. *My* daughters. Do you have any idea how rich you and your sister would have been? You would have lived like princesses.

What father doesn't think their daughter is a princess? And it's not like you were actually married to anyone. Those idiots had you sign the wrong paperwork."

"I'm not married?" Aria asked, her eyes wide in confusion.

"No. And your sister's dead, so the deal was a bust anyway." Her father rolled his eyes.

Now it was my turn to tell that piece of garbage off.

I turned and stepped up to him. Towering over him, I pushed my finger into his weak chest. "You don't even care that your child is dead? You treated your daughters like slaves. You think you're slick because you've done business with the scum of the Earth?"

He tried to step back but fell onto the couch. "Your mom is one of the people I do business with."

"Like I said, you do business with the scum of the Earth. And you're a fool to have anything to do with her. She will chew you up and spit you out worse than anything you can imagine. Even worse than what you did to your own flesh and blood."

Just as Aria's father began to say something the sliding doors opened and out walked my mom, Mr. Dorton, and Alexa.

My eyes widened at the beautiful woman Alexa had become. I had seen a few pictures of her but nothing recent. The only thought I had was she would make a man very happy one day.

The following thought caused my heart to sink. I was going to be that man if my mother had her way. And she always had her way.

Alexa gave me a stiff smile as she fussed with her dark hair. Aria was right, there was no sister. Alexa was the dark-haired woman she saw with my mother.

"Alex, I'm happy you came. But don't you think we should have left Aria out of this," my mom said as she pursed her lips.

"Why? Why would I leave the woman I want to spend the rest of my life with out of anything that has to do with me?"

My heart sped up, not from confronting my mother, but that I spoke out loud what I had been thinking about for the past month.

"What?" Aria's voice cracked beside me.

I didn't want it to be like that. I wanted to whisk Aria off to that island we talked about. Serve her fresh fish, tropical drinks, and a diamond ring while gazing at the ocean.

I turned to her and took her hand. "I think you know how much I love you, Aria. And this is the last place I wanted to do this, especially in front of these people." I glared at Aria's dad as Aria gave my mom the evil eye.

"But, I can't keep this inside anymore. The more time I spend with you, the more I realize that I need to show you, to tell you, how lucky I am to have found you in that art gallery three years ago," I said as I stared into her warm brown eyes.

"You didn't find her, Alex," Aria's dad interrupted me pouring my heart out to his daughter.

I turned my head toward him and regretted holding Aria back when she wanted to attack her father earlier.

He smirked. "Oh, you think you just happened to find my daughter in an art gallery? Your mother and I made sure you 'found' Aria. Mrs. Hawthorne was desperate. Since you refused to be a man and fuck a woman. Even prostitutes who would fuck anything if they were paid enough."

"Dad!" Aria yelled at her father.

"Don't tell me he didn't tell you he was a virgin when you two finally had sex?" He waved his hands in the air in front of him.

"Dad, none of this is appropriate," Aria said.

"Anyway," he said ignoring his daughter's comments, "when Mrs. Hawthorne mentioned her problem with her son, I knew my daughter was perfect for him. She loved art and would have sex with any man with a penis."

I heard Aria and Alexa gasp but I only saw red. I don't even remember moving toward Aria's dad, but I remember punching him in the face. And in the stomach. And finally, shoving him against the window in the room before Mr. Dorton pulled me away.

Pushing Mr. Dorton off me, I turned to my mother. "That's what you want?" I pointed to Aria's dad as he lay curled in a ball on the floor. "You want to surround yourself with those type of people? People who would sell their family, their children for money. Then turn around and call their children whores. But I'm not good enough? I'm a problem to you?"

I could feel the hot tears streaming down my face but I didn't care. My mother was awful and she wanted to be with awful people.

"It's a necessary evil, Alexander," my mother said after a sigh.

She had grown so immune to this sick life that it didn't faze her.

"There is something evil in this room and she has a Botox face and wears diamond rings," I said and smirked.

"Alexander August Hawthorne! That is no way to speak to me. I'm your mother."

It only caused my smile to grow. I never made my mom angry and it felt good. She was always so in control, cool, and rarely fazed. Finally, I found one of her buttons to push and I wanted to take a sledgehammer to it.

"Oh yes, the mother who thinks lying is a form of endearment. Or telling him never to go outside during the day for fear he would be kidnapped and tortured . . . that's what every good mother does. And that anyone who showed me attention only wanted me for my money."

"I told you, Alexander, I did that to protect you. I may not have been a typical mother but it doesn't mean I didn't love you." She stepped forward and tried to touch my arm.

I moved back shaking my head. "Don't. If you loved me, how come you never told me?"

There was silence. My mother frowned and I thought I saw regret in her eyes.

"Mom, just—"

"Alexander, I'm sorry. I do love you, very much," my mother said.

She gazed down at the floor as her shoulders slumped. "I'm tired, Alexander. Tired of fighting and sneaking around. Maybe you do belong to Aria—" My mom was cut off from Mr. Dorton.

"Emma," he said.

She waved her hand at him. "Douglas, it's fine."

My mother nodded and surprisingly, he accepted that.

"Alex, it's been a long time. I have lived like this for so long I forgot what it was like to just love people instead of be weary of them. I don't even know what I am fighting anymore." She gave a sad smile and walked over to sit on the couch.

There was a knock at the door. Mr. Dorton went to answer it. Moments later he came back.

"The car is here to take us to the chapel. For the wedding." His eyes darted between me and his daughter.

"Dad, I can't marry him. I told you that. You told me I was here about a potential job offer. Please, tell me your terrible scheme to marry Alex is over." Alexa waved her hand at me and Aria.

"Don't worry, Alexa," my mom said before standing back up. "We'll go to the chapel, but we will be going to make my son's dream come true because I love him."

My mom took my hand and Aria's hand and held them. "What do you say Ms. Dixon. Do you want to marry my son tonight?"

THIRTY-FIVE

Aria

"The blushing bride," Alex's mom said to me as she led me into the little Vegas chapel's prep room. It was a tiny room with a full-length mirror, chair, and petite round table in the corner. The room had one small window that faced an alley.

"We don't have to get married right now. I appreciate that you want to make your son happy but he just proposed," I said still in shock at her complete turnaround with me.

When Alex's mom asked if I would be open to marrying Alex tonight I wanted to say no but my head nodded yes. In a few months, maybe. Or, perhaps, in a couple of years we could start to plan a wedding.

It's not so much the thought of being with Alex that had my throat tighten until I thought I couldn't breathe, it was the marrying part. If people hadn't noticed, I didn't have the best example of a good marriage growing up.

I never dreamed of being a bride and still don't. I love Alex but I had no desire to have him put a ring on it.

Mrs. Hawthorne pulled a small black leather bag from her purse and placed it on the table. "I'll let you use some of my makeup." She turned to me and pursed her lips as her eyes roamed my face. "You do need to freshen up. I can only hope my makeup can help with that."

I sighed realizing that's probably the best I'd get out of Alex's mom when it came to being nice.

"Thank you. When can I see Alex?"

Mrs. Hawthorne made her way to the door but turned before closing it. "It's bad luck to see the groom before the wedding, Aria. You will see him when the ceremony is to start."

Before I could stop her, she closed the door.

I stared at the makeup and mirror. The more I gazed at them, the more sweat trickled down my neck.

Shouldn't I have friends helping me with this? Like bridesmaids. I opened my purse and pulled out my cellphone.

I called Morgana, no answer.

I called Evaleen, no answer.

Tiffany would help. She's always eager to support people. I called her. No answer.

Crap. Where are my Chicago peeps when I needed them?

I took a few steps toward the table with the makeup, suddenly hyperaware of how suffocating the room appeared. Was it purposely made closet-sized to make sure people raced down the aisle for fear of being consumed by four walls and worn, green carpeting?

I had to get out of here.

Turning I moved to the door but when I tried to open it, the door handle wouldn't budge. I jiggled the handle a few times and realized Mrs. Hawthorne had locked me in here. Could she tell I wanted to escape?

How do I get out of here? Maybe there was a key. I scanned the room and still only saw a small table, chair, and mirror. The key would have to be hidden . . . like on a window ledge.

I walked over to the window and felt around the edge. There was no key to be found, but when I tugged at the window it easily pushed out. I'll escape through the alley.

Since this room was in the basement, the window was small and set high up toward the ceiling. I moved the chair over and climbed up. A whisper of a memory when I had to do this the last time I was marrying someone caused my eyes to burn as I pushed myself through the tiny hole.

I was almost out when I felt hands on my arms. Since I was turned face down I couldn't see who was pulling me. Probably some drunk dude looking for a good time. I'd have to explain that hanging out by wedding chapels wasn't the best place to find a hookup.

When I got free and stood I was shocked at who was standing in front of me.

"Grace?" I said.

Grace Jenkins, Mimir's office receptionist where Morgana and Evaleen both worked, was helping me escape from a marriage in Las Vegas.

"Hi, Ms. Dixon." She smiled and even in the dark light of the alley I could tell she was blushing.

"Why are you here? Did you come to Vegas on vacation?"

If so, that's a really crazy coincidence she happened to be here to help me. Maybe Evaleen was right about Grace, she's a weird stalker-like person.

"I didn't like what they were doing to you. It's not right," she said as she waved toward the chapel.

"Were you inside when we came in? I wish I had known but I didn't see you."

"I don't have time to explain, I need you to come with me."

Grace glanced over my shoulder and her eyes widened. Before I could turn my head to see what was happening, she grabbed my hand and pulled me with her. She was surprisingly strong for someone so petite.

We ran in the opposite direction of what she had seen, to the end of the alley. Once we got there, we were met with a large black SUV and

Alexa holding the door open for us. I hopped in as Alexa got in behind me and shut the door.

Grace hopped into the driver's seat and took off just as I buckled myself in. There was someone in the passenger seat in the front and when he turned I gasped.

"Alex? Did you do this?" I asked.

I was confused. Did he not want to marry me, too? I could understand why, given his family background, but then why did he propose?

"No, Grace did. She saw what was happening and decided to help." Alex turned his head to watch Grace as she focused on the Las Vegas streets while maneuvering the vehicle.

His eyes seemed to soften and he reached over to place a hand on her shoulder. The hairs stood on the back of my neck. Why was he touching her?

"Grace. Why are you here?" I said and I didn't care if everyone could hear the edge in my tone.

I could see her dark eyes flicker up to the rearview mirror. She heard me but there was silence.

"Aria, I wanted to wait to tell you until we got somewhere safe." Alex turned in his seat with a pained expression on his face.

He never wanted to marry me. This was all a setup to get out of marrying Alexa or to get back at his mother or something.

How could I be so stupid not to see it? Alex is a Hawthorne and Hawthornes are some fucked-up people. That's saying something considering my family.

Was Alex using me all this time? Were all his words a lie? And how did he drag poor Grace into all this? Probably saw how she looked at him in the elevator back at Mimir and decided to use her, too.

I felt sick and I had no way out of this car. I went from one trap to another.

"What is it, Alex? Just tell me. I'd rather hear honesty than lies." I wiped at the lone tear as it slid down my cheek.

I pushed back into my seat and folded my arms—the only protection I had for what was about to come. Heartache. Loss.

I will never give my heart to any man again, no matter how much he understands the need to express beauty through art. Was that a lie, too?

"Grace is my twin sister, Aria. My mother wasn't lying. She was at the chapel when we arrived. I finally got to meet her."

My eyes danced between Alex and Grace. Tiny Grace and big Alex. How could they possibly be brother and sister? But then I saw it.

Their nose was the same and their cheekbones. They even had the same dark hair. The only differences, other than height, was eye color and skin pigment. Alex had skin like caramel while Grace's skin was light, creamy.

"I have my mother's complexion," Grace said as if reading my mind.

"I, uh, I can see that. You two just met?" I asked, not really knowing what to say.

"Yes. Grace actually knew for a while but Mom told her it wasn't safe to tell anyone, even me. That's why she stared at me when she met me at Mimir. She knew but couldn't say anything."

"It's not easy keeping secrets but, as our mom said, it can be for the best to reveal them at the right time."

Sounds like something Mrs. Hawthorne would say. Now I felt bad for Grace. Here I was, believing she was creepy and worse, after my man, but she only wanted to know her brother.

"Don't you have parents, Grace? Didn't they ever tell you about your real family?" I had a million questions in my head and barely knew where to start.

She sighed as she maneuvered the SUV away from the bright lights of Vegas and into the dark desert.

"Not really. Yes, I was adopted when I was a kid. But they didn't really love me. I was just an unpaid servant to them. You have no idea how happy I was when my real mother contacted me. It may sound silly but I always dreamed my real parents would come for me."

I noticed her knuckles whiten on the steering wheel before she continued, "When Emma, oh, I mean, Mom. That's so weird to say still, after everything that's happened. Anyway, when she told me about my family, my brother," Grace turned her head to give a quick smile to Alex before focusing back on the road, "I wanted to run off and be with them. But then she told me why I was adopted and that I had to keep it secret, I was willing to do that for my real family. I would do anything for that kind of love."

"Grace, I'm so sorry you had people treat you like that. We seem to be a car full of misfits. All our parents only cared about was using us for personal gain," I said and let go of a cynical laugh.

"That's why I had to get you all out of there. I overheard Mom talking to the other two men about marrying you, Alex, to Alexa," Grace said pointing to Alex. "The things they said. It was crazy what they planned to do. No, this wasn't the family I had in mind. I knew Alex was a good person and figured Alexa was too, so I snuck them out a side door while their parents continued to talk."

"I wanted to come get you but Grace said it wasn't safe. She decided to help you escape. So here we are." Alex smiled at me as if everyone in this car was the perfect family.

THIRTY-SIX

Alexander

I was happy. No, that's not right, I was blissfully content. I had no idea I could feel this way but here I am in a motel room in Sterling, Colorado waking up next to the woman I love with my sister in the room across the hall.

Could I have even imagined this a year ago? No.

This must be what it feels like to have a happy family. To be surrounded by the people you love. Even Alexa, I told her she could come stay with us for as long as she wanted. But she decided to stay with a friend in New York. We dropped her off at Denver International Airport on our long drive back to Chicago.

"What time is it?" Aria asked, her voice rough from just waking up.

She stretched and curled into my arms. I pushed some strands of hair that fell into her eyes before kissing her forehead.

"It's a little after eight in the morning."

We kissed and my hand began to wander down her bare back until it grabbed at her plump ass cheek. She groaned which I have learned was the switch I needed to turn me into the wild animal she loved.

I rolled on top of her and was about to pin her arms back when there was a knock at the door.

"Did you order something?" Aria whispered into my ear.

"No." I lifted my head shaking it and reluctantly, lifting the rest of my body until I left the bed.

Grabbing my jeans that I bought while we were in Denver, as none of us had a change of clothing, I slipped them on before looking out the peephole.

"It's Grace," I said as I opened the door.

It felt like all those missed years were trying to squeeze themselves into my heart whenever I saw her. And when she blushed, I knew it was happening to her, too. Maybe that was a twin thing. That I just knew what she was feeling without having to ask.

But something was a little different. Her eyes wouldn't meet mine and I wondered, was all this too much for her. Not just meeting me but finding out her real mother was a monster?

Everything must all be sinking in now. I wanted to hug her and tell her we had each other but she held her hands up as I moved closer.

"Alex, um, I need to go get something at the store. I'll take the car, just wanted you to know in case you came looking for me."

I nodded. "Okay. Thanks for telling me. Is it okay if I give you a hug?"

Her eyes widened as she glanced around the hall. "Why?"

My heart cracked wondering if she was ever shown affection by the people who raised her.

"Because you're my sister and I love you," I said with my arms open.

Grace turned her head slightly as if she was thinking of something but finally nodded. I enveloped her in my arms and gave her a big squeeze. She made a squeaking sound and I loosened my hold. When I pulled back she seemed confused.

I stepped back. "When you're out can you pick us up some coffee because the stuff here is awful. I can give you some money if you need it."

She shook her head. "No, I'm good. Coffee it is."

With that, she turned and made her way toward the lobby of the motel. Shutting the door, I went back to the bed. Aria was sitting up looking beautiful. She had put on a T-shirt which made me frown but she was gorgeous with or without clothes.

"That was nice of you," she said.

"Nice?"

"Yes. You gave her a hug. Now it makes sense why Grace always acted a bit strange. Because of how she was raised. You're probably one of the first people to hug her because you wanted to, not because you needed to give the appearance that you cared. I have a feeling the few times that woman has been shown affection was because her parents were pretending to care in front of social workers."

I sat on the edge of the bed. The bed dipped as Aria scooted toward me. Her hands warm and needed as they slid across my chest holding me close.

"I thought it would be the best thing in the world to find my sister, but to know she had to deal with that for so long hurts more than when I had no idea she even existed."

Aria tightened her hold. Her warm breath soothed my sore heart. What would I do without her? These past few months, whenever my mother pointed her twisted lies toward me, Aria was the one who knew exactly how to bring my pulse under control. She soothed me with her words, with her art, and with her body.

Now that I found her, I'd be lost without her.

"Did you mean it when you said you would marry me?"

My heart had gotten a little in front of my head when I proposed. I meant every word, but the last place I wanted to express my feelings to Aria was in front of my mother.

"How about we just live together for a while? See how it goes," she said.

I was rubbing the arm she had draped over my chest but stopped at her words. Turning, I pulled her beside me. "You don't want to marry me?"

Disbelief and melancholy clawed at my neck before settling in my heart.

Her jaw firmed and with a flared nose she nodded.

Aria was using me. Was I some fun oddity, the rich recluse virgin? Well, ex-virgin now. Something to have a good laugh about when she saw her friends again?

I was angry, but most of all, I was hurt. I may not have intended to propose, but I still loved her. Those dreams of us being on the beach and spending the rest of our lives together were so real I could smell the salty, beachy breeze in her hair.

Something unexpected happened. I laughed. It's not that I meant to, but when I opened my mouth to speak, laughter poured out instead.

"What's so funny?" Aria asked with rounded eyes.

I stood and waved my hands around the room. "This. This is funny. You run halfway across the country to 'kidnap me,'" I raised my fingers in air quotes before continuing, "tell me you love me but you don't want to marry me. This is farcical, Aria. You. Me. Our lives. If Hollywood made a movie of us, it would be a zany comedy."

Then I lowered my voice. "Can one man escape his evil mother's clutches to be with the woman he loves? Can he stop the woman he loves from running from her past long enough to see happiness is right in front of her? What love story doesn't include kidnapping, discovering long lost family, and escaping arranged marriages."

Aria stood from the bed to pull on her purple panties and jeans. Then there was silence.

"Okay, maybe not a comedy but definitely a soap opera," I said.

I was losing it. It was obvious. But I didn't care. I had enough of people holding love and happiness out in front of me like a carrot stick, only to pull it away when I came near.

There was a knock on the door.

"Grace is back with our coffee," I said as I bent down to grab the brown T-shirt I wore yesterday and put it on.

Making my way to the door, I opened it without glancing at the peephole, which I would discover was a mistake.

"Who are you?" I asked the tall man with the shaggy brown hair and black T-shirt. Something about him seemed familiar but I couldn't place him.

I heard movement behind me and glanced back to see Aria pulling up her jeans.

"Something happened to your sister. You both need to come with me." His voice was deep, almost gravely, as he pinned me with a stare.

The past five minutes arguing with Aria melted away as worry for Grace took over.

"Let me grab my shoes—" I turned but he grabbed me by my arm and pulled.

"Hey, wait, aren't you—" Aria said and was cut off as another man, who must have been standing in the hall, forced his way in and grabbed her.

"Get off of her." I tried to yank my arm away from the guy with the shaggy hair, but he managed to move behind me and pin my arms back.

Before I knew what was happening, a bag had been put on my head and I was being pushed forward.

"Did Tiffany get you to do this? Aria, did you call Tiffany?" I asked hoping Aria was nearby since I couldn't see anything.

If Tiffany was behind this, she was smart enough to get someone much taller to help. And the bag wasn't transparent which made this feel like a real kidnapping.

The guy pushing me halted. "What about Tiffany? What does she have to do with this?"

"I don't even know what this is? Tiffany is Aria's friend. She tried to help me a few days ago thinking I was being forced into marriage. She tried to kidnap me, much in the same way you are doing now. Only she's a lot shorter and not as good at it as you. She seemed to enjoy doing it, though. I thought maybe she was trying again," I said and knew I was babbling.

His grip loosened and I heard the guy chuckle. "Yeah, I can see her doing something like that."

"What? So, she is in on this—" I couldn't finish what I said as I was pushed inside something. I fell on what felt like a cushioned seat.

When I heard a motor start, I knew I was in a car. The guy had tied my hands behind my back and arranged me in the seat before he closed the door.

"Aria! Are you here?" I said.

"Oh, you won't be seeing her again. I don't think Mrs. Hawthorne would like that." I heard the guy say from in front of me.

My head jerked back as the car moved forward.

Now, I didn't care if Aria never wanted to marry me, I only wanted her to be safe. Even if it meant she was without me.

THIRTY-SEVEN

Aria

"You ruined, Alexander," Mrs. Hawthorne sneered at me.

The guy who grabbed me from the motel room finally took the bag off my head. I had been pushed and pulled and shuffled around so much I didn't know where I was.

I was thankful to be able to breathe. That bag was suffocating and I gulped at the cool, dry air around me. My hair was matted to my face and, with my hands tied behind my back as I sat on the metal chair, there was nothing I could do about it.

But the air felt wonderful.

"I don't think I was the one to ruin him. If we are talking about ruining people's lives, Mrs. Hawthorne, you're going to need to sit as we go through the list of lives you ruined."

Just because I was kidnapped, had my hands tied behind my back, had no idea where I was, and almost passed out a few times didn't mean I wasn't ready to take this bitch down.

"I saved lives, not ruined them." She moved toward the desk by the back wall. She was impeccably dressed as usual. The steely Emma Hawthorne had a gray silk blouse on with a pencil skirt and heels. Who dresses like that to kidnap someone?

As my eyes adjusted to the light, I realized I was in a room with a window that overlooked a large warehouse.

I could be anywhere. Even if I screamed, I suspected the only people who would hear me worked for Mrs. Hawthorne.

"Do you really believe that? You kidnapped your son. No mother in her right mind would force her son to marry someone and then kidnap him when he walked away. Can you not see how crazy this appears?" I said as I stared at her.

This woman was so out of touch with reality. Now I know why Alex was laughing back in the hotel room. All of this was absurd.

"You have no idea what we're up against, Aria. The power that these men hold, it's deadly. We need to destroy that. Why do you think I let my son be with you?"

"Because he's an adult and can see whoever he wants," I mumbled as I rolled my eyes.

A loud bang had my eyes flip up toward her. She pounded her fist on the desk as she gritted her teeth.

"No, because you of all people should understand why I need to do this. I hate that I haven't been closer with my son. Despise that, they made me live in fear for so long. But, sometimes, we need to make sacrifices for the greater good." She gazed off into the distance and I wondered what world she saw there.

Maybe she saw her perfect crazy world. A world where she was the hero. Emma Hawthorne really believed that what she did to her son was necessary. She wasn't some bitter woman who took her anger and need for control out on her son. She was like some loony terrorist who believed that something greater than themselves was telling them they needed to destroy innocent lives.

"But your son isn't like those men. He's a good one." I slowed my words.

Big thugs don't scare me. Even when that guy, who I never got a good look at, threw a bag over my head and dragged me here, I wasn't scared. But a delusional person with thoughts of grandeur that involved destroying people's lives . . . yeah, that scared the piss out of me.

And this crazy person had money and power. She had the means to do anything she wanted.

"Of course, he isn't. That's why he's perfect for the plan."

The door flew open and then a man wearing sunglasses and a leather jacket walked in—the same man who grabbed Alex at the motel.

It's over one hundred degrees outside and felt only twenty degrees cooler in here.

"You do realize you are inside or did you just have cataract surgery?" I said because beefy thugs irritated the hell out of me.

He turned his head toward me but ignored my words.

"He's here, Jay. Should we put him in the same room as Alexa?" he said walking up to Mrs. Hawthorne.

Jay? I thought her first name was Emma.

"Yes. Is the minister here?"

I held my breath as I hoped they weren't talking about Alex.

"He's about ten minutes away. Soon your son and Alexa will be married. We haven't found Grace," he said.

My shoulders slumped in relief. I had never been so thankful that anyone had to make a run to the store in all my life. By doing that, Grace saved herself from being kidnapped.

Mrs. Hawthorne slammed the desk again with her fist. "She has the access to what we need. All those resources at Mimir. We need that. How are we supposed to expose and take down those high-powered men? Those politicians, CEO's, media executives, and industry leaders?"

How does Mimir play into this?

"Do you really think Grace can get access to that information at Mimir? She's only the receptionist."

My eyes bounced between Alex's mom and the thug next to her. There was something about that guy that seemed familiar. Then it hit me.

"Hey, are you the guy from the coffee shop?" I said but the guy never answered.

"You can go, Jagger. I have enough people here to help me with my son and his soon-to-be wife. Why don't you head back to Chicago and try to find Grace? I have a feeling if she thinks everyone left her, she'll give up and head home," Mrs. Hawthorne said.

He nodded and kept his head down, turning his back to me as he left the room. He didn't want me to see him. Maybe that's why he wore the sunglasses inside like a douche.

He's the guy that watched Alex and I in Wake Up Joe's a few weeks ago. Mrs. Hawthorne had him follow us. What did he know? Maybe the guy found out about Alex buying Henrik's place. Mrs. Hawthorne knows more than I had hoped.

I had to get out of here.

Closing my eyes, I took a deep breath ready to do and say anything to save us. To get Alex and Alexa to safety.

"Thank you, Mrs. Hawthorne," I said as I willed my eyes not to leak for what I was about to do.

"Thank you? For what? According to you, I'm a terrible mom and a monster."

You are.

"No, of course not. Once you explained why you did what you had to do and from what Alex told me, I get it. I really do."

She narrowed her eyes at me, unsure of my sincerity. "And what exactly do you get, Aria?"

"These people need to be stopped. If I had a chance and the resources to destroy the men who killed my sister, don't you think I would have? But, I'm not you. I don't have billions of dollars at my fingertips. I don't have access to people in high places."

She scrutinized me for a moment. Despite all the Botox that tightened her face I could tell she was considering my words. She had to know what happened to my sister. The woman knew everything. She even had contact with my father.

"That was disgusting what your father did to his children. I hated dealing with your father, but he knew people that could help me. As for the money, well, Alex has it really. My husband left me nothing. That's one of the reasons I needed Alex for this." She shook her head.

"Between the Hawthorne name and money and Alexa's family connection to members of Congress, we can do so much to not only get back at the men who hurt us, but the men who hurt you, Aria. And get the people who want to hurt our country." Mrs. Hawthorne smiled. And she looked unhinged. "If we can get access to the Mimir information then I won't need your father anymore." Mrs. Hawthorne pursed her lips as she leaned against the desk. She muttered something about some Russians but I couldn't make out exactly what she said.

"I could help you." My heart jumped madly in my chest as I pushed out the words.

"How could you help?"

"I don't know what you need, but since both my friends work there, I don't think they would be suspicious of me stopping by."

"Hmm." Emma's brow pinched as she tapped her finger against her chin. "We would need you to gain access to certain files that would only be allowed through a high level executive computer. These files contain very personal data on lots of people including politicians and leaders throughout the country and the world."

Everything was coming together in my head. She was going to use their information against them in some way.

"Morgana is an executive. I could use her computer. Wait until she steps out to use the restroom or something and use it then."

I made fists behind my back as I prayed she believed me. The woman was crazy after all. She could be playing me as I was playing her.

"That does sound solid. We have someone in the company who can tell you exactly what files to download," she said before walking around the front of the desk.

Mrs. Hawthorne removed a cell phone from one of the desk drawers and tapped at it a few times.

"Hi, Trey, this is Jay," she said as she placed the phone to her ear.

"I need you to contact Aria Dixon tomorrow. You are going to help her download the Mimir files. Yes, that Aria. How's Damien doing? Uh huh. Just make sure those cops play their part. I'll contact you tomorrow," she said before putting the phone down.

She smiled at me. Or at least, tried to smile. Her cheeks and forehead were so tight it appeared she was in pain as she curved her lips.

Mrs. Hawthorne strolled over and looked down on me. "You understand Alex has to marry Alexa. He is a part of all this too. You will have to sacrifice him for the greater good."

Her finger pushed away the hair that had dried to my face. I turned my head up and forced myself to keep my eyes on her.

I cleared my throat and took a deep breath. "Yes. I'm actually glad he's marrying her instead of me."

Her fingers pulled away from my head. "What?"

"Don't get me wrong, Mrs. Hawthorne, I care for your son. He is a good guy, but I don't ever want to marry anyone. Life has shown me that nothing good comes from marriage. When your son asked me, I didn't want to hurt his feelings. That's why I said at the chapel that we didn't have to get married that day. I was trying to get out of it."

I took a deep breath before forcing the worst of my words out. "I wanted to break up with your son anyway. He's good looking and it was nice having fun with him with the money, but I'm going to get rich from my artwork now. I really don't need him. I already had a few galleries in New York and London contact me."

A lot of what I was telling her was the truth, but when I said it out loud, it didn't feel like the truth. Especially the part about wanting to break up with Alex. Because I didn't. And it was hard not to let my tears show knowing he was about to marry Alexa and I would lose Alex forever.

THIRTY-EIGHT

Alexander

I wasn't happy.

"I'm so sorry, Alex. I can't believe she said that. Maybe this is another trick from your mom," Alexa said as she placed a soft hand on my shoulder.

We both sat on the concrete floor in a storage room of a warehouse. When I was brought to this room and had the bag taken off my head, I was happy to find I wasn't alone—Alexa was here. But when I realized seconds later she was trapped too, all the happiness turned to anger.

There was no window, just a florescent overhead light and one door. I threw my body against the door at least twenty times before I gave up. As I rubbed the pain away from my arm it dawned on me that there was no way out. I opened every box I could find, which contained remote control toy trucks.

At that moment, I wished I had watched *MacGyver* instead of *Get Smart*. At least I might be able to make a small bomb using only AA batteries, some wire, and a plastic toy.

What was worse than being trapped with no way out? Hearing every word Aria said to my mother about not wanting to marry me. We must be near where she's located and heard her heartbreaking words through the vents.

Alexa wanted to scream to let Aria know we were here but I stopped her. What could Aria do? She was trapped like us. Instead we sat quietly, hearing the woman I loved tell the woman I hated that she wanted nothing to do with me.

I already knew anyway. It shouldn't be a surprise. Aria told me that when we were kidnapped.

But it didn't stop it from hurting.

"It's okay. Who can blame her? Look at what being with me brought her." I waved my arms around the room.

"But it's not about that. If you love someone, then you do anything for them. Even put up with their crazy mother." Alexa elbowed me and smiled.

She understood. Laughter was necessary for sanity with families as messed up as ours.

"I would have for her. When she first started to tell me back at the motel, I laughed. Because I was willing to let her go to make her happy. Of course, I was hurt. Of course, I wanted to beg and plead for her to stay. But when I really thought about it I knew we would never be able to lead a normal and safe life with my mother around. Because I love her I was willing to let her walk away. It hurt so much that all I could do was laugh for fear if I didn't, I would cry."

I rested my head against the wall as I closed my eyes to the world. Maybe if I had done what my mother wanted from the beginning and left Aria out of it, we would be safe.

The door flew open and standing there was my mom and Aria. Her platinum hair in disarray and her clothes dirty, wrinkled, yet she looked like my first breath of air after being held down by water. I hated that despite what she said, I still loved her.

"The minister is on his way. In less than an hour, you two will finally be man and wife," my mom said as she walked in, folding her arms.

"Husband and wife," Aria said. She came to stand next to my mom.

"What?"

"You said man and wife. Alex is already a man, but after the ceremony he becomes a husband as well. I mean, she becomes a wife so it only makes sense that he becomes a husband," Aria said.

Even in that moment, knowing she didn't love me, I couldn't help but smile at her adorableness.

"Yes, yes. It doesn't matter. Husband, whatever," Mom said before waving her hand at Aria.

I stood. "Mom, please, at least let Alexa and Aria go. You want me to do something to help you, fine. But let them go."

She shook her head, laughing.

"Now why would I do that, Alexander? Aria is going to help me. She's part of my team now." My mom gave Aria a side hug. It was weird and both women appeared uncomfortable.

"As for Alexa, well, her plan was put in place a long time ago. With her by your side, after I take down all those men, it will be easy for you to become a senator. Alexa is practically political royalty. Who doesn't want a nice, good-looking, young senator that hasn't been tainted from years of politics? And then, if everything goes well, you can announce your intention to run for president."

"I'm not even thirty. I'm twenty-six. How can I become a senator?"

"It's going to take a few years to build your image and work the right angles. Anyway, this marriage is important. With the Dortons, you can meet with just about any politician you want. You see why this is necessary, right, Alexander?"

Whenever I overheard my mother talking on the phone growing up she mentioned politics, but I never put it together. I figured, since she was friends with the Dortons, she was speaking to them. It never occurred to me that she had plans for me to enter politics.

"I don't want to be a senator or the president, Mom. You can't force me into a career that I have no desire to be a part of."

"It's not about what you want, Alexander. I wanted a normal, happy family where I could raise my children in peace, but your grandfather made that impossible."

"But Grandfather is dead. Who are you trying to get back at? The men who hurt you are dead."

My mom frowned as her nose flared. "Don't you think I know that! Who do you think made sure they died?"

Deep in my heart I knew it was true but refused to acknowledge it. My hand went to my forehead as I rubbed the deep ache that had been building all day.

"You killed them," I said and was surprised she heard my whisper.

"No, I didn't lay one finger on them. But I knew people who would make sure they didn't live any longer. Your grandfather was easy. Most of his servants hated him and were happy to slip the drug into his nightly whiskey. They thought it was a sleeping medication. I told them I needed to get my hands on the paperwork he had in his bedroom. They drugged him so he wouldn't wake when I did that. They didn't realize he would never wake up. They were upset but I told them I would turn a blind eye if any jewelry found its way into their pockets."

She laughed and shook her head. "When the police found he had been poisoned and some of his diamond cufflinks and an antique pocket watch in the cook's home, it was an open and shut case. Of course, the cook tried to blame me, but really, who were the police going to believe? Especially, when I donated so heavily to their annual Widows and Orphans fund. Not to mention I 'helped' a few of the cops working on the case."

My mouth hung open but she kept talking. "As for your uncle, who you thought was your father growing up, well, he proved to be more difficult. I didn't want to have to kill him but he was going to take you from me. I had to make sure his plane went down. I knew why he suddenly showed interest in you that Christmas twenty years ago. It wasn't because he cared—he knew you weren't his. It was your grandfather whispering in his ear to take you away from me."

"Look at what you did? You have blood on your hands, Mom. How can you say what you want to do is for the best when so many lives have been taken?"

My mother's eyes grew wide and I believed in that moment what I said might have gotten through to her. I saw horror on her face but it disappeared as quickly as it came. Covered up by her usual steely façade.

She opened her mouth to speak but Aria's hand on her shoulder caused her to turn. "Mrs. Hawthorne, why don't you go check on the minister. See if he's here yet. I'll keep an eye on them. Make sure they understand why we are doing this."

I saw the same hardness in Aria's eyes as she held my mother's gaze. This was a nightmare. It was one thing to lose Aria but to watch her turn into another version of my mother was unbearable.

"Good call, Aria," my mom said and Aria followed her to the door, closing it behind her.

"Why, Aria? I get that you don't love me, but why help her?" I stared at Aria's back as she faced the door.

She stood there because she couldn't answer me. Aria couldn't face the truth that by helping a monster, she was turning into one herself.

After a moment, she faced me. I stared into her large, chocolate eyes and found nothing but fear mixed with determination.

"It's not about me, Alex. This is about the bigger picture," Aria said.

Alexa gasped. I should have been angry. Maybe screamed to wake her from this horrible dream. But I didn't. Even after all that has happened, I walked over to her to put my arms around her.

Maybe if she felt my love she'd wake up.

But Aria held out her hand to stop me.

"Please, no, Alex. You don't understand."

"Then help me understand! I don't want to marry Alexa," I said as I glanced over at Alexa before turning back to Aria, "and Alexa doesn't want to marry me. I want to be with you, Aria. But if you really don't want me, then I'll walk away. But please, don't help my mother. She doesn't care about you. Emma Hawthorne only cares about herself and her sick need for power."

Aria smiled and placed her hand on my chest. "I'm not helping your mother. I'm feeding into her gruesome fantasy to help us escape. I love you, Alex, and I think it's time to leave."

I hadn't noticed but she had placed her bare foot, as neither of us had shoes on when we were kidnapped, between the door and the wall so it wouldn't close completely.

Aria opened the door and waved for us to follow her out.

THIRTY-NINE

Aria

"She saw us," Alexa said in a hushed tone.

We were huddled behind some large crates after we heard some noise a few moments after leaving the storage room.

I held my arm out to stop them from moving and peered over the corner of the crate. Something moved but I held still. Then it jetted toward me like a missile.

I quickly moved back, pressing my back against the crate. It flew by missing us completely.

"It's a bird, not Emma Hawthorne. Let's keep going. There should be a way out in the back. By law, every building has to have at least two exits," I said.

Alex grabbed my hand and brought it to his lips, kissing my dirt-covered fingers. "I love that you are filled with random knowledge. It's cute and lifesaving at the same time."

"Less kissing and more getting the hell out of here," Alexa said as she made a move past us.

We followed her advice even if my heart was still racing from relief that my plan worked. It was hard not to run and jump into Alex's arms when he said I didn't want him anymore. I wanted to give him a thousand kisses and tell him it wasn't true.

The pain in his eyes almost broke me, but I knew if I gave anything away we would never have a chance to escape.

I wanted to take him right there when I saw the love and relief in his eyes after his mother left and I admitted the truth. But it's not always the right time to have sex. Like when we are escaping a crazy woman who had us kidnapped and is hell-bent on taking over the country by murder, bribery, and lies.

It felt like we were making our way through a maze as we moved farther toward the back of the building. Just as we saw the door with a red, glowing exit sign overhead, we heard loud voices.

"They're gone! Quick, search everywhere," A male voice came from the middle of the building.

"We have to run. There's no other way. If we hide, they'll find us," I whispered.

"I'll stay and distract them. You two run," Alex said as he placed his hands on our backs.

"Absolutely not! I didn't just tell the devil herself a pack of hateful lies and risk myself, just so you could get caught again. We all go," I said as I glared at Alex.

"Aria, no. You two need time to flee. Who knows what's out there. We could be in the middle of the desert. Where will you hide? At least if I distract them, then you two can assess the area and find some place to go. It gives you time."

I could feel the tears burning my eyes as I shook my head. I refused to leave behind someone I loved, again.

"No, I'll stay. You two get help. At least, Alex, you can protect Alexa. You might need to climb over a fence, you can use those big arms of yours to help her out."

"They're coming. Why don't we all just make a dash for it? If we stay and argue, we all will be caught," Alexa said, her eyes wide in frustration.

"I don't like any of this. Why are you being so stubborn?" Alex said and gritted his teeth.

"Because I love you, that's why. I will fight them for you. Now, both of you, go," I said pointing to the door.

Alexa started to make a move but Alex grabbed her and kept his eyes on me. "Oh, and I don't love you enough to fight them? I will fight them until the ends of the Earth and into the stars. So, *you* go with Alexa."

"How about all of you come with me?" A deep voice came from behind us.

We turned and looked up from our crouched positions to find the douche, Jagger, standing there.

As we stood, Alexa turned to us, pointing her finger in our direction. "I'm never speaking to either of you again. Who has a fight about who loves whom more as they try to escape a kidnapping? Idiots, that's who."

She was right. I glanced at Alex and his pitiful expression matched how I felt.

"This was all my fault," both Alex and I said at the same time.

"Damn straight it is," Alexa said as Jagger pushed us forward.

We walked past the storage room and dread filled my chest. This was it. I would have to witness the man I loved marry the woman he didn't love.

Mrs. Hawthorne must be with the minister right now telling him exactly what to say, even if the two people getting married tried to say no.

We kept walking and noticed more people mulling around the area. More of Mrs. Hawthorne's thugs. We probably wouldn't have had a chance of escape even if we tried. She must have a bunch of help both inside and outside the building.

"Go out the door," Jagger said as we came to the front.

Alex pushed open the door and we all shielded our eyes to the bright light. Once my eyes adjusted to the light, I noticed we were surrounded by green. I could see a farm off in the distance and wondered if we could have made it to that farm in time before being caught.

More 'what ifs' weighed me down as I tried to get by in this world. Would I even have any desire to paint anymore with so many people I loved being taken from me?

Jagger stood in front of a large black SUV and opened the back door, waving for us to get inside. We were probably going to be taken to some church Mrs. Hawthorne gave a lot of money to so this forced marriage could take place.

I felt sick. And when I saw Grace in the front passenger seat, my heart hit the floor. They got her.

Mrs. Hawthorne won. There was no beating her.

"Thank goodness you all are all right," Grace said as we took our seats.

I nodded and didn't have the energy to even fake a smile.

"Did Agent Chance explain everything to you?" Grace asked as she turned in her seat to face us.

The driver's side door opened and Jagger got inside.

"Agent Chance?" Alex said.

Jagger turned, finally taking off his ridiculous sunglasses to stare at us with his cool, green eyes. "I'm Agent Jagger Chance with the United States government."

"The CIA?" I asked.

"Something like that. We work with the CIA and FBI. We are here to arrest Emma Hawthorne, Douglas Dorton and his wife, Sofia Dorton. Emma Hawthorne, who goes by the name Jay to cover her tracks, is head of a criminal organization to infiltrate the government. We had the warehouse bugged and heard everything she said to you. Don't worry, you all are safe, thanks to the help of Grace here."

My eyes widened. "Grace? How did you help?"

Grace blushed and shook her head. "It was nothing. I told Jagger when he reached out to me a few months back that I would help him.

When I met you, Alex, I knew you were a good guy. I can sense it, you know?"

She shook her head. "Anyway, I made sure he kept an eye on you two when our mom was going to make you marry Alexa. I couldn't reach him when she first brought you all to the chapel in Vegas."

I noticed some pink filling Jagger's cheeks as he cleared his throat.

"So, I took it upon myself to get you out of there. But, of course, Mom found us so I called Jagger to make sure he got to you before she sent someone else to kidnap you."

"Unfortunately, we needed the kidnapping to happen in order to get more information from Emma Hawthorne. I made sure my team was waiting to stop everything on my call."

"You've known about this for months?" I asked Grace.

"Yes, but I had to keep everything a secret. I meant it when I said I was happy when our mom reached out to me. I thought I finally had a family that cared about me. But when she explained what happened and what she planned to do about it, I wanted no part of that. In fact, I was angry. I didn't want anyone to be hurt ever again. These people she's trying to hurt, while they may be bad, have families. They have children. She's not God. She can't decide who lives and who dies. I had to do something."

Alex reached over the seats and kissed Grace on the cheek. "You're my hero, Grace."

"And my hero, too," I said and reached over to put my hand on her shoulder.

"And mine. Thank you so much, Grace, for what you did," Alexa said with tears rolling down her face.

I glanced over at Agent Chace and saw him pull the glasses back over his eyes. Leaning forward, I whispered in his ear, "Don't think I can't see you crying. You try so hard to act tough, but inside you're a big softy."

He cleared his throat, buckling his seatbelt clearly ignoring me.

"Everyone, buckle up. It's a nine-hour drive to Chicago so get comfortable," Jagger said.

I sat back in my seat. We put our seatbelts on as the car moved forward. I held Alex's hand and rested my head on his shoulder. I had no idea I fell asleep until the car stopped.

We were at a gas station.

"Where are we," I asked as my voice rumbled to life.

"Just outside of Des Moines. Still have a way to go," Alex said and I could feel something tickling my neck.

Alex was playing with my necklace.

"With all that has happened, this necklace never got lost or broke. It always stayed with you."

I instinctively reached up to touch the gold heart and dusted Alex's fingers in the process.

"Yeah, for a cheap necklace my sister saved up for to buy when she was thirteen, it has held tight."

"Because it's her heart," he said and I gazed up at Alex. "You never left her behind, Aria. She's been with you the whole time."

I nodded as my face crumbled. He pulled me into his arms and let me cry. All those tears I held inside me, all those years I pushed the thought of her away—they were finally free.

We were all finally free.

EPILOGUE

6 Months Later

Aria loved me.

At least, that's what she told me every day. And when I told her I was taking her on a trip to a secluded tropical island for the last two weeks of December, she said she loved me then, too.

Even now, as we sit and watch the waves crash on the beach, sitting under palm trees on a double lounger that fit both of us, she whispered those words.

"I love you, too," I told her and tried to control my hand as it trembled reaching to push a few strands of bright blond hair out of her face.

I couldn't handle the pressure. Every time she told me she loved me, my throat tightened and I wanted to run into the ocean to get away.

"Is anything wrong, Alex? You look nervous."

Forcing a smile, I shook my head. "No, of course not. This is our dream remember?"

My cheeks felt like they were going to crack as I held the grin. She nodded and sat back, gazing at the waves once again.

I deflated in relief that she bought it. It was a lie and she believed me. But for how long?

A male voice came from the side of our lounger. "Would you like to order drinks, maybe a snack?"

It was the butler that came with the home we rented on the island. He's a nice guy. Very accommodating and seemed to know our needs before we did. But I'm not ready yet.

I mean, yes, technically, everything is in place, but emotionally, I didn't think I was ready yet.

Aria started to say something but I cut her off. "No, Tyler, not just yet. I'm still full from breakfast."

I chuckled as Aria knitted her brow.

"Maybe I want something. I'll have the—" Aria said as I sat up cutting her off from Tyler both verbally and physically.

"No, don't. I, uh, we should do something first. Like sex. We should totally have sex." I sort of half-frowned half-smiled.

Everyone was quiet.

"I'll come back later," Tyler said and I heard sounds of sand shifting as he scurried off.

"Are you sure you're okay?" Aria reached over, placing her hand on my forehead.

I grabbed her hand and pulled her close. "It's just, I've been thinking. With everything that has happened to us, and even your friends, this year, I wonder if we should have more sex."

My words were broken. Nothing coming out of my mouth made sense.

"I like the part about having more sex but what does that have to do with what happened this year? And if you really wanted to get me in the mood, you'd feed me first. Hence, why we should have ordered when Tyler was here. You know I'm easy when it comes to good food."

I groaned. She was too good. Even when we got home from being kidnapped by my mom this past summer, she insisted on finishing the mural. Even if I only used that mural as an excuse to get near her, she wanted it there to reflect our crazy journey together.

It somehow changed as she finished painting it. There were still elements of old master paintings but instead of it being a history of art, it was a car on a highway with art along for the ride.

"This is hard," I said as I pounded a fist on the thick striped padding that covered the chair.

"No, it's not," Aria said as she stared at my swim trunks.

"I mean this. Us." I gave up trying to delay. It was time.

"Tyler! We're ready," I yelled and within seconds he appeared.

I hope he wasn't listening. What if we had decided to have sex?

He placed a silver tray down on the small table beside me and left.

I grabbed the silver bowl. It was cold but I held on. Taking the lid off I presented it to Aria.

"Oh, shrimp! I love shrimp. Perfect. Wait. Is that . . .." She lifted the gold necklace from the center of the ice. "This is my necklace but there's something else there."

I put the silver bowl back on the platter and turned to Aria.

"It's been exactly six months since your birthday. And since I missed it because of my crazy mother, I wanted to make up for it. Sort of a half birthday," I said and released a deep breath.

"There are two hearts on here, instead of one. The new heart is covered in diamonds," Aria said as she cupped the pendants and brought them closer for inspection.

"I added the other heart," I said as my own heart beat wildly in my ears. "It's there because you already have your sister's heart and now, I wanted to give you my heart. I made the heart out of diamonds because I want to make sure you have it forever."

I took the necklace from her and placed it around her neck. It sparkled in the sun but not as brightly as her beauty.

"Aria, I know you don't want to get married. And now that you have explained why, I get it. But, I still want you to have something to show you that I will always be yours. You not only helped me break free from all the things holding me back, but you showed me how beautiful life and love really is. I may be blood related to my mom, but you're my family. I want us to live together, forever."

She sat there staring at me like I just told her I liked to fart only in bathtubs because it turned it into a sauna.

I knew I was asking too much by wanting to live with her and telling her that I wanted to be with her forever.

"This is all, uh . . ." She took her hand from me and fiddled with the hearts on her necklace.

When her eyes darted away, I knew I lost her. Fuck. I can't believe I did this. I couldn't just leave well enough alone, could I? We were fine the way things were. Some nights she stayed at my place, other nights I stayed at hers. About once a week we would sleep in our own condos.

"Of course, I want to be with you forever, Alex. I love you. And this pendant, it's so beautiful. When we head back to Chicago, we can figure out which place we want to move into."

I gave her the biggest, most goofy grin before I pulled her into my arms. She curled into me, her leg wrapping around my hip. It was like her body was made for me.

My lips descended to her neck and I refused to stop kissing her until she finally pulled me away.

"Alex, stop. I want to give you something, too." She flashed a wicked smile before hopping up from the lounger and going back inside our house. The wall of the living room was made of sliding windows that we kept open during the day so it was as if we were always outside even when we went into the house. I watched her pull a large bag from behind the couch before she came back to the lounger.

"I wanted to give it to you on Christmas in a few days, but since you gave me a gift, I thought it fitting I give you one. I hope you like it." Aria placed the holiday-themed bag in front of me.

I kept my eyes on her as I pulled a shoe box out of the bag. She was bouncing up and down on her haunches in excitement.

While it was a shoe box, the way she was acting, I thought shoes would be the last thing in the box. I was wrong.

It was a pair of sneakers. Not even expensive name-brand sneakers, but some brand I had never seen before. The logo looked like cell reception bars.

"Thank you," I said.

I wanted to say more but what else could I say. Thank you for a pair of sneakers when I have ten more pairs at home.

This was our first test as a couple. She buys me an average gift after I poured my heart and soul into her gift. I needed to learn to act like it was the best thing ever.

I smiled and stared at her. She giggled. The more I smiled, the more she giggled.

Then she reached over to the small table by her side of the lounger and tapped her phone a few times.

My shoes vibrated.

"Are these massage shoes?" I flipped them over.

"No, here let me show you." Aria reached forward and pressed the back part of the sneaker that on some shoes were an air pump.

But the button didn't pump air into the heel, it caused the bottom part of the shoe to flip open. There was a keypad inside.

I was confused as I looked up at her. Her grin was wide and open—like a clown—and she had her arms out.

"Alex. It's a shoe phone. Just like *Get Smart*."

My dick hardened.

"It's a tech gadget. A sneaker. And a reference to one of the best shows of all time, all in one," I said as I stared into her smart, sexy, perfect eyes. "I love you so much right now."

Then I tackled her. I didn't let go of the shoes right away, but as we rolled around and I tried to slip off her violet bikini top sacrifices had to be made.

"Aria, you're going to have to undress yourself and me, too," I said as I sat up on my knees while clutching the shoes to my chest.

She rolled her eyes as she reached for my swim trunks. "What I do for love."

THE END

BEHIND THE SCENES

This is the part of the book where I tell you little factoids about different parts of the story and/or why I wrote the book. As I write, I throw in things that have happened to me, to people I know, or stuff I witnessed in life. Some of it is crazy and some is dorky, but that's me – crazy and dorky.

Let's get started!

In chapter two, Aria was angry with Alex and makes up a fake award rich people get for being terrible. It's a golden statue with the biggest dick. Well, folks, I have that statue. Honestly. Not making it up. My statue isn't gold. It's bronze, I think, but it looks like the Oscar statue took some performance enhancing drug, got a mohawk and decided to grow a beard.

The story behind that statue goes back about ten years when I was living in Chicago with my hubby and we hadn't had kids yet. Having all that free time we decided to enter the 48-hour film project. That's where you get a genre, a line of dialogue, a certain character and a prop that must be used (if I remember correctly). Then you have 48 hours to film, edit, and turn in a 5-7-minute film. Our friends, my husband, and I went for it. Our genre was time period (which was one of the worst genres you can get for a 48-hour film because it's hard to make the world around you appear from a different era in that short period of time). But we went for it. I chose 1980's After School Special as inspiration for the film.

And it worked, because we got an audience favorite award. That's where the statue came from. Now, it didn't have a giant penis or mohawk or beard when we received it, that's where one of our friends came in. He was an artist and did some metal work. He made a mold of the statue and gave it all those features. Don't ask why. We all thought it was funny at the time. Now you know I have a biggest dick statue.

In chapter twenty-nine, Morgana's mom has a room that's decorated year-round for Christmas. That was inspired by a woman I used to work with. I used to be a medical photographer at a medical school. There was a woman who worked down the hall for the head of the medical school. I think she was his assistant, but that was a long time ago so I'm not sure. What I do remember of her, was how proud she was that she had a room devoted to Christmas. She always had a Christmas tree up and the entire room decked out in green and red and gold. When I asked what she did at Christmas time, she told me she put up a tree in every room (even the bathrooms got small, tabletop trees). If there was such a thing as Christmas addiction, she would be a full-blown addict.

In chapter thirty, Alexa mentions an old tv show from the early 90's called Get A Life which featured Chris Elliott. That whole scene was inspired by me and how I used to be a mega couch potato. Meaning, I had the tv guide schedule memorized from 1978 through the 1990's. Seriously, if you named a show from that time frame I had probably watched it. and I LOVED GET A LIFE.

It was absurd, immature, and ridiculous and I was crushed when it got cancelled. I remember going on a rant on the phone with my first boyfriend because I was so angry it got cancelled. I mean, the main character dies 10 times during the course of the series. Who does that? Yet, he would be back to life the next episode. I'm still a little angry they cancelled that show.

That ends the Behind the Scenes of One Wild Ride. I may lose fans from this but I did warn you I was a crazy dork.

ABOUT THE AUTHOR

Elizabeth Lynx was a printer. She was also a graphic designer, photographer, actress, comedic improviser, merchandiser, and now she is adding author to that extensive list of professions.

She has written an erotic romance called Her Night with Him. Since she spent a lot of time training and moved halfway across the country to pursue comedy (much to her husband's chagrin) only to change her mind and take up writing, Elizabeth decided to write a romantic comedy series called Cake Love.

Follow Elizabeth Lynx:

Website: www.elizabeth-lynx.com

Fan Group on Facebook: Elizabeth Lynx's SWIM Meet

Goodreads: http://bit.ly/ELynxGdReads

THANK YOU

I would like to thank the people who made this story look presentable. Silvia & Marla, without you I think most people would believe I threw rocks at a keyboard and then tried to publish it as a book. Your 'I'm not sure about this' comments are more helpful than you know.

And thank you to all the Swimmers! I have so much fun with all of you. Whenever I need help you are there and when I am having a bad day, your kind words always make me feel better. And I loved the cover. Thank you so much for your help with the design!

Finally, to my family. To my mom and dad for always believing in me and pretending you skip over the sex scenes when you tell me you read my books. To my husband for your support and understanding that this is what I must do. And, to my boys, I love you so much. You make me feel like the smartest, most beautiful person in the world. For that I am forever thankful for giving me the confidence to follow my dreams.

www.ingramcontent.com/pod-product-compliance
Lightning Source LLC
Chambersburg PA
CBHW050734230626
47052CB00002BA/131